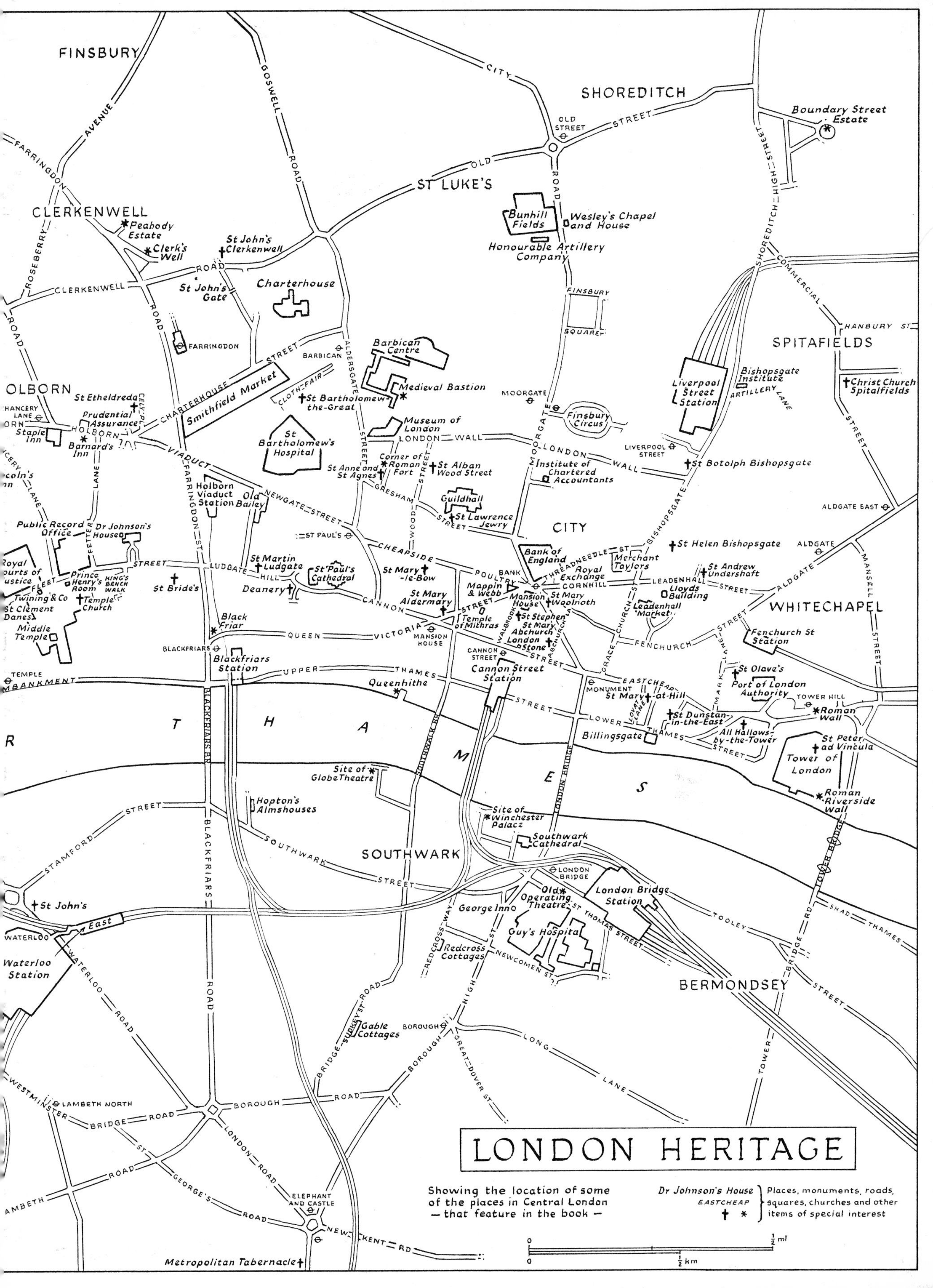
LONDON HERITAGE
Showing the location of some of the places in Central London — that feature in the book —
Dr Johnson's House
EASTCHEAP
Places, monuments, roads, squares, churches and other items of special interest
FINSBURY
SHOREDITCH
CLERKENWELL
ST LUKE'S
SPITAFIELDS
CITY
WHITECHAPEL
SOUTHWARK
BERMONDSEY
Boundary Street Estate
Bunhill Fields
Wesley's Chapel and House
Honourable Artillery Company
Charterhouse
Smithfield Market
Barbican Centre
Medieval Bastion
St Bartholomew-the-Great
St Bartholomew's Hospital
Museum of London
Liverpool Street Station
Bishopsgate Institute
Christ Church Spitalfields
St Botolph Bishopsgate
Institute of Chartered Accountants
Guildhall
St Lawrence Jewry
Bank of England
St Helen Bishopsgate
Royal Exchange
St Paul's Cathedral
St Mary-le-Bow
Tower of London
Southwark Cathedral
London Bridge Station
Guy's Hospital
Site of Globe Theatre
Site of Winchester Palace
Metropolitan Tabernacle

LONDON HERITAGE

also by Michael Jenner

SCOTLAND THROUGH THE AGES
YEMEN REDISCOVERED
BAHRAIN – GULF HERITAGE IN TRANSITION
SYRIA IN VIEW

LONDON HERITAGE

The Changing Style of a City

Written and photographed by

Michael Jenner

MICHAEL JOSEPH
London

To my father

MICHAEL JOSEPH LTD

Penguin Books Ltd, 27 Wrights Lane, London W8 5TZ (Publishing and Editorial)
and Harmondsworth, Middlesex, England (Distribution and Warehouse)
Viking Penguin Inc., 40 West 23rd Street, New York, New York 10010, USA
Penguin Books Australia Ltd, Ringwood, Victoria, Australia
Penguin Books Canada Ltd, 2801 John Street, Markham, Ontario, Canada L3R 1B4
Penguin Books (NZ) Ltd, 182–190 Wairau Road, Auckland 10, New Zealand

First published in Great Britain 1988

Maps by Boris Weltman

Typeset in 11½/13pt and 11/12pt Cheltenham Light
by Goodfellow & Egan Ltd, Cambridge
Printed and bound in Italy by Olivotto

British Library Cataloguing in Publication Data

Jenner, Michael
London Heritage: the changing style of a city.
1. Architecture — England — London
2. London (England) — London
I.Title
720′.9421 NA970

ISBN 0-7181-2903-2

Page 1: a giant Ionic capital from Smirke's General Post Office at St Martins-le-Grand has found a resting place in Walthamstow.

Title page: Pickering Place, St James's

Contents

Burlington's Chiswick House set new standards of Palladian perfection.

Acknowledgements

Most of the research and photography for this book was carried out from vantage points ordinarily accessible to members of the public, but I am most grateful to the following for special facilities and permissions which were invaluable in the course of my work: All Hallows by the Tower; All Saints, Margaret Street; Bank of England; British Federation of University Women; British Rail Property Board; Canonbury Day Nursery; Canonbury Tower; Charlton House; the Clermont Club; the Clothworkers' Company; Corporation of the City of London; Courtauld Institute of Art; Eagle Star Insurance; Eltham Palace; English Heritage; Finsbury Public Library; Friends of the Old Palace, Croydon; Hall Place; Mr and Mrs Hollamby, Red House, Bexleyheath; the Honourable Society of Lincoln's Inn; the Honourable Society of the Middle Temple; House of Commons (Serjeant at Arms); House of Lords (Gentleman Usher of the Black Rod); Lambeth Palace; Lansdowne Club; Leighton House; London Borough of Camden; London Residuary Body; Merchant Taylors' Company; Museum of London; Museum of the Order of St John; National Maritime Museum, Greenwich; National Trust; Post Office; the Richmond Fellowship; Royal Academy of Arts; Royal Courts of Justice; Royal Naval College and Chapel, Greenwich; St Andrew Undershaft; St Augustine's, Queen's Gate; St Bartholomew-the-Great; St Dunstan's, Stepney; St Helen's, Bishopsgate; St James-the-Less, Pimlico; St Mary-at-Hill; St Mary Magdalene, East Ham; Mr Dennis Severs of 18 Folgate Street; Sir John Soane Museum; Southwark Cathedral; Temple Church; Thames Water Authority; Tower Bridge; Victoria & Albert Museum; Victorian Society; Westminster Abbey; Whitgift Hospital, Croydon.

Special thanks are due to the staff of the Museum of London, the Guildhall Library and the British Library. Any researcher on London owes a debt to all those who have already published their own works; and a small number of the huge range of books are mentioned in the bibliography.

Monument to John Stow, the great chronicler of Tudor London, in St Andrew Undershaft.

Introduction

London may no longer rank as the world's largest metropolis – and indeed it has now slipped out of the top ten in the league of the most populous cities – but it retains its leading status as a great city with a phenomenal wealth of historic content accumulated over a period of almost 2,000 years. That urban heritage is the subject of this book, which aims to show in contemporary photographs the evocative relics of London's growth through the ages and to interpret in a concise text the shaping circumstances behind each phase. The resulting story is essentially the changing style of the city landscape. Architecture and design are naturally at the centre of this account rather than sociology and politics, for the main thrust of this portrait of London is to focus the spotlight on those physical elements of the metropolis which survive to tell the tale of centuries past.

Unravelling the past is no easy matter. The remains of the Roman period, for example, have been mostly eradicated by subsequent rebuilding in the City, where in London's most valuable archaeological site the latest buildings jostle for space within the original square mile. Only occasionally is London's most ancient past given room to co-exist alongside the modern, as at the Barbican Centre which has preserved within its confines some of the medieval bastions of the old city wall built on Roman foundations. Usually the reality nowadays is of rapid operations of rescue archaeology when a site is about to be redeveloped before even the remains below ground are obliterated for ever. Thus in 1985-6 a corner of the Roman Basilica next to Leadenhall Market was briefly uncovered, but such excavations are only temporary and tantalising glimpses of fragments of the past.

The medieval period is also elusive. Timber-framed houses are extremely vulnerable and the Great Fire of 1666 was but the worst of many conflagrations. Nevertheless, the Middle Ages cling on obdurately in ghost-like form in the shape of some streets and even in the dimensions of house-plots. Fleet Street, despite its modernity, still retains a medieval feel in parts due to the narrow frontages which have been inherited from previous structures over the centuries. Such pointers are invaluable in recreating in the imagination the texture of the lost urban fabric.

It is natural to look for history in the obvious places, such as the Tower of London and Westminster Abbey, but often the humbler structures are more eloquent in evoking the everyday life and style of the city. The old gables of Staple Inn in High Holborn, although heavily restored, convey a precious image of the London streetscape of almost five hundred years ago; Covent Garden, despite all the changes, is still highly significant as a forerunner of the London square. Of course, the evidence becomes more tangible and abundant as one moves forward in time; there are buildings of many types from the seventeenth century. Georgian London, although often jerry-built, still does service as homes and offices; and Victorian and Edwardian elements constitute the underlying style of London today.

Redevelopment has been a greater destroyer of the old structures over the centuries than such cataclysmic events as the Great Fire and the Blitz, and it is exceedingly rare to find an ancient monument not hemmed in by subsequent building. One notable exception is the much disregarded twelfth-century Lesnes Abbey, a lovely if scant ruin set in open grassland on a slope overlooking the new settlement of Thamesmead.

The homely clutter of a Victorian bedroom at 18 Stafford Terrace.

Old buildings are occasionally removed to new locations, such as the Temple of Mithras foundations, transferred some 250 feet to Queen Victoria Street in the 1950s, and the splendid medieval Crosby Hall which was brought from Bishopsgate to Chelsea in 1908.

In addition to such anomalies our historical senses have to contend with the din and clamour of the present. Heavy traffic, parked cars, unsympathetic street furniture and advertising hoardings are the main intrusive elements which make it difficult to appreciate the flavour of the past. To a certain extent, the camera can isolate period scenes and produce cameo-like effects, but wider views are generally out of the question. There are, however, a number of remarkably preserved authentic interiors in London, of which the most complete is the nineteenth-century Linley Sambourne House in Kensington, now in the care of the Victorian Society.

There is no end to the story of London. Already we can perceive the outlines of dramatic new developments in Docklands which promise to make a significant twentieth-century addition to London but the planning and architectural values of this great venture have yet to emerge. The main story of this book stops in 1914, not just because of the inherent problem of according historic status to our own era, but because London had certainly reached a natural summit of urban achievement at that time; since then there has been an overall loss of cohesion, and many fine neighbourhoods have been destroyed or mutilated. But although this account is concerned with London's past its message is not anti-modern. It is only a matter of time before the closing decades of the twentieth century themselves pass into history. An appreciation of London's inherited urban characteristics is a pre-requisite to the building of a worthy future which lives up to a notable metropolitan tradition.

There can be no specific definition of the ideal nature and shape of London: on the contrary, for dynamism and continual change is the lesson. London has always been a living city rather than a folk museum. It is full of ambiguities. Although without an overall plan, it contains many planned neighbourhoods. Though not renowned for its beauty, it is crammed with items of charm and distinction. Complexity and diversity are its hallmarks, which reside in small pockets and enclaves of amazing individuality. London's past is not neatly arranged for convenient inspection and it takes a small effort to seek out and savour the many historic faces of the city which are often hidden or subtly disguised.

Retrochoir of Southwark Cathedral, the pristine grace of Early English Gothic.

1 From the Romans to the Middle Ages

The evolution of London during its first fifteen hundred years is a tale not of steady growth but of erratic fluctuations from peaks of prosperity to troughs of decline. The city came into being around the middle of the first century AD as an entirely new settlement on a 'green-field' site which was in fact still partly forested. Much uncertainty surrounds the history of this initial version of Londinium which was burned to the ground by Queen Boudica in AD 60. That its subsequent meteoric growth was due to its strategic value as a centre of imperial communications is generally recognised; but that also implies that London came into being only because it was conveniently located between the important tribal centres of the day, notably Silchester and Colchester. The alignment of the road network has raised the possibility that the direct route between the two places passed to the north of Londinium, and if this was so then the reason can only be that the future capital of Britannia did not yet properly exist when the first roads were built. This remains a matter of conjecture but it serves to underline the fact that London arose from a specific set of circumstances and not from an ancient human settlement lost in the mists of prehistory. From the very beginning the purpose of the city was as a communications centre, and from that commerce and ultimately political power accrued. However sudden its birth, London rapidly drew to itself all the Roman land routes like so many threads through the eye of a single needle. It was above all the fixed bridge over the Thames which gave the city its unique strategic importance; and this encouraged the arrival of the first generations who hailed mainly from other parts of the Roman Empire and not from the region itself. The first Londoners were predominantly foreigners, entrepreneurial types anxious to make a profit from the new province of Britannia. Their city was an instant Roman enclave importing everything from its institutions to its pottery in the early stages. As things settled down so native Britons were attracted to the benefits of Roman civilisation and Londinium forged ahead to reach an early summit in its fortunes when it supplanted Colchester as the provincial capital by the end of the first century.

But although Londinium acquired the trappings of imperial bureaucracy it entered a period of economic and political decline, eventually administering only a quarter of Britannia as a result of the country's first reorganisations of local government in the third century. Archaeology has revealed a conflicting picture of the later phases of Londinium. Although the overall population would appear to have shrunk and there were large areas of unoccupied land within the walls, several of the villas excavated show all the trappings of great wealth. Bricks, tiles, carved stone and marble, window glass and fine mosaic pavements speak of a sophisticated building technology. The metalled roads and imposing city wall, baths, basilica and governor's palace show that Londinium was a fully evolved Roman city with all the amenities. It set standards of comfort and hygiene which were not to be attained again until after the Middle Ages.

However, the cultural legacy of the Romans in London was to amount to nothing. It became a ghost town after the Saxon invasions in the middle of the fifth century. Nor did the urban layout leave its imprint, except for the wall and gates which remained *in situ* throughout the Middle Ages. The exact nature of Londinium's Saxon successor Lundenwic has been the greatest mystery in the history of the city. Archaeology has failed to locate an early Saxon settlement on the site; and it is only as recently as 1984 that research and excavation have shown convincingly that the Saxons elected to establish themselves outside the Roman walls at a riverside location centred on Aldwych where they might easily beach their craft. It thus appears that the London of the Romans ceased utterly to exist as a city until the ninth century when Alfred, for reasons of security, ordered the resettling of the city within the walls. Alfred's London was essentially a new creation with its own street pattern and building style. It borrowed from the Roman city only some building materials which it recycled from the ruins. Londinium served as a quarry rather than a model.

The Saxons' contribution to the shaping of London, despite or perhaps because of their lack of grandiose urban concepts, proved to be decisive and enduring. It is quite remarkable how this race of farmers and warriors applied themselves to the creation of what became a major medieval city prior to the Norman Conquest. They evolved the basic structure of London from its street plan to the roots of its administration in the wards and parishes. By the time of the Conqueror's arrival in 1066 London had grown into a robust and resiliently English city, too formidable not to be handled with respect and possibly too complex to be included in the Domesday Book. While the rest of the country swiftly passed into Norman ownership London remained resolutely English, gradually absorbing Norman influence rather than being the object of a takeover.

It is interesting to reflect on the Saxons as rustics in an urban context. It is possible that the small-scale neighbourhoods they created as the tiny cells in the city organism were but replicas of ancestral villages. The spirit of the Saxons is arguably still present in the village structure of London today, a feature which has been defined as the main characteristic of the scattered metropolis by contrast to the 'planned' cities on the continent, such as Paris and Vienna. The average size of parish in the City itself was as small as 3½ acres until as recently as 1907. Saxon settlement was not just within the walls, for there were many villages dispersed over the entire region we now know as Greater London. Many of the names of today's suburbs go back to before the Conquest and have their origins in Saxon villages such as Haveringae, Upmunstre, Grenviz, Bronlei, Croindene, Cambrewelle, Fuleham, Totenham and Cheiam. Not surprisingly, outer London has retained more ancient parish churches than the city centre; and the pattern of medieval settlement is still apparent in such places as Ruislip, Walthamstow and Kingston – the latter retaining the shape and function of its originally Saxon market-place even if the buildings have all been rebuilt.

Although the impact of the Normans as city creators was limited by the existing achievements of the Saxons they made an outstanding contribution as the builders of

Window of Winchester Palace, marooned relic of a bishop's residence.

great monuments of stone. Compared to the paucity of Roman and Saxon remains the Norman era is splendidly tangible in London. The great buildings such as the White Tower and St Bartholomew-the-Great are as solid and serene as have ever been built. But London was not overawed by these symbols of Norman power. In fact the period

Late medieval hammerbeam-type roof of Eltham Palace.

witnessed the consolidation of the City as the financial and commercial centre as a counterbalance to the political arena of Westminster. In the graphic if somewhat fulsome description of London in the 1170s by William Fitz Stephen there is a reference to the freemen as 'barons', a word which aptly conveys the standing of the merchants *vis-à-vis* the Crown. Fitz Stephen shows an unalloyed enthusiasm for the urban apparatus of London. Although the city was still a fairly modest settlement of about 25,000 inhabitants, it was a time of great economic and demographic expansion. The idea of the city as the very expression of human progress was not yet open to doubt, but the vices of London had already been remarked by another commentator of the period: 'Whatever evil or malicious thing that can be found in any part of the world, you will find in that one city.'

As the Normans were followed by the Plantaganets so the Middle Ages matured both politically and architecturally. The influence of the Church was paramount with new monastic foundations appearing within as well as outside the walls such as those of the Black Friars (Dominicans), Grey Friars (Franciscans) and White Friars (Carmelites) whose presence has survived only in street names. In central London only at Westminster can the complete range of monastic buildings be seen. There is a fragment of the old Charterhouse in the shape of a fourteenth-century door to a monk's cell; notable remains in outer London include the foundations of Lesnes Abbey and the 1460 gatehouse of Barking Abbey. A by-product of the Church were the palaces of the bishops of York, Ely, Winchester and of London, for example, and those of the Archbishop of Canterbury at Lambeth and in Croydon. The thirteenth-century Palace of the Savoy began the trend of a noble faubourg outside the walls along the Strand. Its strategic location between the City and Westminster also attracted the lawyers to establish their Inns of Court and of Chancery, placed symbolically as well as geographically between the poles of finance and government.

Medieval London must have been a city of a thousand architectural delights; but the contrast between the noble precincts and the hugger-mugger of the poor districts was certainly extreme. The congested areas of London became really urbanised with the construction of multi-storey dwellings. The last square foot of living space was eked out by the practice of overhanging 'jetties'. Many families were restricted to a single room in tenements above the shops. But, for all the problems, the overcrowded streets of London in the Middle Ages must have presented a fascinating sight as a teeming hive of human activity. Along the waterfront, commerce was a colourful and tangible reality, a complete contrast to the scene of today when the only vessels using the moorings within the City are the pleasure launches and a fleet of barges which take away some of London's rubbish from a small dock near Southwark Bridge.

The Middle Ages were the formative period in the making of London. The outline of the future metropolis was sketched out by the street plan of the City, the establishment of Westminster and the scattering of village centres in the region. It was in the fourteenth century that London's first great and prolific architect Henry Yevele applied the stamp of individual genius on a series of notable buildings. He stands at the beginning of a tradition which extends via Sir Christopher Wren and John Nash to the present day. The Romans may have given London its foundations but its form and substance have grown from medieval roots.

Roman Londinium

Roman Londinium has been likened to a 'city of the mind' because the imagination has to recreate an entity for which there is not much obvious physical evidence. Indeed, as one walks about on the surface of twentieth-century London there is precious little reminder of a Roman predecessor. This is hardly surprising since the original ground level of Londinium now lies buried as much as six metres beneath the streets of today. Yet there remains just enough both *in situ* as well as in museums to conjure up a vivid, albeit fragmentary picture of this first city on the banks of the Thames.

The outstanding progress made by archaeologists in recent years has enabled a precise enough dating of the sites and finds, coupled with documented historical facts and events, for an outline chronology of Londinium through the four centuries of its existence to be pieced together. The most important finding to emerge from the debris of the past is that we are dealing not with one single Londinium but with several, or at least various distinct phases of the evolution of the city which reflect the ups and downs, sometimes extreme, of its early fortunes. The known relics of Londinium provide historians with fairly reliable navigational aids through the murky waters of the city's Roman origins.

A collection of human skulls on display in the Museum of London is a grim reminder that the infant settlement was set on fire and razed to the ground, only ten years after its foundation by the wrathful Boudica, Queen of the Iceni, in around AD 60. The skulls, which were discovered in the Walbrook stream, now a part of London's sewage network, are believed to be those of the unfortunate victims of Boudica's act of revenge against the Roman occupiers. The burning of the city can also be detected in places in a stratum of burnt material which represents the consumed remains of Londinium's houses, which would seem to have been modest timber-framed constructions with walls of wattle-and-daub and roofs of thatch. It was an inauspicious beginning for what was eventually to become the capital of the province of Britannia.

This ruined Londinium was probably not the first Roman settlement in the area after the invasion of AD 43, for there must have been a military camp to guard the river crossing; and this, judging from the alignment of Watling Street, was almost certainly at Westminster where the Thames in those days might still be forded. Londinium, roughly corresponding to the territory of the City of London as it exists today, acquired significance as a potential site for an urban settlement with the building of the first permanent bridge from Southwark to the north bank of the Thames. The presence of firmer gravel deposits in the midst of so much clay and marshy ground at what was precisely the tidal limit of the Thames made this the ideal location for the bridge which was so essential for the Roman subjugation of Britannia. Since there is no evidence of any previous native settlement of consequence in the vicinity it must be assumed that Londinium was a deliberate act of town planning on a green-field site, chosen simply on account of its strategic location at the heart of the Roman communications network. Camulodunum (Colchester) was the first capital of conquered Britannia, established at the existing capital of the tribe known as the Catuvellauni. At the outset of the Roman occupation what mattered most was access from the Channel port at Richborough in Kent to the military headquarters in Colchester. The bridge over the Thames came as a consequence of

A nineteenth-century reconstruction of a Roman statue at Tower Hill.

that imperative; and thus the first foundation of Londinium's future commercial and political ascendancy was laid. This wooden structure was probably located about 20 to 30 yards east of London Bridge, and the remains of one of its timber piers has been excavated at Fish Street Hill.

Whatever the decision-making process which led to the creation of Londinium, the choice was evidently a good one and the economic potential of the city drew merchants and traders from the heartland of the Roman Empire, anxious to make a profit by supplying the soldiers and administrators with all the luxuries of Mediterranean civilisation. Recovery after the disastrous fire of AD 60 was largely due to a certain Gaius Julius Alpinus Classicianus, the far-sighted 'procurator' who persuaded Rome to a policy of reconciliation rather than repression after the revolt led by Queen Boudica. Fragments of the tombstone of this enlightened official, London's first known distinguished resident, have fortunately been discovered and are on display in the British Museum. The city familiar to Classicianus would have been that described by Tacitus as 'a place not indeed marked out by the title of "colonia", but was crowded with traders and a great centre of commerce'. Very soon, under the governorship of Julius Agricola, AD 77 to 93, Londinium was launched upon a course of expansion. It was again Tacitus who reported that 'Agricola gave private encouragement and official assistance to the building of temples, fora and private mansions . . . the Britons were gradually led on to the amenities that make vice agreeable – arcades, baths and sumptuous banquets. They spoke of such novelties as "civilisation", when really they were only a feature of enslavement.'

This construction boom at the end of the first century carried over into the second. The major known monuments of this period include a forum, basilica and temple complex, storehouses and a quay along the riverfront, a governor's palace and public baths. Sadly, there is nothing to be seen of all this impressive apparatus, with the possible exception of the London Stone in Cannon Street which may have come from the entrance to the governor's palace; but in 1985–6 there was a rare and brief opportunity to view the north-east section of the second basilica, which with its immense forum occupied a square of almost 8 acres and ranked as the largest Roman structure north of the Alps. The basilica itself measured more than 152 metres in length, about the same as St Paul's Cathedral, and was a noble forerunner of the Guildhall and Royal Exchange combined and a bold symbol of Londinium's economic pre-eminence both in the context of Europe and of Britannia. All that remains of the latest excavation are some boxes of artefacts, pottery sherds and fragments of the painted wall plaster which once decorated the interior of this mighty edifice. The masonry has now been used as rubble for landfill, possibly in the docks, thus presenting a future generation of archaeologists with another small problem.

The only structure from the beginning of the second century still visible in places is the fort at Cripplegate. Portions of its wall, surmounted by later medieval stonework and bastions, can be viewed from a window in the Museum of London as well as from the Barbican Centre. Nearby in Noble Street the foundation of one of the internal corner towers has been preserved, and part of the fort's west gate can be inspected under London Wall. It has been noted that the fort was probably not intended for the defence of Londinium, which was still an unwalled city at the time, but as a garrison for troops in transit to the trouble spots on the northern frontier.

Londinium's finest hour must have been in AD 122 when the Emperor Hadrian visited Britannia. Indeed, the possibility is strong that it was none other than Hadrian who ordered the construction of both the fort and the forum with its basilica. We are lucky to have a fine souvenir of Hadrian's

A fleeting glimpse of the basilica during the 1985–6 excavations close to Leadenhall Market.

passage through Londinium in the shape of a noble bronze head of the Emperor which was fished out of the Thames in 1834. Larger than life, it probably formed part of a grand statue which might have been set up in the forum or on the bridge itself. This important relic of Hadrian deserves more prominent display than it currently enjoys in an obscure glass case in the British Museum.

The Londinium as witnessed by Hadrian, with its booming commerce, fine buildings and cosmopolitan citizenry, appears to have been devastated around AD 125 to 130 by another great fire, this time accidental. The evidence of the debris shows that Londinium was now roofed with baked tiles rather than thatch; the floors were of concrete with crushed red tile fragments and occasional mosaics. The full extent of the damage has not been determined but at least 100 acres were consumed in the flames. The basilica survived the conflagration but the subsequent recovery was apparently slow and patchy. A layer of what the archaeologists call 'dark earth' has been discovered on many sites, indicating a break in human occupation. Was the great basilica a white elephant? For a trade slump would seem to have occurred very soon after its completion. The situation of Londinium from around the middle of the second century is indeed hard to make out as there is much conflicting and ambiguous evidence.

On the one hand there are definite signs of a decrease in the population, due perhaps to a combination of economic decline and possibly an epidemic. But at the same time there are some magnificent testimonials to the wealth and artistic taste of at least some of the better endowed citizens in the form of a series of brilliant mosaic floors which adorned some of the houses of the period. Examples are on view in the British Museum and the Museum of London, showing a high degree of craftsmanship and aesthetic merit. These were not provincial versions by unskilled local workers but confident productions of the current imperial fashion, evidently intended to make the occupants of the houses feel at home in the familiar surroundings of Roman civilisation. In this respect as in others Londinium was planned as a faithful replica of the standard Roman urban model. Perhaps the street-plan of the city deviated somewhat from the strict rectilinear prototype in its apparent compliance to some of the natural features of the site, but Londinium was generally an authentic Roman design with no marked native characteristics.

Available evidence from building fragments indicates that interior design conformed to the Roman norm with coloured panels, friezes and naturalistic painting applied directly to the plaster walls. The Museum of London has recreated two typical Roman dining-room interiors from AD 100 and AD 300 using the appropriate utensils and food vessels excavated in London. The basic style appears to have remained essentially unchanged over two centuries. As for the architecture of Londinium, stone was used only in the more important buildings. Otherwise the houses were of London's clay and brick-earth. Thus already in Roman times the true character of London, the city of brick rather than stone, had revealed itself. It is indeed noticeable how little masonry has been discovered. Kentish ragstone was the most readily available material but it was hardly the stuff for the monumental architecture of antiquity. Nevertheless, it was ideally suited for that most enduring of all Roman constructions to be found in London, the great wall constructed around the city about the year AD 200.

It has been estimated that 13,000 barge loads of the stone – similar in size to that excavated at Blackfriars – would have been needed to transport the material from the quarries along the Medway near Maidstone to the site of the wall. This most important physical relic of the Roman presence can be seen at various locations in London. The most impressive remains are just south of Tower Hill Underground where the Roman portion of the wall still stands to a height of 4.4 metres with medieval stonework above. The characteristic construction technique was to build up a layer of rubble core faced with squared blocks of ragstone which would be levelled off with a course of flat red tiles to create an even and rigid foundation for the next layer. The bands of red created by the tiling courses provided a striking visual motif that was to re-emerge centuries later as a purely decorative idea in the alternating strips of variously coloured stone or brickwork so fashionable in the Byzantine-inspired buildings at the close of the Victorian age.

But it is the engineering achievement rather than the stylistic merit of the wall of Londinium which still commands respect. This was no hurried defensive measure organised by a beleaguered population.

Fragment of London's Roman wall at Tower Hill, revealing details of the fine construction.

This huge project required immense resources of finance and manpower which would have been hard to find, given the relative decline of the city at the time. Since parts of the area encompassed by the wall were no longer in occupation at the time of its construction it is difficult to believe that this was the initiative of the citizens themselves. The conclusion is almost inescapable that the order came from very high up; and the circumstantial historical evidence points to the Governor of Britannia, Clodius Albinus, who would have needed to fortify Londinium as a power base in view of his daring challenge to attain the imperial purple for himself. As it turned out, Albinus died in battle at Lugdunum in Gaul against the triumphant emperor Septimius Severus and Londinium acquired a mighty city wall as a result of this otherwise fruitless enterprise. It may also be seen at Cooper's Row and further remnants are dotted about the City, preserved in such unlikely locations as an underground car park and the yard of the General Post Office. A cross-section of the wall has been recorded in an imaginative modern mosaic in a pedestrian subway which runs beneath Houndsditch.

The redoubtable Septimius Severus continued his military campaigns and passed through Londinium in AD 208 on his way north to tame wild Caledonia. His Syrian wife and family would have stayed behind in Londinium and it is possible that the presence of this lady, Julia Domna, might have prompted some of the major architectural works such as the monumental arch and the screen of the gods, of which frag-

The relocated Temple of Mithras at its new home in Queen Victoria Street.

ments have been discovered. Certainly third-century Londinium had the trappings of a refined urban culture. Although Septimius Severus divided the province of Britannia and created a rival capital at York, Londinium must have remained a worthy city of the Roman Empire with its imposing public buildings such as the basilica and wealthy villas nestling within a majestic stone wall.

An exotic souvenir of this period was excavated in 1954 in Walbrook. A modest structure, it was identified as the Temple of Mithras which housed the cult of this deity, originating from the lands beyond Mesopotamia. Mithraism, with its emphasis on pure, honest and courageous conduct, had many adherents in the army, civil service and the trading community. Several items of statuary, including a head of Mithras himself, were recovered and are now in the care of the Museum of London. However, it was not possible to preserve the building *in situ* and a massive public outcry assured its reconstruction at a nearby site in Queen Victoria Street, where it now lies rather incongruously between the heavy traffic and a towering office block. Archaeologists are generally dismissive of the value of this reconstituted Mithraeum but it is at least a tangible piece of Roman Londinium and an indicator of one of the cults in favour in third-century Britannia.

By the end of the third century there were definitely some threatening storm clouds on the horizon. The city had considered it expedient to defend its exposed underbelly along the Thames, even at the expense of some ambitious quayside facilities, which were now rendered useless by the riverside wall. Clearly, Londinium was now more apprehensive of an attack than in the past, as is evidenced by the more hasty construction. That the danger loomed in the east can be seen in the fact that it was that sector of the city wall to be reinforced with circular towers towards the middle of the fourth century. These bastions were filled in with items of masonry taken from the cemeteries as well as from some of the grand public monuments, such as the arch. Defence now took clear precedence over pomp and prestige. The base of one of these solid bastions can be seen at Emperor House in Vine Street.

Although Theodosius managed to restore order after the massed attacks on Britannia around AD 367 by Picts, Scots and Teutons, the confidence of Londinium must have been badly shaken by the distant rumblings. A further sign of the mounting crisis was the strengthening of the riverside wall at the eastern end around AD 400. The alignment of this structure has given rise to some speculation that this was perhaps the beginning of a citadel, a precursor of the Norman and medieval fortifications of the Tower of London, where part of the base of the riverside wall has been exposed to view. In AD 410 the citizens of Londinium were informed that they would have to be responsible henceforth for their own defence, and by the middle of the fifth century the erstwhile capital of Britannia was to disappear from the historical records for about 150 years. Londinium was no more.

Although the visible remains are meagre fare by comparison with certain other Roman cities in Europe, the picture of Londinium can be added to by the collections of artefacts on display in the Museum of London and the British Museum, such as the small personal items of daily use, from footwear, cooking pots, glasswear and jewels to the intriguing lower half of a leather bikini, presumed to have been worn by a dancing girl or acrobat. But so much of Londinium still lies underground or has been totally destroyed; the theatre, temples and sports arena are yet to be discovered and there is no trace of a Christian church, although the city had a bishop as early as AD 314. Thus vital areas of Roman Londinium remain elusive and without substance, truly more a city of the mind than a living presence.

In Search of Saxon Lundenwic

If Roman Londinium leaves much to the imagination then Saxon Lundenwic must be described as downright elusive; for the historical and archaeological record from AD 450 to about 600 is remarkably blank, and thereafter until 1066 still very patchy. The immediate aftermath of Londinium is still enshrouded in mystery. There is the enigmatic brooch of Saxon design, dropped in the ruins of an abandoned Roman dwelling around the middle of the fifth century in what is now Lower Thames Street, which has been interpreted as a sign of the passage of a group of Saxon scavengers picking their way through the ruins of a deserted city. But at the same time we are informed by the *Anglo-Saxon Chronicle* that the defeated Britons took refuge in the walled city of Londinium after a battle at Crecganford (Crayford?) in AD 457.

The debate about the state of Londinium in the post-Roman era has been variously pursued. Some have argued for a continuing occupation and attribute the lack of archaeological evidence to the nature of Anglo-Saxon buildings which, being of wood, leave only faint traces in the soil, easily obliterated by the work of subsequent ages. Some point to the accumulated layer of 'dark earth' overlying Roman occupation in many places and propose that the city was largely avoided by the Saxons. Others have postulated a 'sub-Roman slum' in which the inhabitants squatted amidst the ruins of the sophisticated urban apparatus which they could no longer maintain. Recent researches, now confirmed by excavations in the Covent Garden area, have helped cast light on this dark chapter of London's history. It now appears that the Saxon successor settlement to Londinium was not within the old Roman walls but a mile or so to the west, along the Strand where the incline of the foreshore would have been convenient for beaching vessels. Lundenwic of the fifth to seventh centuries was probably a straggling riverside community whose centrepoint corresponded to what is today called Aldwych. Indeed, the very name of Aldwych, meaning 'old town' in the language of the Saxons, has also been interpreted as further proof of the Saxon occupation on this spot. It might well have acquired the description of 'old town' in the late ninth century when the walled precinct of Londinium became once more the focus of London's development.

Whatever the precise circumstances, the idea of a largely abandoned Londinium with a primitive riverside settlement nearby founded by the Saxons coincides neatly with what we know of these Teutonic invaders. They were farmers and pastoralists as well as warriors, preferring small rural clusters of housing to anything remotely urban. Indeed, the early Saxons in Britain can be seen almost exclusively as countryside folk, the founders of most English villages. The names of many London suburbs and of entire boroughs go back to the Saxon proto-villages established in the region which have been swallowed up by the rampant growth of London since the nineteenth century. We can therefore imagine a liberal sprinkling of villages around London in early Saxon times with the most important settlement along the Strand by the Thames, well placed to serve the trade with Europe. This would have been the London described by Bede in around AD 731 as 'a mart of many people coming by land and sea' and not the area within the walls which was still largely derelict.

Further evidence of the essentially rural nature of the Saxon presence in the London region may be adduced from the 'Saxon farm' excavated in Whitehall and in the

Profile of Saxon barrows still clearly visible in Greenwich Park.

recorded distribution of Saxon burials, mostly far away from the old city centre. The outlines of Saxon barrows are still visible at Farthing Down in Croydon and in Greenwich Park to the west of the Observatory; and a Saxon burial has been preserved in the Bromley Museum in Orpington. At Grim's Dyke in Pinner lies an enigmatic earthwork, considered to be no later than the sixth century, which has been interpreted as a territorial marker dividing the lands of the Saxon farmers from those of another people, presumably Britons, who occupied the uplands. Grim's Dyke can still be traced for several miles, but its major part runs through a private golf-course where it shows its profile most clearly against the close-cropped sward of the greens and fairways.

The first historical fact to be recorded after the long post-Roman silence around Londinium is the founding of St Paul's

Cathedral by Mellitus in AD 604. This can be seen as a recognition of the renewed importance of the walled city but it is by no means certain that this was so, for the archbishopric was established at Canterbury by Augustine, which reflected the power and influence of the Kingdom of Kent. Presumably London prospered under the kings of Mercia who controlled the city until about AD 800 when it passed to Wessex; but the real revival of the ancient area of Londinium was brought about by a dramatic shift in the political circumstances of the ninth century. Following the Danish invasions the Anglo-Saxons united under Alfred and brought the expansion of the Danelaw to a halt. The new frontier of Wessex included London, but only just, for the Danish realm extended right up to the River Lea. For the first time in its history London found itself on the front line. It had been the target of Danish raids in 839, 851 and 872 and had been occupied for fourteen years by the Danes before Alfred regained the city in 886 for the Anglo-Saxons. Not surprisingly, the defensive possibilities afforded by the old Roman walls persuaded Alfred to reoccupy the city and to initiate the redevelopment of London on its previous Roman site. This momentous event of 1100 years ago marks a most decisive turning point in the history of London.

Sadly, there is not one structure remaining in London, even as an outline, as a testimonial to the work of Alfred. He is credited with the rebuilding of the city walls and tradition associates him with the early patching of the Roman wall at Cooper's Row, but this is mere conjecture. It is possible that the recently excavated stakes at New Fresh Wharf may indicate a repair of the Roman riverfront in Alfred's time. Of greater and more lasting significance were the land grants made by Alfred for the development of mercantile areas along the river which combined port facilities with market privileges in the neighbourhood. It is strange to think of Alfred as a pioneer among the commercial developers of London but the signs of his enterprise have been discovered at Queenhithe and at Billingsgate. These trading zones, as we would describe them today, helped lay the foundations for London's economic resurgence in the tenth and eleventh centuries. They have also left their imprint in a new grid arrangement of narrower streets which supplanted their Roman predecessors. Excavations have shown that it was common Saxon practice to build houses directly over the metalled streets of old Londinium so that the basic rectilinear layout imposed by the Romans was gradually obliterated in the course of time. Alfred also had a new intramural road constructed which followed the length of the city wall, and this has best survived in the modern roads between Moorgate, Bishopsgate and Aldgate. Alfred's waterfront development at Queenhithe may still be detected in the indentation of the riverbank at this point which is a noticeable feature.

Although London became the most important, and certainly the wealthiest city in England, Winchester remained the official capital of Wessex; and it was here that most coronations were enacted. However, several Saxon kings were crowned in Kingston in the course of the tenth century; and there is still a rare and remarkable relic of those days in the sacred stone which has been preserved for about a thousand years. It is now kept in a fancy cage of Victorian date placed to the east of Kingston's medieval Clattern Bridge. The royal presence in London itself is presumed to have been lodged in a palace situated within the confines of the old Roman fort at Cripplegate until this was abandoned by Edward the Confessor in favour of a new kingly residence at Westminster, but once again archaeology has drawn a blank in attempts to identify such a building.

In fact there is very little of definite Saxon origin in the form of stone structures. It is assumed that early Saxon churches were of

The Saxon crucifixion in St Dunstan's, Stepney.

The Saxon arch of All Hallows by the Tower makes use of Roman bricks.

wood and there is even documentary evidence that this was so in the case of the first church of St Andrew's, Holborn, as mentioned in a charter of 959. For an example of the type it is not necessary to go far from London: the church of St Andrew at Greensted near High Ongar in Essex possesses a nave of split oak trunks dating back to the middle of the ninth century. But there was a gradual transition to stone which often involved the recycling of Roman material, notably the red tiles familiar to us from the surviving portions of the city wall. The most famous example of re-used Roman material in London is the Saxon arch of the church of All Hallows by the Tower. This sole remaining relic of a Saxon structure above ground level in London itself would point to the existence of a sizeable if simple building. The eleventh-century crypt of St Mary-le-Bow also contains Roman fragments, as do other churches further away from the centre of London, such as the old parish church of Kingsbury and St Paulinus at St Paul's Cray. There is evidence of Saxon work at All Saints in Kingston and at All Saints in Orpington which has a Saxon sundial, upside down, with some inscribed runes still legible. St Dunstan in Stepney houses a fine late Saxon carved crucifixion. Saxon foundations have been preserved in the crypt of St Bride's in Fleet Street. Other known Saxon churches, such as St Alban Wood Street, of which only the later Wren tower still stands, serve to remind us how little of Saxon Lundenwic has survived. There is no record even of the first St Paul's Cathedral, destroyed by fire in 1087.

It is not easy from the fragmentary evidence available to picture the exact course of London's steady progress from post-Roman dereliction to pre-Conquest prosperity. But we know that London's growth was often interrupted, even after Alfred's day, by further Viking attacks, notably in 982 and 994. In an unlikely alliance King Olaf of Norway helped Ethelred expel the Danes for a short while in 1014, but the Danish King Cnut reigned in London from 1016 to 1035. There are reminders of this tumultuous period with several churches dedicated to St Olaf as well as St Clement Danes in the Strand. The Museum of London has a chilling display of Viking battle-axes and spears found in the Thames near London Bridge and a carved stone from a tomb in St Paul's which may have been that of one of Cnut's Danish courtiers. Yet throughout the often violent events of the tenth and eleventh centuries London increased in economic stature due to its strategic location between the wool-producing pastures of England and the manufacturing towns of the Low Countries. With wealth came self-confidence and a strong tradition of local democracy characterised by such institutions as the 'folkmoot' and the 'husting', the one Saxon and the other Scandinavian in origin.

As for the physical appearance of Saxon London, we know something of the house styles, such as the sunken-floored hut excavated in Milk Street and a larger hall near St Martin's-le-Grand. These were wooden structures, presumably with thatched roofs; it would appear that stone was not used for domestic buildings as it was for churches. For all its burgeoning commerce Saxon London must have been a primitive city compared to its Roman predecessor. Population statistics estimate a figure of 10,000 to 12,000 inhabitants just prior to the Conquest, which is about a third of the 35,000 citizens living in London at the peak of the Roman occupation. Nevertheless, it was during the Saxon period that the basic structuring of London into administrative wards was laid down and the boundaries of most of its parishes drawn out. The medieval city existed on the eve of the Norman Conquest, albeit in embryonic form. The centralised bureaucracy and rectilinear street pattern of the Romans had been erased and the almost organic cluster of small neighbourhood units and scattered villages, which are a feature of London to this day, had been indelibly imprinted on the landscape. Saxon Lundenwic is thus the direct genetic ancestor of today's city, rather than Roman Londinium. The Saxons may not be represented by much in the way of artefacts and monuments but the essential structure of their town is still with us; and indeed it was Edward the Confessor, last of the Saxon kings, who, by moving the royal palace from the City to Westminster, helped to create the two poles of monarchy in the west and business in the east which has been the most enduring aspect of London's subsequent development for almost a thousand years. It may not be possible to see Saxon Lundenwic but it can be felt as an inherited urban pattern.

The Impact of the Normans

The Norman Conquest of 1066 was probably the most decisive event in British history, for the Normans, in contrast to the Romans, were here to stay; their language, culture, laws, institutions as well as their genes were to be grafted on to the Saxon and Celtic stock. While most Norman features have been so mixed and mingled endlessly with native elements over the centuries as to become almost indistinguishable, examples of their imposing architecture have survived to convey at least a partial impression of the great impact of Norman civilisation at the time. However, the idea of a sudden and complete Normanisation occurring in the aftermath of 1066 which effectively closed the Saxon chapter is misleading, especially so in London, which witnessed the advent of Norman culture well in advance of the Conquest and continued to cling to the inherited Saxon fabric long after it.

London, appropriately so for an embryonic capital city, found itself placed in the architectural avant-garde by the style of Edward the Confessor's new Benedictine Abbey of St Peter, constructed between 1050 and 1065 on Thorney Island. Later to achieve fame as the Abbey of Westminster, this magnificent stone edifice on a gravel eyot between two branches of the Tyburn as it entered the Thames was from the same design mould as the great Abbey of Jumièges in Normandy. Sadly, an idea of its external appearance can be gained only from the evidence of contemporary artists, for Edward's abbey church was progressively demolished from about 1245 to make way for the present building. Some fragments of the old Westminster survive, notably in the Chapel of the Pyx and adjacent museum which once served as the undercroft of the east range of monastic buildings, most probably the monks' Common Room; and the present library has been identified as the former dormitory of the Benedictines. A tantalisingly fine fragment of the original building fabric, a capital with a splendid carving of the Judgement of Solomon, has been preserved; and this serves as a small but potent reminder of the artistic quality of the Anglo-Norman abbey. Close by, Edward ordered a new palace to be constructed but this was rebuilt as early as 1097–9 by William Rufus who created a mighty hall measuring 240 feet by 67½ feet, these dimensions being exactly those of the Westminster Hall of today. However, neither monarch would recognise it now, for the Middle Ages saw it transformed internally from an aisled hall resting on a forest of pillars to a vast open space under a revolutionary new design of roof whose weight was carried by the walls themselves. The work of William Rufus is still apparent in the lower part of the masonry, although the building as a whole must be assigned to the achievements of a later age. It is interesting to note that William Rufus expressed himself dissatisfied despite the great length of the hall. He is alleged to have remarked that it was 'too big for a chamber and not big enough for a hall'. Is it possible to read into this peevish comment the burning ambition of the Normans to impress on the locals their power and permanence through the sheer weight and size of their architecture?

Such ambitions were most dramatically realised in the White Tower, the most enduring and obvious symbol of the Norman occupying power in London. It is recorded that the purpose of this fortress was 'against the restlessness of the large and fierce populace'. Commenced around 1078 some twelve years after the Conquest, the White Tower conveyed the unmistakable message of the dominance of Norman

The White Tower, the original Tower of London, an enduring symbol of Norman power.

civilisation. Much of the stone was imported from Caen in Normandy to give dignity as well as strength to the great edifice, the like of which had not been seen before in London. This was no mere military fortification but a splendid palace-castle in the best Norman tradition which can be traced back to Rouen in the tenth century. Rising ninety feet from the ground to the top of the battlements, the castle of the Conqueror soon became known as the Tower of London to the suitably impressed populace. This name was later transferred to the entire, medieval complex of fortifications, and the original castle or keep has since been known simply as the White Tower because it was kept whitewashed to intensify the overwhelming effect. The mighty Tower must have utterly dominated the lowly buildings of late-Saxon London, serving both as a warning and as an inspiration.

The White Tower has come through nine centuries remarkably unscathed, but its external appearance was modified in the early eighteenth century with the conversion of the narrow Norman windows into the more generous and classical ones of today. The authentic character of the original can best be sampled within the walls, which contain one of the most perfect examples of early Norman church architecture. The Chapel of St John is an austere composition of heavy round arches, groin-vaults in the aisles and a barrel-vault over the nave resting on solid, robust, circular pillars with simple cushion capitals of spartan adornment. This is an essay in the pure style of the rounded, perfectly semicircular arch, the basic structural element of the style known as Romanesque or Norman. Nowhere in London does the quintessence of early Norman building achieve such uncompromised expression. The huge rounded forms convey a reassuring sense of strength, repose and stability; it is as if the circular arch is closer to the natural shape of things than the pointed arch, the product of Man's increasing ingenuity. However, the structural limitations of the rounded arch are all too apparent. The sheer weight of the stone and the unbending logic of the equation that the height of the arch was dependent on the breadth of its span meant that if buildings were to grow higher without becoming even more bulky then technology would have to change. And that is precisely what happened in the course of the twelfth century.

It was the transition from the rounded arch to the pointed arch, from Norman or Romanesque to Gothic, which liberated architecture from the seemingly absolute dictates of gravity. Henceforth, the building mass was no longer in repose block upon block but the weight was carried on ribs of stone which concentrated the downward force at precise points. The outward thrust of one pointed arch was counterbalanced by that of its neighbour so that only where the arch came to rest on an external wall was any buttressing needed. The new structure was thus held in place by the precisely calculated distribution of the thrust and counterthrust through a seemingly delicate web of stone ribs joined together in a series of pointed arches. The new Gothic style swept across Europe from the twelfth century on, and its actual appearance in London may still be witnessed in two remarkable buildings.

In the crypt of St John's Clerkenwell, the Church of the Knights of St John of Jerusalem founded by the Order of the Hospitallers, ribbed vaulting was employed in 1140, but the shape of the arches had not yet evolved from the Romanesque. But these early examples of ribbed vaulting in the rounded arch are contained within a later rebuilding of the crypt in about 1185 when the pointed arch was introduced. The transition is perhaps not such a spectacular sight to behold but the crypt of St John's Clerkenwell is one of those important turning points in the history of architecture, for it shows a process in the making. Equally fascinating is the Temple Church of 1185 which reveals behind a typically Norman round-arched doorway a full-blown Gothic interior arranged as a circular nave. It has been emphasised that there is nothing transitional in the pointed arches themselves which are fully evolved but that the switch from the Romanesque to Gothic is evident in the juxtaposition of obviously Norman elements such as the blind arcading of intersecting round arches of which the triforium is composed. At the Temple Church the architects had availed themselves of the revolutionary new technology of the pointed arch but had not yet parted company with the familiar and trusted decorative motifs of the old style.

Pointed arches – possibly London's earliest – may also be detected in parts of the crossing of that gem of a Norman church belonging to the Priory of St Bartholomew in Smithfield, constructed between 1123 and 1145. The remains are but a part, namely the choir of the original edifice, but

St John's Chapel, a jewel of Norman architecture within the White Tower.

The Temple Church shows an early use of the pointed arch in London.

the scale of the building is breathtaking nonetheless. There is a crescendo of rounded forms rising from the huge circular pillars supporting recessed arches with a fine billet moulding which rest on well-defined cushion capitals. Above that a series of equally large arches shelter a space divided into four bays each with a semicircular arch resting on round pillars. This composition of spherical shapes, entirely devoid of artifice, is taken to a triumphant conclusion in the rounded apse where an ambulatory forms a perfect continuation of the groin-vaulted aisles. As one makes the tour, a variety of enticing vistas between the pillars is successively revealed. St Bartholomew-the-Great, as the church is now called, presents a grand display of architectural strength contained in simple but adequate harmony, a telling contrast to the more graceful, almost ethereal effect of Gothic's soaring vaults or the rational

St Bartholomew-the-Great. Only the choir remains of London's finest Norman church.

The characteristic rounded apse of the Norman parish church is preserved at St Mary Magdalene, East Ham.

church interiors typical of the Age of Enlightenment.

Notable examples of Norman architecture on a more modest scale are to be found in other churches, such as the late eleventh-century crypt of St Mary-le-Bow, as well as in a prolific scattering of parish churches in the villages which have since been engulfed by the rampant metropolis of Greater London. Norman works occur at some unlikely locations: within a stone's throw of Heathrow airport and the M4 motorway are the essentially Norman churches of St Mary's Harmondsworth, St Peter & St Paul Harlington with good features still much in evidence and St Mary's at Bedfont Green which has retained its Norman doorway within a much later building. But one has to cross to the other side of London to find London's finest surviving Norman parish church. St Mary Magdalene in East Ham has not been extended beyond the original simple structure of nave, chancel and sanctuary, except for the sixteenth-century tower at the west end and a small porch, so that the impression is overwhelmingly Norman. The interior has been modified by the enlargement of some of the windows but the timbers of the roof are partly the originals of 1130, held together by the wooden pegs placed there by the Norman carpenters. A fragment of blind arcading with an evidently freehand version of the familiar zig-zag decoration evokes the rough but effective handiwork of less skilled stonemasons. The building materials came from a variety of sources: Kentish ragstone, flints and chalk from Purley, pudding stone from Norfolk, Roman tiles and finer stone from Caen were gathered together and held in place by good Norman mortar. An anchorite's cell within the thickness of the walls and the moulding of the west doorway are further delightful features

The blind arcading is a notable feature of the interior of St Mary Magdalene.

of this small Norman church in East Ham.

Another fascinating relic of the Norman period in London is the original Clerk's Well to which Clerkenwell owes its name. One of the three wells mentioned by Fitz Stephen, the Clerk's Well fell into disuse as recently as the middle of the last century, was filled with builder's rubbish, built over and then forgotten. It re-emerged to the light of day during reconstruction work at 14-16 Farringdon Lane in 1924 where it may still be inspected, courtesy of the London Borough of Islington. The visible brickwork is sixteenth century and later but the well itself was in use in Norman times and probably earlier. The Clerk's Well bears witness to a chain of human occupation on the site going back at least a thousand years.

However, churches have left the strongest imprint of Norman London. The contemporary description of London composed by William Fitz Stephen in 1180 noted that 'there are both in London and the Suburbs 13 greater Conventual churches and 126 lesser Parochial'. There had clearly been a tremendous burst of building activity over at least two centuries extending back to before the Conquest but reaching its peak in the eleventh and twelfth centuries. Among the 'greater Conventual churches' of Fitz Stephen's account there remain substantial parts of the Church of the Knights Templar, the Priory of St John of

The Clerk's Well has a documented history of 900 years.

St Pancras Old Church, one of the earliest sites of Christian worship in London, was re-Normanised in the nineteenth century.

Jerusalem and the Priory of St Bartholomew mentioned above, and to the list one might add the scant remains of St Mary Overie, now incorporated within Southwark Cathedral, and the fragments of the Clerkenwell Nunnery. At the site of Bermondsey Abbey, a Cluniac foundation of 1089, recent excavations have unearthed some distinctly Norman items of carved masonry and a gilded bronze figure from an early thirteenth-century crucifix. Other great religious foundations which Fitz Stephen would have seen but which are now entirely lost to view include St Mary Spital which gave its name to Spitalfields and the vast Augustinian Holy Trinity Priory at Aldgate. Others were to follow in the course of the Middle Ages but these early ones in Aldgate, Spitalfields, Clerkenwell, Smithfield and Temple Bar north of the river and

Lesnes Abbey, a twelfth-century Augustinian foundation, provides the clearest groundplan of a monastic ruin in London.

in Bermondsey to the south were all deliberately placed according to the custom on the outskirts of the urban area and thus indicate the extent of London's growth at the time. How far Fitz Stephen's concept of the suburbs stretched is difficult to say, but probably not as far as Merton, where the twelfth-century doorway of the Priory has been re-erected in the nearby churchyard of St Mary's, or to Lesnes Abbey near Thamesmead, which was founded in 1178 by the Lord of the Manor of Erith.

The remains of Lesnes Abbey represent London's most intelligible outline of a monastic settlement in Norman times. Although the ruins are modest in height, they are unencumbered by any subsequent development and the layout of the conventual buildings is clearly revealed in the shortly cropped grass. In places more substantial parts of the masonry are still intact, such as the arched doorway to the monks' dormitory and the stone benches or seating ledge which form an integral part of the rectangular chapter house. The commanding view down the slope of the hill towards the Thames shows that the monks did not despise a healthy location and a fair prospect. The ruins of Lesnes Abbey, well maintained and undefiled, provide the most evocative spot to conjure up an image of the monastic movement in its early years.

As for the city of London as a whole in Norman times, one has to imagine a slowly changing scenario with only the wealthier citizens starting to acquire houses of stone in lieu of the traditional wooden dwellings inherited from the Saxons. Although none has survived, it is most likely that London's stone houses were broadly the same as the known examples in Lincoln and Norwich, which have attracted the name of 'Jew's House', probably because Jewish financiers did particularly well during the Normanisation of England. Fitz Stephen notes the 'lordly habitations' of bishops, abbots and magnates and it may be assumed that most were still within the confines of the city inside the walls, although the attractions of the Strand for noble residences may already have been discovered since Fitz Stephen mentions that the royal palace at Westminster is joined to London 'by a populous suburb'. This development would have centred on the Aldwych, thereby reviving the fortunes of the Early and Middle Saxon settlement of Lundenwic. It is thought that any surviving stone undercrofts of Norman buildings would have been finally destroyed in the course of the nineteenth century when the foundations of Victorian developments in the City were dug. One such was identified as belonging to the residence of the Prior of Lewes in Southwark. It was recorded before its demolition but a further example has survived, thanks to its transfer to a site in Mark Lane by the Clothworkers' Company.

It is difficult to come to an accurate assessment of the impact of the Normans on London. Available evidence shows that the city had already developed a forceful personality by late Saxon times and that the Norman penetration of London institutions was minimal during the first century after the Conquest. Neither did the Normans exercise a shaping hand in the structural development of London's street plan which followed its own pre-established course. But the construction of the Tower and old St Paul's, which lasted until the Great Fire of 1666, must have dominated the skyline of the city. The major contribution came, however, with the implantation of the French monastic orders in the eleventh and twelfth centuries. Their mighty buildings set within vast precincts introduced the latest in architectural styles, such as the round naves of the Temple Church and of St John's Clerkenwell based on the Church of the Holy Sepulchre in Jerusalem. These ordered communities living in sophisticated isolation were certainly in stark contrast to the early medieval congestion wherein dwelled the average order of Londoners. The Normans may thus be credited with the introduction of a monumental architecture of stone and the development of native skills in masonry and carpentry. Equally important was the associated notion of a more refined urban culture. Fitz Stephen had made exalted claims for London in 1180: 'Among the noble cities of the world that are celebrated by Fame, the City of London, seat of the Monarchy of England, is one that spreads its fame wider, sends its wealth and wares further, and lifts its head higher than all others.' But London at the end of the twelfth century was poised for more glorious achievements which would make it truly one of the great centres of civilisation in the Middle Ages. The Normans had bequeathed the city some magnificent buildings but London was probably not yet in the vanguard of urbanism in Europe.

Monuments of the Middle Ages

By the end of the twelfth century London was physically as well as spiritually impregnated by the many manifestations of the Church. The walled city was almost encompassed by a monastic girdle formed by a series of religious houses set within their own precincts. These majestic buildings in self-contained enclaves were outposts of a superior European culture which set new standards of architecture and planning. The further extension of ecclesiastical foundations was to be the leitmotif of development in the Middle Ages, with the establishment of new monastic houses continuing unabated until the end of the fourteenth century; and the religious spirit found a further outlet for its energies in the fifteenth century with the rebuilding of many parish churches. Both materially and culturally the Church was in the forefront of progress; and if the architectural history books appear to be obsessed with ecclesiastical monuments in their chapters on the Middle Ages, this is not just because more examples of religious than secular character have survived but also because the Church, with its vast wealth and possessions, was the major patron of architecture; and its constant search for more exalted structures aimed at bridging symbolically the gulf between God and Man created the climate for the most revolutionary developments in the design and technology of building. It was only natural that London, the emerging political as well as undisputed commercial capital of the kingdom, should acquire some of the finest realisations of the new styles. Church architecture was by no means a matter of marginal interest at the time; it was the central issue and its lessons and example were applied often unmodified in buildings of lesser stature in the secular domain.

The transition from the rounded Norman arch to the pointed version of the Gothic school had already made its impact in London in the second half of the twelfth century. The opening of the thirteenth century was to witness the first pure flowering of the style known as Early English. Here the newly discovered freedom of the mason-architects found simple but eloquent expression in the chaste structures of the unadorned shafts and vaults. The nakedness of the structural elements must have been a source of great satisfaction to the builders, a pleasure that architects were soon to forego and not rediscover until the advent of iron and glass constructions such as the Crystal Palace in the nineteenth century. But in the Middle Ages it was not as a result of a deliberate act of will that form followed function but as a natural artistic impulse. Such a happy economy of means coincided with the austere idealism of the reformed monastic orders, notably the Cistercians; but their London foundations, of which the Abbey of St Mary Graces was the foremost, have all fallen victim to the depredations of time. It is to an Augustinian house, St Mary Overie (now Southwark Cathedral), to which we must turn for one of the finest specimens in London of the Early English style.

The choir and retrochoir grafted on to the Norman church fabric between 1215 and 1235 is a work of startling simplicity. Here all the technical skill of the new style is revealed with pride and without any dissimulation. There is an obvious delight in the apparent defiance of gravity with the stone roof appearing to float as effortlessly as the leaves and branches of a mighty forest. One has only to compare the slender supporting columns to the heavy cylinders of Norman design to realise the overwhelming joy at the novel technical mastery it must have inspired in its creators. A

The retrochoir of Southwark Cathedral forms a canopy of Early English pointed arches.

similar freshness of touch is evident in the choir added to the round Temple Church in about 1240. Here the array of pointed arches on elegant shafts with no architectural crescendo, the aisles being of the same height as the nave, create a modest space but one with an impressive degree of unity. The narrow lancet windows and the square east end, in contrast to the French preference for the rounded or polygonal apse, are the hallmarks of Early English.

Westminster Abbey, the greatest of London's medieval monuments, shows important developments and variations which mark its departure from the relatively unadorned and straightforward architecture of the Early English type. It is a highly complex building, essentially constructed over a period of 300 years, that is, without taking into account the controversial

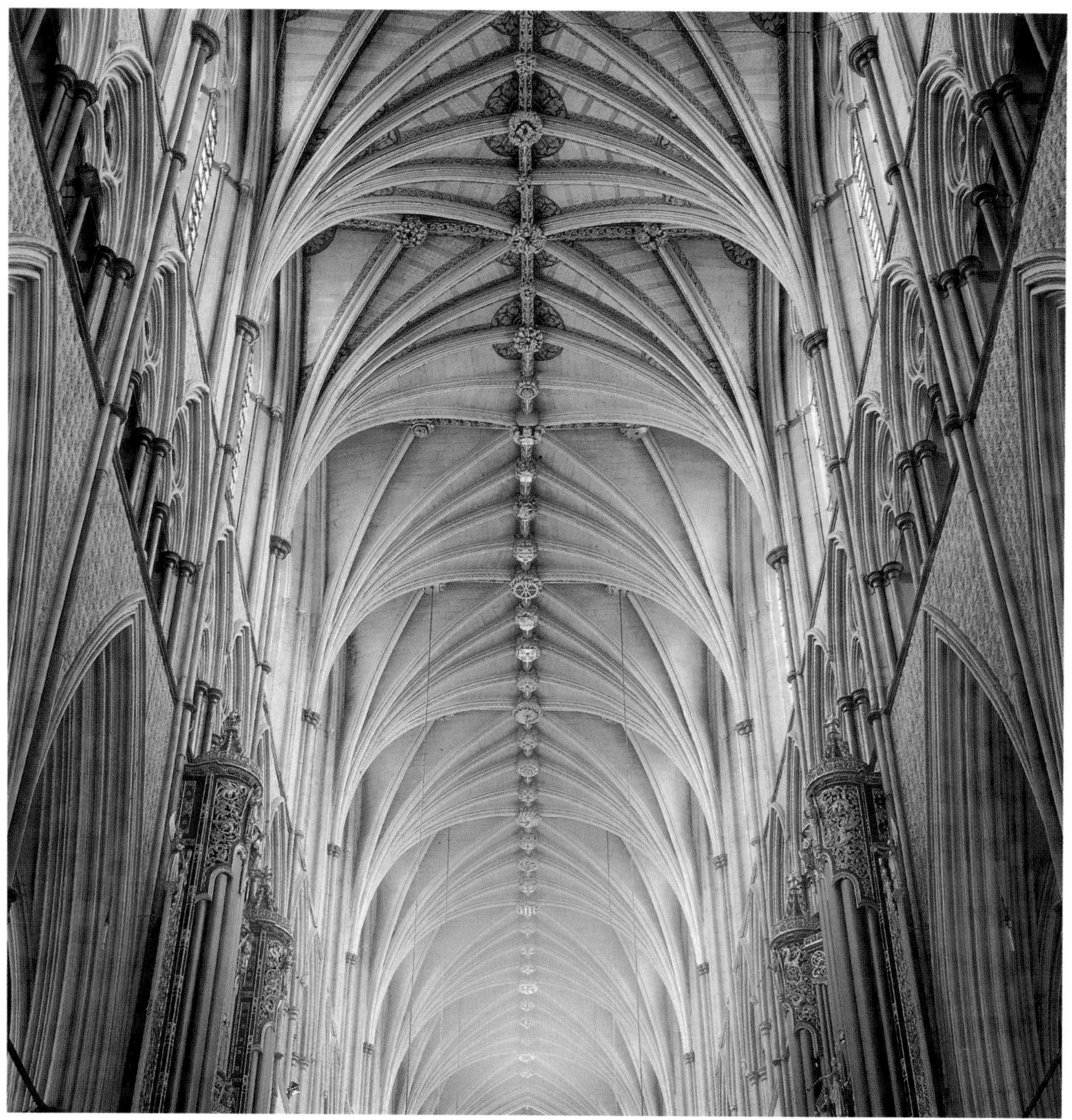

The nave of Westminster Abbey demonstrates the soaring quality usually associated with French Gothic.

'restorations' of Hawksmoor and Scott. The present edifice, which gradually supplanted the Norman church of Edward the Confessor, was begun in 1245 by that most prolific of royal builders, Henry III (1216-72). The first part of the work to be accomplished was the east end which followed the French tradition of the polygonal apse with ambulatory and radiating chapels. Henry III's Lady Chapel of 1220, built prior to the general reconstruction, was demolished in the sixteenth century to make way for the spectacular Henry VII Chapel which belongs decidedly to the Tudor period. By 1255 the chancel, transepts and the first bay of the nave had been built. The work has noticeable French affinities in the decoration and in the markedly narrow proportions of the edifice in relation to its great height. This graceful loftiness of

Westminster Abbey is also the major feature of the rest of the nave which was for the most part completed from 1375 onwards under the direction of Henry Yevele. The first architect of renown to have substantially shaped the face of London, he assiduously followed the proportions laid down over 130 years previously. This was a remarkable phenomenon, given the tendency throughout the Middle Ages for new variations of Gothic to be added to existing buildings with a blithe disregard for overall effect. Yevele might thus be acclaimed as the first architect in London to respect the scale and harmony of the inherited fabric and to design in sympathy with it. Nonetheless, there are differences in treatment of a specifically English character so that the nave qualifies as a sort of stylistic hybrid.

There is also evidence of two national styles at work in the Chapter House, completed in 1255. Although extensively

The floortiles of Westminster Abbey's Chapter House convey an idea of medieval design.

restored by Scott in the nineteenth century, this wondrous structure might still be hailed as the *tour de force* of the Early English skill at suspending vaults with daring and a dose of showmanship. A single central shaft supports no less than eight bays which radiate grace and energy. Six of these are filled with high broad windows which flood the space with light. Yet there is not a hint of artifice in this dramatic arrangement but a grand simplicity deriving from the logic of the structure. In terms of architectural evolution the size and decoration of the windows prefigure the subsequent shape of Gothic design. Westminster Abbey was revolutionary in its day and a highly influential trend-setter.

The question of French stylistic input at Westminster Abbey is unresolved. The cathedral at Amiens and the Sainte Chapelle in Paris have been identified as the antecedents of the Chapter House windows, for example, yet the octagonal shape of the building is resoundingly English; and while the flying buttresses are thought to be an inspiration from France there are sufficient stylistic details of acknowledged English origin to establish the fact that the Abbey was no mere copy. Nevertheless Westminster Abbey remains the most French of English cathedrals and this may well be due to the cultural orientation of its royal sponsors. It is interesting to note that the 'new work' on the old cathedral of St Paul's was commenced in the 1250s at exactly the time when Henry III's work was being completed at Westminster. By contrast the new east end of St Paul's was in the square, resolutely English mould. Can one detect here a direct challenge of the City of London to the 'foreign' church erected by the king? Certainly the great spire of old St Paul's, rising to over 450 feet, must be seen as an expression of London's self-confidence *vis-à-vis* the Crown, the two poles of the future London standing perhaps both culturally as well as geographically apart.

A less controversial aspect of Westminster Abbey lies in London's greatest collection of medieval floortiles still *in situ* in the Chapter House. These magnificent glazed examples of the tilemaker's art use the technique of clay inlay to create decorative designs of a buffish yellow against a reddish-brown background. Thanks to the royal patronage of Henry III a flourishing tile industry was launched and similar products have been excavated at several thirteenth-century sites in London, both in palaces and monastic settlements. The tiles are outstanding both for their figurative and abstract designs as well as for their obvious bearing on the early form of such popular heraldic devices as the lion and the fleur de lys. Since similar pavements were also used in noble abodes, they help convey a material impression of the furnishings of domestic residences of the finer sort during the Middle Ages.

Sculpture, that other great artistic legacy of the Church in the Middle Ages, presents only fragmentary evidence in London of its achievements. Centuries of neglect, combined with the notorious acts of national vandalism perpetrated under the sponsorship of such political opposites as Henry VIII and Oliver Cromwell, have reduced what must have been a stunningly rich array of statuary to a few isolated examples. Westminster Abbey, thanks to royal protection, has by far the most splendid and best-known collection of medieval sculpture in London. However, in the Chapter House are two fine figures of around 1250 which are often overlooked. These elongated carvings of the Virgin Mary and Archangel Gabriel enacting the Annunciation possess the ethereal, archaic beauty of the Early English period. One has to imagine many such works, albeit on a more modest scale, adorning London's churches at the time. They vividly demonstrate one of the features of medieval sculpture: the idealisation of the human figure. The same tendency can be seen in the funerary monuments, such as the effigies of the knights in the Temple Church. In Southwark Cathedral there is a notable thirteenth-century wooden effigy of a knight, somewhat over-restored, but still a good illustration of the idealised image of the noble deceased so popular at the time. Nearby is a stark reminder that this was but one extreme aspect of the medieval vision: a recumbent stone carving of a naked man whose body displays the crude physical torment of death with the ribs of the corpse already moulded hard against the skin and the head more of a skull than a human face. This naturalistic portrayal of the body's material decomposition, of which another gripping specimen can be found in the crypt of St John's Clerkenwell, is a recurrent theme in the art of the Middle Ages which presents the exact counterbalance to the sweet images of sanctity. Also in Southwark Cathedral are some impressive wooden bosses, originally from the roof, which form a gallery of grotesque faces, each no doubt

Partly restored effigy of a medieval knight in Southwark Cathedral.

containing specific references intelligible to the congregation of the day. That it was thought fit to have such leering grimaces hovering over the nave may be seen as another example of that curious juxtaposition of the divine and the profane which seems to have presented no conflict in the minds of our ancestors in the Middle Ages.

The general tendency of church architecture in the fourteenth century was away from the purity and simplicity of Early English to the more elaborate and artful forms of Decorated Gothic. London possesses few examples of this period and the best are the window of St Etheldreda, in Holborn (new glass), and the east range of the cloister at Westminster. At the same time an increasing number of rib vaults were employed largely for decorative effect, the intersections providing a convenient pretext for fanciful carved bosses. This can be seen in the nave of Westminster Abbey, as in the nearby Jewel Tower of about 1380 which was almost certainly the work of Henry Yevele. This demonstrates how techniques devised in the ecclesiastical context were readily applied in the secular domain.

Out of Decorated Gothic evolved the Perpendicular in the last quarter of the fourteenth century, which was to have a longer run, until the sixteenth century, thereby imparting a much more substantial imprint on the design of London's buildings. The Perpendicular style takes its name from the device of introducing a large number of vertical lines in both window and wall tracery which were extended in length so as to almost eliminate the curved arches altogether. The larger windows in fashion were divided into an increasing series of narrow perpendicular spaces. However, the accompanying feature of the style was the containing of arches within a square which made for lower structures and a greater stress on the horizontal. The Perpendicular was thus more on the human scale, a down-to-earth version of the loftier forms of earlier Gothic; and as such it was a convenient and practical variant which could be applied with ease to a multiplicity of more modest, even workaday structures. It became the style *par excellence* of the parish church, not only in London but indeed throughout the country. Such churches can be recognised by their generally low and squarish external aspect. Inside they are well lit, harmonious and roomy without overawing their parishioners. St Dunstan's Stepney, St Margaret's Westminster, St Olave's Hart Street, St Helen's Bishopsgate and St Peter ad Vincula all demonstrate this restrained and humanised late Gothic style.

Although the Church and its works loomed large in medieval London, there was no shortage of noble edifices of a secular character. Fewer have withstood the depredations of time than the religious buildings but it is still an eloquent architectural collection. Pride of place must go to the restructured Westminster Hall of 1394 to 1401, a joint effort of the mason Henry Yevele (as ubiquitous in the fourteenth century as Wren in the seventeenth) and the carpenter Hugh Herland. Its interior is still one of the great building achievements in London. The magnificent oak hammerbeam roof was as revolutionary to carpentry as the earlier pointed arch to masonry. The new construction technique allowed a span of 67 feet 6 inches which carried the 660 tons of the roof to the walls without any internal support. With a length of 240 feet there emerged a vast open space, a radical improvement on the lines of pillars which had previously divided Westminster Hall in the days of William Rufus. It still ranks as the finest as well as the earliest structure of its kind. It is ironic that it now serves no precise function, but that is perhaps all for the good. The emptiness of furniture and fittings simply enhances the immense feeling of spaciousness. The only distraction for the eye, apart from the carved angels of the hammerbeams themselves, is the series of statues of kings of late fourteenth-century style set up along two sides of the hall.

The institution of the Great Hall was not

The great roof of Westminster Hall by Hugh Herland is a masterpiece of the art of the Middle Ages.

reserved for kings as at Westminster but lay at the heart of noble and even lesser homes in the Middle Ages. Although the communal life once shared by the lords with their retinues gradually gave way to a more intimate lifestyle in private apartments, the hall remained as the focal point of the household, used on ceremonial occasions such as feasts and receptions and expressing symbolically the status of the owner.

The hall was also the ideal venue for the evolving institutions such as the guilds and the 'inns' of the students of law. Indeed, it is thanks to the legal profession that the hall of a medieval house just off Holborn has been preserved in the building known as Barnard's Inn which goes back to the late fourteenth century. Part of the roof is original, although this and most of the later panelling is currently obscured.

Ribbed vaulting of the porch of the Guildhall goes back to the fifteenth century.

Sadly, almost the entire original stock of halls of the various London guilds has been destroyed, notably in the Great Fire of 1666 and the Blitz of the Second World War. Only the hall of the Merchant Taylors' Company, largely rebuilt, and part of the crypt, are testimonials of original medieval architecture. More has survived of the Guildhall itself, although the present building is a distinct hybrid with its late eighteenth-century front, Victorian interior and post-war roof. Much of the masonry dates back, however, to the beginning of the fifteenth century and there is good detail in the old vaulting inside the porch. Here the stone bosses bear the coat of arms of Edward the Confessor, which has been interpreted as a sign that the previous Guildhall may trace back its roots to the reign of that monarch. One of the original windows has survived, complete with a stone bench built into the bay. The undercroft has come through the ages surprisingly intact and is a glorious example of the sort of vaulted crypt which would have formed the foundation of many London halls in the Middle Ages. Four of the stone statues representing the Civic Virtues which once adorned the exterior of the Guildhall have been rescued from a garden in Wales and are now on display in the Museum of London.

The Great Hall of the Middle Ages has endured as a building form into the twentieth century, mainly in colleges and universities where it freely admits to its historical references. It seems quite possible that it was considered an ancient form and a partial anachronism as early as the second half of the fifteenth century when there was a great revival of the previous values and imagery of the earlier age of legend and chivalry. This perhaps was part of the

The bridge over the moat at Eltham Palace employs the Perpendicular style of arch.

inspiration behind Edward IV's work at Eltham Palace of 1479, of which the Great Hall is the notable survivor of a complex of buildings sited romantically as much as defensively within a moated enclosure. The original bridge with its pointed arches set within a square form is a perfect illustration of the style of Perpendicular Gothic, as are the doorways which show the successful application of this highly convenient architectural design. However, it is the roof which is the crowning glory of Eltham Palace; although not such a daring hammerbeam as that of Westminster Hall it is a strong and rich composition of considerable impact (see page 16).

Just across the moat of Eltham Palace is an interesting timber-framed building known as the Lord Chancellor's Lodging which repeats in a more modest version the hall and other elements of its grander neighbour. An even smaller model of the medieval hall-house may be seen, at least from the outside, in the old village of Walthamstow, which is referred to quite simply as the Ancient House. These are the two best examples in the London area of fifteenth-century domestic dwellings of the middling sort and it may be assumed that many such homes were crammed into the streets of London along with narrower structures of a more obvious urban type. But London's oldest timber structure, which covers a vast space measuring 120 by 30 feet, is no baronial hall but a simple barn in Ruislip. Fittingly known as the Great Barn, it has been dated on the evidence of its carpentry to the thirteenth century. The excellence of the workmanship is a sign of wealthy patronage, which was by no means the preserve of kings but in this case that of the Abbey of Bec in Normandy.

An even more miraculous survival of the Middle Ages is Crosby Hall of 1466 which was removed in 1908 from Bishopsgate to Chelsea where it now serves as the refectory of a hostel of the British Federation of University Women. The reconstructed hall is all that remains of what was an extensive establishment with generous private apartments. The 69-foot hall was evidently a matter of great prestige for its merchant owner Sir John Crosby and it is easy to imagine the potential of the premises as a stage for business and diplomatic entertaining. The most striking feature of Crosby Hall is the splendid roof in which the crossing of the tie-beams is a technically unique arrangement. The gilt and bright colouring of the woodwork may appear fanciful but it serves as a reminder of the medieval taste for polychromatic decoration. This was a society that preferred a riot of colour to the simplicity of naked natural materials so much in favour nowadays. Crosby Hall is thus an authentic if somewhat bizarre example of its times. It also shows to what heights of luxury and refined living a successful London merchant might aspire in the fifteenth century.

Military architecture, on the other hand, was largely financed from the royal purse; and it was Henry III, the moving force behind the rebuilding of Westminster Abbey, who initiated much of the work which transformed the Tower of London from a fortified keep to a great concentric castle. During his reign the inner wall running from the Wakefield Tower in the south via the Salt Tower in the south-east, the Martin Tower in the north-east and the Devereux Tower in the north-west was constructed. The circuit was completed during the reign of his son Edward I (1272-1307) who also added the outer circuit wall. The fortifications of the Tower have lost much of their medieval aura but the gloom and suffering which so many people endured within its confinement can still be sensed when one sees the poignant graffiti the prisoners scratched on the stone walls of their cells. There are also some pleasant features such as the stone fireplaces of the Salt Tower and the Byward Tower which are unexpected reminders of physical comfort in an otherwise forbidding setting.

Perhaps it was also Henry III who added the ten hollow bastions to the western

Crosby Hall, brought from Bishopsgate to Chelsea, boasts a magnificent roof.

sector of the city wall for it is recorded that in 1257 he 'caused the wall of this Citie, which was sore decayed and destitute of towers, to be repaired in more seemly wise than before'. Good examples of these bastions have been preserved, especially in the garden landscape between the Barbican Centre and the Museum of London. The grafting of the medieval bastions to the Roman wall may be studied to best advantage at a site beneath the yard of the Post Office in Newgate Street. There is a remarkable contrast in construction techniques: the Roman wall with its straight course of levelling tiles and the round bastion of random rubble, both equally effective.

Most of London's gateways were rebuilt more than once in the course of the Middle Ages but not one has survived. The only visible relic of this type lies at Tower Hill

A medieval bastion on Roman foundations is preserved at the Barbican Centre.

where the foundations of a thirteenth-century postern were excavated as recently as 1979. It was a well-built structure, using stone from Caen in Normandy for the finer parts. Two arrowslits and a slot for the portcullis have been identified. It is likely that this small gate was accessible only for foot traffic. Further repairs to the city wall were ordered once again as late as the last quarter of the fifteenth century after the attack on London in 1471 by the Kentish rebels. This time the sense of urgency was not so great that it precluded a minor artistic indulgence. A diaper pattern of darker brick on a lighter red background is still visible at the section of the wall preserved in the garden of St Alphege by London Wall. It is a very pretty device which is still employed occasionally in modern brickwork. Decorative impulses are also evident in some medieval stonework, such as the pleasing chequerboard motif of the boundary wall of the Charterhouse which may date from 1405.

The appearance of brick in London was a sign of the changing times. The move from stone and timber to brick towards the end of the fifteenth century was one of the great turning points in the building history of London. Henceforth, brick was to alter radically the face of London as it was employed for houses great and small. The humble brick was already present, although invisible, in the undercroft of Crosby Hall and behind the ashlar masonry of Eltham Palace. Its triumphant emergence as a noble external finish coincided neatly with the dawn of the Tudor era in 1485; and so virtuoso a performance did it deliver in the sixteenth century that Tudor architecture is still the source of the most accomplished feats of brickcraft in the land. The role of

Recently excavated postern gate at Tower Hill, probably built in the late thirteenth century.

the brick in the future appearance and growth of London can hardly be overestimated.

Conversely, associations of medieval London are inextricably bound up with images of stone architecture, from the elegant Gothic arches of cathedrals to the heavy vaults and dark dungeons of the Tower. But it must not be thought for all that, that London in the Middle Ages was a city of stone. Wedged between the city wall, the churches, monasteries and noble mansions, the common reality was one of timber and wattle-and-daub. The frequency of fires noted by Fitz Stephen in the 1170s was still the norm in spite of the more stringent building regulations which banned thatch and prescribed stone instead of timber for party walls. By all accounts the architectural delights of the city were offset by unspeakable squalor and chronic overcrowding which was relieved only by the outbreak of the bubonic plague known as the Black Death in 1348 when some 30-40 per cent of London's estimated 50,000 inhabitants fell victim to the scourge. A grim reminder of the period was unearthed in 1986 during excavations at the site of the Abbey of St Mary Graces to the east of the Tower; archaeologists came across a mass of bodies in what must have been one of the huge cemetery pits where the deceased were dumped in their thousands during the height of the Black Death.

Although it is as well to be mindful of the horrors of medieval London, no survey is complete without mention of some of the vanished glories. Old St Paul's Cathedral would have been an amazing sight, both higher and longer than today's, completely dominating the city. A rival attraction would have been the stone London Bridge, built between 1176 and 1209; its nineteen arches came to support an entire community of shops and houses as well as a chapel dedicated to St Thomas. It was one of the liveliest parts of town, along with the waterfront and its teeming wharves. The two great markets at Cheapside and Eastcheap were the popular commercial centres, of which nothing has survived but some street names such as Milk Street, Bread Street and Ironmonger Lane. Property-holding records of the period reveal, however, something of the physical nature of medieval trade in Cheapside where there was a proliferation of tiny shops with the average frontage as small as six feet and entire families crammed often into single rooms above. In addition there were even smaller retail units in the form of trading areas known as 'selds', covered markets sheltering a number of 'stations' which might be just large enough to accommodate the wooden chest of a trader. It has been estimated from the documentary records that *c.* 1300 some 5000 people may have been employed in the commerce of Cheapside alone.

Congestion and smallness of scale appear to have been the rule in medieval London's tiny shops and houses in narrow streets, trade regulated by a multiplicity of guilds, and the administration divided into small wards and parishes with correspondingly small churches. The whole must have been a rich and colourful urban tapestry in which each thread had its own vibrancy and personality. The 'rationalising' of myriad individual cells into the present amorphous City where memories of the Middle Ages are overshadowed by monolithic office blocks has been the inexorable trend of the intervening centuries. Surprisingly, the medieval labyrinth of the street pattern can still be read in many places and the spirit of the age which founded the City is not entirely extinguished but lingers on in archaic-sounding institutions, such as the guilds, which make a triumphal annual stage appearance in the grand procession of the Lord Mayor's Show. With the golden coach and its escort of pikemen and company upon company of liverymen parading in their ceremonial garb it might seem that medieval London is still lurking in the wings waiting to reclaim its own.

The Jewel Tower, designed by Henry Yevele, London's first known architect.

Monument in Southwark Cathedral to Lockyer,
a London pillmaker who died in 1672.

2 Tudor and Stuart Expansion

The period encompassed by the Tudor and Stuart dynasties from 1485 to 1714 was one of the most eventful and decisive in the shaping of London. Dynamic growth and a remorseless increase in population was halted only momentarily by such catastrophic events as the Plague and the Great Fire. Already at the end of the sixteenth century John Stow, the chronicler of Elizabethan London, looked back with regret to the green fields of his youth which had been swallowed up by housing; and in 1684 the diarist John Evelyn noted that London's population had doubled in the course of his own lifetime. From the estimated statistics we can follow a tenfold increase from around 50,000 in 1530 to 500,000 in 1660 just prior to the Plague of 1665 in which more than 100,000 Londoners perished. The demographic explosion was largely due to the phenomenal wealth of London as the City flexed its muscles in international trade and finance, drawing countless hopefuls from the provinces as well as providing sanctuary to many refugees from the religious persecutions in Europe. Behind the statistics there were radical changes in most aspects of urban life.

Probably the most dramatic development was the end of London as a walled city. Even during the late Middle Ages London had been bursting at the seams; now it spilled out during the sixteenth and seventeenth centuries, not in an ordered way but all over what is now the metropolitan region, creating a patchwork of scattered communities. This far-flung pattern of growth was made necessary initially by the stranglehold of the monastic properties which barred the expansion of London in the areas immediately touching on the city walls. But the Dissolution of the Monasteries by Henry VIII completely revised the scheme of things. The lands of the abbeys and convents came into the possession of a new class of Tudor aristocrats who were eager to derive profit from their valuable acquisitions. However, it was not until the middle decades of the seventeenth century that men such as the Earl of Bedford with the Covent Garden piazza in 1631 and the Earl of Southampton in Bloomsbury in 1665 were able to cash in on the monastic lands they had inherited and to introduce to London the concept of a planned urbanism. Between the two schemes there occurred the Civil War which interrupted the process of growth, although London was spared any destruction in the fighting.

Such orderly developments around a formal square were the shape of things to come, resulting from the individual initiatives of landowners and speculators. Apart from the flurry of utopian schemes for rebuilding London immediately after the Great Fire of 1666 there was never in practice any hint of a masterplan for the metropolis.

Only in the Covent Garden of Inigo Jones did the notion of Classical formality appear to take precedence. With Henry Jermyn's prestigious faubourg around St James's Square the prime objective was to provide a fitting milieu for the wealthy and aristocratic residents whom the speculator hoped to attract as leaseholders. By the end of the seventeenth century the London square had been repeated many times over and was a definite planning success on account of its suitability to the basic requirements of its inhabitants. In contrast to the Baroque squares of Europe, the London square did not evolve as a showplace or a status symbol but as an efficient solution to the practical needs of urban living.

The new enclaves of orderly houses in self-contained communities represented an extreme reaction against the crowded, often ramshackle conditions prevailing within the City. Already in Tudor times the congested and insanitary heart of London inside the

St Peter ad Vincula, a Tudor example of Perpendicular Gothic, in the Tower of London.

walls was avoided by those with the means to afford a country residence outside. This drift to the countryside had a negative effect on the nature of the City, which became even less desirable as a residential area and subsequently evolved more as a business centre with industrial appendages. The essential oneness of the medieval city with rich and poor living in the same neighbourhoods was gradually destroyed as the wealthy headed out to dream homes in the West End and beyond, leaving behind a social divide which has remained to this day.

In terms of building evolution in London the Tudor and Stuart eras witnessed the definitive triumph of the common brick as the universal material of construction. First ennobled by its use in the palatial projects of Henry VIII, it proceeded to become the stuff of all but the most modest of houses. Availability of local supplies of brickearth gave London the means to provide for its own growth. The brick, the use of which made steady progress during the sixteenth and the first half of the seventeenth century, partly promoted by Royal Proclamations, really came into its own in the aftermath of the Great Fire. The new London was built essentially of brick with some stone dressing, but there were exceptions to the rule: timber-framed houses continued to appear in places, as is evidenced by the survival of examples of the period in Cloth Fair and in Middle Temple Lane.

In terms of architectural style, the versatility of brick, often in combination with stone, opened the way for experimentation and innovation. The stylistic possibilities of the timber-frame had been well-nigh exhausted by the second decade of the seventeenth century when the concept of Classical architecture was brought to London by the Surveyor General, Inigo Jones. However, Jones's rigid adherence to the tenets of Palladianism put him somewhat out of tune with contemporary taste and his works did not have much influence at the time. It fell subsequently to Sir Christopher Wren, the Surveyor General during the period of reconstruction after the Great Fire, to produce a comfortable, non-doctrinaire and pleasing version of Renaissance Classicism which was more acceptable to the English and also better suited to the light and climate of the country. In the latter half of his long career Wren turned increasingly to the Baroque but he was not dogmatic in his views. Only with the rejection of his Great Model for the rebuilding of St Paul's do we sense the frustration of a thwarted idealist. Otherwise he proved himself to be a man of the age, a scientist, pragmatist and artist of the real world who was capable of producing a seemingly endless stream of brilliant solutions to the manifold architectural tasks entrusted to him. However, Wren – as an urbanist – did not leave his imprint on the map of London, for his Baroque masterplan for London's rebirth in 1666 was rejected along with the rest.

The Londoners' successful resistance to all the masterplans put forward at the time is significant, for it shows the strength of the citizens as a social force and their commitment to the inherited pattern of London, the product of incidental growth. It also highlights the struggle in London between the Absolutist tendencies of the Stuart monarchy and the democratic institutions of the City. The battle was finally lost by the Stuarts with the departure of James II in 1688, and the change is marked by the new architectural values of the Court under the regime of William and Mary. The power of the people also made itself felt in the fight for the preservation of open spaces for sport and recreation. The very existence of Finsbury Square and Circus, Red Lion Square,

Schomberg House, a seventeenth-century mansion. The caryatids are a later addition.

Leicester Square and Lincoln's Inn Fields is due to popular pressure, including some physical protests, in the seventeenth century. The larger expanses of parkland such as Hampstead Heath, Richmond Park and Hyde Park owe their survival, on the other hand, to the protection of Henry VIII who reserved for his own hunting vast areas of the country around London.

As for the business of architecture, it was not yet the preserve of a professional élite but was open to those with the talent of producing good designs. Inigo Jones came to architecture via stage design, and Wren via mathematics and astronomy. Although the tradition of the gentleman amateur was to persist into the eighteenth century both Jones and Wren schooled other architects in the persons of John Webb and Nicholas Hawksmoor respectively. Wren's style can still be discerned in some works of the twentieth century but the influence of Inigo Jones faded along with the decline of Palladianism itself. Wren's immediate legacy at the time of his death in 1723 was, however, the style of English Baroque, which lasted only until the 1730s and in London was mainly confined to a few churches.

The underlying message of the period was the transition of London from the medieval to the modern. The city was the centre of a tremendous expansion of trade and finance, symbolised above all by the founding of the East India Company in 1600 and of the Bank of England in 1694. This was also the Age of Discovery, of the Reformation and the Renaissance as well as of rapid advancement in the sciences. Technology was essential to the growth of London as early as 1613 when Sir Hugh Myddleton's New River, which Wren called 'this noble aqueduct', brought fresh water to London from springs in Hertfordshire through an artificial waterway forty miles in length with an average drop of only five inches per mile. The present headquarters of the Thames Water Authority stands on the site of New River Head in Rosebery Avenue where the water was distributed from a reservoir through conduits of elm. The sumptuously carved panelling and the intricate plaster ceiling of the New River Company dating from the second half of the seventeenth century has been reconstructed in the Oak Room of the present building. It is vastly more lavish than anything built by William III himself, to whom the directors respectfully dedicated their new boardroom.

The Tudor and Stuart period, which takes us from the London of William Shakespeare to that of Samuel Pepys and beyond, was characterised more by the dynamism of change and progress than by any enduring features. Nevertheless, there appear in retrospect to be a number of qualities which constitute part of the spirit of the age. With the passing of the Middle Ages London experienced a release from the domination of the Church and developed its own secular institutions. Architecture reflected the change with a steady move away from Gothic to a lighter mix of Renaissance and Dutch influence. Most of the productions of the time display a carefree mood, a vivacity born of wit and freedom to experiment, and a delight in surface decoration which culminated in the carved swags, garlands, fruit and cherubs' heads from the chisel of Grinling Gibbons and the almost playful use of Classical devices by Sir Christopher Wren. All this would soon be frowned upon by the more earnest minds which shaped Georgian London, bringing a more regimental discipline to the task of urbanism and a more purist philosophy to the question of artistic and architectural style.

The Tudor Style from Cottage to Palace

Without doubt the greatest single architectural achievement of Tudor London was the Henry VII Chapel at Westminster Abbey. Its miraculous fan-vaulting stands for the culmination of the Gothic style, where the delicate tracery of the stone appears transformed into a web of weightlessness. But despite its wondrous majesty it was to have no enduring influence, for this was the grand finale of the Gothic age rather than the start of a new movement. On the other hand, the first rays of the Renaissance in England have been detected here in the masterful funerary sculpture by the Florentine Pietro Torrigiano, most notably in the tomb and screen for Henry VII himself. But the Italian contribution lies in decorative detail rather than architectural style and it was destined to have no immediate effect. It is somehow ironic that it was Henry VIII who was responsible for the completion of the Henry VII Chapel commenced by his father, for his main claim to renown in the ecclesiastical domain is destructive rather than constructive. But there it stands, an ecstatic as well as enigmatic building, a stunningly beautiful continuation to the east end of Westminster Abbey. Its original quality is more readily appreciated from within, since it has retained its rich array of statuary which the iconoclasm of the Reformation eliminated elsewhere without hindrance.

London experienced very little new church building in the sixteenth century. Possibly the need had been met by the products of the preceding generations, but this decline in religious architecture coincided with the spirit of the age, which was shifting away from the ecclesiastical to the secular, from cathedrals and churches to palaces and mansions. The emergence from the Middle Ages is most obviously expressed in the ebbing of the dominance of the establishment devoted to the works of God in favour of that promoting the material interests of Man. In this great transition of values Henry VIII looms large, symbolising the fact that Man, with all the faults of his condition, has at last come into his inheritance. In Henry VIII we can see the building energies of his predecessors, which had been mainly directed to castles and cathedrals, now diverted into a proliferation of palaces where pleasure and the parade of majesty take over from any more serious or nobler purpose.

In a sense Henry VII had given the lead with his stylish rebuilding of the old house at Sheen, relaunched and renamed as Richmond Palace, where Henry VIII was brought up. All that now remains is the gatehouse bearing the recently restored coat of arms facing towards Richmond Green and parts of the building fabric in the houses known as the Wardrobe. However, Henry VIII's prolific output of palace-building in and around London was more inspired by the example of Cardinal Wolsey; his sumptuous palace at Hampton Court was already far more royal than anything in the possession of the King, but when Henry VIII took it over in 1525 it was to be enlarged and to receive the further adornment of a Great Hall with a mighty hammerbeam roof. Quite apart from its implicit moral lessons to aspiring politicians, Hampton Court is an instructive piece of architecture, representing some of the most significant trends of the age.

The Gothic tradition still underlies the basic design but the details are weaker, the arches flatter. The resulting void surfaces of the exterior invited decoration, and Wolsey filled them with terracotta medallions portraying Roman emperors. This can be claimed as an early sign of the Renaissance, but if so then it represents a false start

Henry VII Chapel, a magnificent Tudor extension to the east end of Westminster Abbey.

which does not in any sense indicate the absorption of the spirit of the Renaissance but merely the importation of a decorative device quite literally stuck on the façade of a traditional structure. When the appetite for Classical motifs resurfaced later in the century the English went for the relatively ornate and debased versions supplied by the publishers of engravings in the Low Countries. The medallions at Hampton Court, and the geometric ceiling designs as well, are a tribute more to the taste of Wolsey than to any general artistic awareness at the time in England.

The real interest at Hampton Court resides in the transformation of the Gothic tradition itself. The idea of the castle as fortress has been transmuted into that of the castle as palace. The gatehouse, towers and battlements, even the moat, have no

Hampton Court witnessed the first flourishes of the Renaissance.

serious defensive capability; and as if to make up for it they are almost puffed up into ornamental features of obvious artifice. The message of Hampton Court is to impress the onlooker with the trappings of wealth and power, a game later played by the nobles of Elizabeth's reign whose 'prodigy houses' are still a source of delight. At Hampton Court the sense of gaiety and exuberance abounds even in the fanciful, convoluted shapes of the chimney stacks which demonstrate the artistic versatility of the new building material, brick, which here receives the royal seal of approval.

Little remains of the rest of Henry VIII's many palaces. Of the enormous and rambling Whitehall Palace, basically a series of extensions to the York Palace of Cardinal Wolsey, only a part of the royal wine cellar survives beneath the Ministry of Defence. Of St James's Palace there is the imposing gatehouse of 1532-40, its octagonal towers a characteristic feature of Tudor castellar design. But of Bridewell Palace at Blackfriars and the Palace of Placentia at Greenwich nothing remains above ground. Likewise the fantasy palace of Nonsuch near Cheam is now only to be encountered below ground. This last of Henry's fourteen royal abodes in the London area has a special significance in that it was an unashamed attempt to upstage François I of France with stylistic borrowings from Chambord and Fontainebleau. The name of Nonsuch itself proclaims the ambitions of the builder. As with Hampton Court, the Renaissance design was superficial, for the entire façade was dominated by vast stucco reliefs of classical subjects framed in carved and gilded slate. Fragments recovered during the 1959 excavation are on display in the sixteenth-century timber-framed house in Cheam known as Whitehall. The Palace of Nonsuch has been criticised for its lavish and ostentatious decoration, but it was a plaything more than a serious work of architecture, being intended as a convenient hunting lodge within a day's ride of Hampton Court and London.

There was a grimmer reality behind Nonsuch for much of the building stone was robbed from the ruins of Merton Priory, which had been forfeited to the Crown along with the rest of the monastic property in England. Thus the Dissolution, which occurred between 1535 and 1540, had the greatest imaginable effect on building throughout the land, and especially in London. Huge areas of today's inner London, which had been held since the early Middle Ages by the monastic orders and formed an impregnable obstacle to urban growth around the City, were suddenly released by Henry VIII to his accomplices to develop as they felt disposed. Some used the monastic buildings as a quarry for stone; and thus the first Somerset House arose on the Strand in 1547-52 from material taken mainly from the Priory Church of St John in Clerkenwell. This great town mansion, which was a pioneer of classical style in England, was created symbolically, it might almost seem, out of the spoils of the Middle Ages. Holy Trinity Priory in Aldgate was given to Thomas Audley who tried all ways to turn his new property to easy profit before installing a house in the crossing of the church and subdividing the choir into small tenements, while the nave and chancel were opened to the sky to serve as courtyards.

The lone survivor, and hence best known example of a converted monastery in London, is that of the Carthusians at Smithfield. Today's Charterhouse shows how a noble residence was fashioned from a monastic complex. The Washhouse Court is a blend of Tudor brick and medieval stonework, a true fusion of material and social values. Charterhouse is an interesting study of how the residential requirements of the sixteenth century, such as the long gallery and the grand staircase, were accommodated in the ecclesiastical structure inherited from the Middle Ages. Another relic of the monasteries is the new gate of 1504 of the Priory of St John in Clerkenwell which has come through the ages intact thanks to its suitability for a number of practical purposes including that of offices for *The Gentleman's Magazine*.

A most fascinating testimonial to the effects of the Dissolution is to be found in Islington, which was well outside the bounds of sixteenth-century London and still surrounded at that time by open fields. Canonbury Tower is a dramatic survival of Canonbury House, built by Prior William Bolton between 1509 and 1532 on estates originally bequeathed to the Augustinian Canons of St Bartholomew's Priory in 1253.

Bolton was one of the last and most energetic of the monastic builders in the period just before the Dissolution. He served as Henry VIII's Master of Works for the building of the Henry VII Chapel; and the delightful oriel window, a rare specimen in London, inserted into the Norman arcading of the triforium in the church of St Bartholomew-the-Great, is but a token of the works he initiated at the Priory. Of his building at Canonbury House the tower is the most substantial relic as the rest of the property has been variously redeveloped over the centuries. Some forty years after the Dissolution, Canonbury House was acquired by the cloth merchant Sir John Spencer whose conversion works and improvements may still be seen as most impressive examples of the new fashions of interior design so popular with the rising merchant class of Elizabethan London.

Within the tower itself the Compton Room contains the elaborate panelling and ornately carved chimneypiece which is such a feature of late sixteenth-century rooms of the better sort. Other examples of Sir John Spencer's taste in décor must be sought in what are now separate dwellings in Canonbury Place but which once formed the east range of the courtyard. Number 5-6 contains, along with an original wooden door bearing the rebus of Prior Bolton, a tun pierced by a bolt, the most accomplished and best preserved late-Elizabethan plaster ceiling in London. This great composition of 'strapwork' design, dated 1599, displays a series of medallion portraits of classical figures such as Alexander the Great and Julius Caesar. It shows what a gulf in time – more than seventy-five years – separated the individual artistic taste of Cardinal Wolsey from that of a successful businessman; the Renaissance flourish of Hampton Court had at last found wider acceptance.

This fine ceiling disappears abruptly where it meets the wall to the north but it re-emerges in the neighbouring house, more precisely in the staff room of the Canonbury Children's Day Nursery. Elsewhere on the premises are two further excellent specimens of Sir John's plaster ceilings. One has rather ponderous pendants, but the other is a delightful sight with its beautifully moulded images of Elizabethan galleys, their sails swelling with a full wind. This is an obvious reference to the international maritime trade which made the fortune of Sir John Spencer and many other of his business contemporaries. Canonbury Tower is thus the perfect spot to evoke real memories of the link between the builders of the monastic properties such as Prior William Bolton and the new class of merchants who eventually profited from the spoils of the Dissolution.

It is instructive to follow the trail of Sir John Spencer a stage further to the church of St Helen in Bishopsgate where he lies interred with his wife beneath an imposing double monument. It is remarkable that the Reformation, which caused the destruction of so much religious imagery, appeared to condone the setting up of the vainglorious funerary sculptures which wealthy folk in the Elizabethan and Jacobean periods endowed with such obvious delight. Whatever pious intent may have lain behind such monuments, their overwhelming message today is one of great artistic indulgence. Charming as they are to behold, they detract from many a church; none more so than the huge Neville tomb crammed into the tiny round Norman apse of St Mary Magdalene in East Ham.

Almshouses, too, became a popular endowment in Tudor times among nobles and successful businessmen alike. At Harefield, still a rural village although part of the London Borough of Hillingdon, there is the small group of almshouses endowed in 1600 by the Countess of Derby. The Church of England also set a fine example with the establishment of almshouses such as the Whitgift Hospital of 1597 by the Archbishop of the same name. This is a lovely complex of Tudor buildings set around an intimate quadrangle which is entered through a

Renaissance-style archway. Education as well as charity passed from the control of the monks; and the sixteenth century witnessed the birth of a rash of grammar schools such as Highgate in 1562 and Harrow in 1572. The original Tudor hall of Barnet, founded in 1573, is now used by Barnet College; and Enfield Grammar School still contains fabric of the first schoolhouse dating back to 1555.

The educational establishments of the legal profession in London have their architectural roots in the late fifteenth and sixteenth centuries. The hall of Lincoln's Inn is the oldest, going back to 1490; its brick gatehouse was built in 1518. The hall of the Middle Temple of 1562-70 is the grandest of all with a double hammerbeam roof and a magnificent Elizabethan screen, reconstructed after damage during the last war,

The Spencer monument in St Helen's, Bishopsgate, a splendid piece of Tudor work.

but still acclaimed as a stylistic landmark on account of its abundance of Renaissance motifs. However, the halls of the Inns are really more significant as enclaves of architectural conservatism; their rigid adherence to the medieval Great Hall ran counter to the trend of the times.

Although the role of the established Church as a patron of architecture was severely reduced, at least the buildings in possession of the Archbishop of Canterbury and the Bishop of London managed to weather the storm. Thus the great gatehouse to Lambeth Palace, built in 1495 by Archbishop Morton, remains as a lovely specimen of early Tudor style with its red brick enlivened by darker brick diapering. The archiepiscopal palace at Croydon, parts of which belong to the Middle Ages, also bears signs of Tudor additions; and

The Tudor gatehouse of Lincoln's Inn dates back to 1518.

Middle Temple Hall, constructed 1562–70, is famous for its double hammerbeam roof.

Fulham Palace shows in the most complete form the restrained domestic features of the smaller type of stately Tudor residence. The courtyard with its fountain is remarkably intact and offers a milieu extremely redolent of the period especially in the charming view through the characteristic Tudor arch of the gatehouse.

It is in the smaller productions such as the manor house of the gentry that the Tudor style is most effective, as exemplified in the London region by Eastbury House in Barking. The economy of scale is matched by a thoughtful use of space and the decorative detail is pleasing without being flamboyant. The splendid octagonal chimneys are the most striking feature of the exterior, which has managed to retain its discreet charm in spite of the unsympathetic environs of a pre-war housing estate.

The intimate courtyard of Fulham Palace, a delightful Tudor residence.

Hall Place in Bexleyheath is another modest mansion of the period exposed to the onslaught of modern development – in this case the A2 runs through the grounds – but it too is a house of great appeal. Hall Place grew from the house built in around 1540 by Sir John Champeneis, Lord Mayor of London. Its attractive chequered front contains a great deal of carved medieval stonework, which indicates that the source of the material was one of the monasteries in the vicinity, probably Lesnes Abbey. In line with the changing fashion of the second half of the sixteenth century, the north front was extended along one of its wings so as to present a symmetrical face. The steady move towards external symmetry was a significant step in the Elizabethan adoption of a more authentic Renaissance style. Accordingly, Hall Place also received a second oriel to match the existing one, which was off-centre, as in the Middle Ages; and the doorway precisely between the two provided for perfect balance. Inside, a Long Gallery of sorts was inserted in the upper floor of the extended wing, but downstairs the medieval arrangement of the Great Hall lingered on.

The stonework of Hall Place was in contrast to the building practice within the City of London at the time. Indeed John Stow states in his *Survey of London* of 1598 that Thomas Audley did not find it an easy task disposing of the stone from Holy Trinity Priory, 'for all the buildings then about the city were of brick and timber'. Unfortunately, the Great Fire of 1666 and the unrelenting pressure of redevelopment have all but eradicated the timber-framed dwellings from the map of Greater London which were such a familiar sight to John Stow. Only isolated examples of the half-timbered

Eastbury Manor House in Barking, a typical Tudor design with prominent chimneys.

Elizabethan or domestic Tudor type still survive, mainly in the suburbs; but there is just enough left to illustrate this phase of London's housing evolution.

The much restored front of Staple Inn in High Holborn is dismissed by the purists as an unreliable specimen of Tudor building, but for all the modifications it has received it is nonetheless London's main clue as to how entire streets must have appeared in the sixteenth century. Owing to the congestion within the city, street frontage was at a premium and it was common practice to point the narrow gable end of the house towards the street. The apartments within would extend back as far as possible, sometimes a great distance, and thus offer fairly commodious accommodation. At Staple Inn, where one building occupied a number of housefronts, it was arranged with a number of separate gable ends giving on to the street. Such an expedient must have created an impressive uniformity of scale in the streets of Elizabethan London where three or four storeys was about the limit in height.

Most of the houses, however, would have been humbler affairs, such as the Old Cottage of around 1500 in Cheam. Also in Cheam is the weather-boarded house known as Whitehall which conceals a timber-framed dwelling of the same period. Some of the most significant parts of the structure have now been exposed to view, such as the curved bracing timbers used for the jettying of the upper storey. The roof can also be readily inspected from the loft, and a line on the floorboards marks the rectangular space originally occupied by the simple staircase which was probably no more than a fixed ladder. Here one is able to appreciate the as yet spartan domesticity of the more modest Tudor home with no chimney, no drainage and no glazed windows. By the end of the sixteenth century Whitehall had been improved and extended, its fortunes perhaps lifted by the proximity of Nonsuch Palace.

Ruislip, to the north-west of London, still possesses its Manor Farm House of Tudor date, albeit with later windows; this is a close-studded construction: that is, the timbers are tightly spaced, and the infill is with brick nogging rather than lathe and plaster. An interesting aesthetic detail is that where brick is used the timbers are left in their natural colour in order to blend, whereas they are painted black when alongside white plaster to create a striking visual contrast. Also of note in Ruislip are the Church Houses, originally built in 1570 as one unit but converted in 1617 into ten two-roomed dwellings for the poor. A sheltered enclave of an expanse of grass opposite the medieval church provides an evocative environment in which to appreciate this vernacular specimen of Tudor architecture.

A grander timber-framed house is Southall Manor, a quite unexpected sight on a busy shopping street, which now serves as offices for the local Chamber of Commerce. In Chingford on the north-eastern fringe of London is a Tudor building in a class of its own. Commonly known as Queen Elizabeth's Hunting Lodge, although its origin is firmly in the reign of Henry VIII, this most attractive four-storeyed edifice was referred to in contemporary documents as the 'Great Standing', indicating its main purpose as a lodge-cum-grandstand. As first designed, the top storey was left open between the studs to permit as good a view as possible of the hunt in progress on the plain below which bordered on Epping Forest. The lodge received a certain amount of restoration in the Victorian period but the timber framing is essentially authentic and conforms to the standards of Crown carpentry under Henry VIII. The structure is straightforward, basically a single block with a projecting staircase wing. Unlike most Tudor dwellings, the upper storeys are not jettied out – presumably there was space enough for the occasional use to which it was put. In south-east London there is also a Tudor building of unique interest. The Tudor Barn in Eltham is the surviving brick and timber building of a moated manor which belonged in the first half of the sixteenth century to the daughter of Sir Thomas More. The manor house itself is gone but the entire inner moat remains and provides a most attractive setting for the surviving range which now accommodates a restaurant and an art gallery. The interior is well preserved, with its fine timber roof and original fireplaces, two of brick and one of stone.

In central London itself there are some fine Tudor buildings tucked away within the Tower precincts. The Queen's House on Tower Green of 1540 once contained a spacious hall two storeys in height. The superstructure of the Byward Tower commanding the entrance to the outer fortifications is another fine creation of the sixteenth century; and there is a pretty timber-framed apartment which adorns St Thomas's Tower above Traitor's Gate,

Staple Inn, High Holborn, a precious survival of London's sixteenth-century streetscape.

Queen Elizabeth's Hunting Lodge in Chingford dates back to the reign of Henry VIII.

dating from 1532. A further addition to London's stock of Tudor building relics was made during the Great War when a Zeppelin raid damaged the gatehouse of St Bartholomew-the-Great, revealing a neat dwelling which would have been occupied by a London merchant of the middling sort around the end of the sixteenth century. But to get an idea of the physical appearance of Tudor London it is necessary to multiply such isolated and marooned examples by several thousand and imagine them packed in tightly together, huddled eave to eave, and, despite the overall uniformity of style, each with its own personality.

But not even collectively can the mass of timber-framed buildings convey the reality of Tudor London, which was by all accounts, most notably that of John Stow, engaged upon a most frenetic course of development. The ravages of the Dissolution were all too apparent, according to the

Venetian Ambassador who wrote in 1551 of 'many large palaces making a very fine show, but . . . disfigured by the ruins of a multitude of churches and monasteries'. Stow's *Survey* is full of nostalgia for the more pleasant, less noisy and less congested city in which he spent his younger days. Estimated population statistics show a veritable demographic explosion in London from around 50,000 in 1530 to some 225,000 in 1605. Despite the release of the monastic precincts for housing there was still not enough space for healthy accommodation within the City. Overcrowding in unsanitary tenements was the order of the day. Many of the streets were not paved and even those that were served as open sewers and rubbish dumps, thereby blocking the drainage which was supposed to run through a gully in the centre. Lovat Lane in the City is the one surviving street of this type in central London. Outbursts of plague

The Tudor barn is all that remains of the moated manor of Well Hall in Eltham.

were frequent, and the problems of rampant urban growth were hotly debated in Parliament and occasioned several royal proclamations by Elizabeth I which sought to check the spread of the city, which was perceived with horror rather than admiration. But the measures ordained were largely ineffectual and only encouraged the worst sort of jerry-building. Henry VIII's declaration of his exclusive hunting area did more to safeguard for posterity such open spaces as Hampstead Heath than any of the Elizabethan bans on new building.

For all its inconveniences, the London of Good Queen Bess is associated in the folk memory as a merry place; and this is largely due to the vivacity of the Elizabethan theatre which blossomed above all in Southwark in an enclave outside the jurisdiction of the puritanical city fathers, in houses such as the Rose, the Hope, the Swan and the famous Globe whose site is marked by a plaque in Park Street. The form of the Elizabethan theatre, with its rows of

A picturesque group of timber-framed houses around Tower Green.

The George Inn, Southwark, gives an idea of the galleried coaching inn of Tudor London, although the present building dates from 1676.

galleries disposed almost in the shape of a horseshoe around the stage, was clearly related to the galleried courtyards of the inns where dramatic spectacles were first performed. The only relic of such a structure in London is the George Inn, fittingly in Southwark. Only one side remains of the galleries, dating from the last quarter of the seventeenth century, to remind us of the origins of London's theatre buildings whose basic design is still alive today in the many traditional establishments still in use.

The Tudor gatehouse of Lambeth Palace shows the fine brickwork techniques of the period.

Both the theatre boom and the overcrowding of London had a common cause: money. Elizabethan London had wrested from the European centres of Paris and Antwerp the mastery of both international finance and commerce. The Thames provided a convenient harbour for the fleets of trading ships, as depicted on Sir John Spencer's ceiling in Canonbury. Without doubt the greatest symbol of London's pre-eminent commercial status was Sir Thomas Gresham's amazing Royal Exchange.

Opened in 1560 by Queen Elizabeth herself, this great complex involved the demolition of some eighty houses, destroying four entire streets. It was a vast colonnaded building set around a courtyard, inspired by the Bourse at Antwerp which it was designed to outshine. It was London's grandest business centre since the Roman Basilica of almost 1500 years previously. It marks the beginning of a process whereby the business institutions gradually ousted the craftsmen and manufacturers from the City itself; and there was a corresponding growth of industrialised settlements in the flat fields of the Essex borders which grew into the East End of later centuries. For the time being the City was still the place of residence as well as of business for the merchant community but there was a strong increase in the number of country houses, such as Hall Place in Bexleyheath, owned by men whose livelihood was in the City. The establishment of an aristocratic ghetto along the Strand where the nobility resided in fine mansions such as Somerset House marked a class divide in London between the West End and the East End. In the general surge of development one can sense that the medieval structures, notably the wall, could no longer contain the urban dynamism of Elizabethan London. It was a hallmark of the age that the expansion of settlement was still unplanned and organic, a state of affairs that was soon to change with the more orderly concepts of the seventeenth century.

In spite of the Tudor enthusiasm for brick the vernacular form of timber-framed construction was still widespread in London at the end of the sixteenth century. One of the advantages of the technique was that buildings could be prefabricated elsewhere and simply reassembled on site. Houses could also be moved with ease – as John Stow's father discovered to his cost when his home was dug out of the ground and moved on rollers a distance of twenty feet to suit the convenience of Thomas Cromwell, the chief henchman of Henry VIII at the time of the Dissolution. Likewise many of the houses removed to make way for the Royal Exchange were re-erected on new sites; and the entire Globe Theatre was dismantled in Shoreditch and reassembled in Southwark to escape the clutches of a difficult landlord. The timber frame continued to thrive throughout Jacobean times becoming more and more ornate with the years, until the Restoration, when the relative cheapness of brick was ousting it in the course of the seventeenth century as the common building material of London.

The notion of architect was not yet established in the modern sense. There was the builder and his client who together would devise a house. The proto-architect might have been more akin to a design consultant who would propose decorative elements gleaned from one or other of the books of Classical engravings mainly published in the Low Countries. There must have been a buoyant demand for works of conversion as Elizabethan features such as the Long Gallery, the Great Staircase, plaster ceilings and carved chimneypieces were installed in existing houses. Water closets were not yet in use and London's houses suffered terribly from the stench of their own cesspits. Cardinal Wolsey's superior plumbing at Hampton Court was not even emulated by Henry VIII in his own palaces such as St James's and Nonsuch. In all there was still a very haphazard approach to the challenge of house design. It is hardly surprising that London can boast no great architect in the sixteenth century. But the situation was to change dramatically in the seventeenth century when the spirit of Renaissance architecture, rather than its misunderstood decorative details, came to preoccupy the minds of the next generation of the builders of London.

Inigo Jones and the New Trends of the Jacobean Era

In terms of London's general appearance the reign of James I (1603–25) did not bring about the wholesale transformation that the Stuart monarch wished to achieve. In one of his proclamations on building he expressed the desire to have it said of himself that 'we had found our citie and suburbs of London of stickes, and left them of bricke, being a material far more durable, safe from fire and beautiful and magnificent'. Despite a ban on wood, which was later relaxed, the advantages of the traditional timber frame were so great, especially in the jettying of the upper storeys to achieve maximum living space, that even people of substance continued to build in this manner well into the seventeenth century. The City of London that was consumed in the Great Fire of 1666 was still predominantly medieval in appearance with its tightly packed labyrinth of half-timbered houses.

Prince Henry's Room is central London's last surviving Jacobean timber-framed house.

In Fleet Street there stands the sole survivor in central London *in situ* of a timber-framed Jacobean townhouse. The Great Fire stopped but a few yards away from this handsome three-storey structure perched over the gateway to the Middle Temple which is known as Prince Henry's Room. This Jacobean building of 1610–11, somewhat restored, is still firmly in the Elizabethan tradition, although it does display some of the stylistic innovations of the age. The extent and regularity of the fenestration, arranged in a double front of two tiers of jettied bays, and the balustraded gallery, which partly masks the pointed gables, combine to achieve a greater balance and a stress on the horizontal plane, thereby marking a clear departure from the narrow vertical effect so typical of the Elizabethan streetscape. A more spectacular example, which shows how Jacobean builders could play with the inherited aspect of the timber-framed house, can be seen in the front of Sir Paul Pindar's home in Bishopsgate of 1624, which was fortunately rescued by the Victoria & Albert Museum in 1890 where it is still on display. This flamboyant composition of 36 lights and 18 fancifully carved wooden panels is an unashamed parade of wealth by a London merchant and diplomat who made his fortune in the Levant. Pindar's house was one of the last of its type before brick and stone took over entirely from wood; and it was also one of the last generation of quality residences to be built within the City. Already the congestion, pollution and fear of the plague in London were driving the better-off to the healthier environs in a

The ceiling of Prince Henry's Room is a rich display of Jacobean plasterwork.

quest for a more rural lifestyle, setting in motion a process of dispersion that has been the leitmotif of London's evolution ever since.

An idea of the style of Jacobean interiors may be gained from Prince Henry's Room which contains its original moulded plaster ceiling, one of the finest specimens of the period. This complex series of interlocking geometric shapes formed by bands of strapwork adorned with foliage and portrait medallions carries as its centrepiece the richly framed initials of Prince Henry, who was acclaimed as a 'Universal Man', the ideal of the Renaissance, and whose tragic premature death was to pave the way to the throne for the ill-fated Charles I. The interior of James I's palace at Bromley-by-Bow of 1606, to judge by the one room preserved in the Victoria & Albert Museum, must have been a showcase of the Jacobean style. Here one sees the early Renaissance adornment of the voluptuously carved overmantel of the fireplace as the symbolic as well as artistic focal point of the room. In accordance with the status of the owner, the royal coat of arms dominates the apartment. The plaster ceiling provides the perfect light accompaniment to the dark panels below, as simple and pleasing a combination as could be achieved before the taste for polychromatic interiors took over. Other splendid examples of plaster ceilings are to be found at Forty Hall in Enfield of 1629, perhaps lacking in the finesse of the royal works at Bromley-by-Bow but certainly not in the exuberance so characteristic of the period.

A more fundamental change during the Jacobean era lay in the underlying trend towards symmetry of appearance and layout. At Holland House of 1607, where only the east wing has survived and which now serves as a youth hostel, the hall was in the middle of the façade, entered by a central door. Thus the medieval dining hall

Charlton House is London's finest complete Jacobean mansion.

The staircase of Ham House marks an early appearance of the Baroque interior.

had become transformed into a vestibule. Symmetry is also the message of the main front of Charlton House of 1612 which has been acclaimed as 'the only Jacobean mansion of the first order remaining in the precincts of London' (Cherry & Pevsner). The centrepiece of this overall balanced composition is formed by an extravaganza of carved stone ornament which is a unique direct imitation taken from the engravings of Wendel Dietterlin's book of grotesque Italian designs first published at the end of the sixteenth century. A further remarkable feature of Charlton House is the dramatic use of the hall as a two-storeyed vestibule which in turn called for the provision of more generously proportioned apartments elsewhere in the house with fine plaster ceilings and ornately contrived chimneypieces. In line with the fashion, the staircase is especially prominent at Charlton House; this is a mighty structure rising in ornamentation through the orders of Doric, Ionic and Corinthian.

The great staircase at Ham House, an addition of 1637–8 to a mansion of 1610, is particularly instructive about the changing style of seventeenth-century interior design. Here the richly carved panels displaying the noble trophies of war, the garlands of foliage in moulded plaster and the overflowing baskets of fruit on the newel posts all herald the heroic Baroque fashions of the Restoration in 1660. The broken pediments over the doors were, however, already part of the stock-in-trade of the artisan builders of the day.

The type of architecture popular in London during the first half of the seventeenth century, which has come to be known as Artisan Mannerism, was an unformulated concoction of stylistic devices, notably the Flemish gable, elaborated by the craftsmen such as masons, bricklayers and joiners. These men had general charge of the design of buildings

Kew Palace, formerly the Dutch House, was originally built in 1631 for a London merchant.

Cromwell House, Highgate, of 1637–8 shows an imaginative use of brick.

before specialist architects, theoreticians such as Inigo Jones, took over the task of making aesthetic decisions. The basis of the artisans' style was non-doctrinal; they delivered what their clients wanted, namely homely buildings with a liberal sprinkling of fashionable decorative motifs. The taste, especially of the businessmen, was still essentially conservative. The mansion of Swakeleys built in 1629–38 at Ickenham for Edmund Wright, an alderman of the City of London, still has its roots firmly in the Middle Ages with its asymmetrical hall. Indeed, it was only the Flemish gables, themselves no longer a novelty at the time, which gave at least a contemporary flair to the house. Artisan Mannerism was also noted for the endeavours of the bricklayers who sought to outdo the masons with their fanciful adornments. The Dutch House at Kew of 1631, now known as Kew Palace, was originally built as the country residence of the Flemish London merchant Samuel Fortrey. It shows just how fine an effect could be achieved, even on a modest scale, by skilful and inventive brickwork. Here even the areas of plain brickwork are distinguished by the use of the technique of 'Flemish bond', according to which 'headers' and 'stretchers' (end-facing and side-facing bricks) alternate within the same course, a marked departure from Tudor practice. Cromwell House in Highgate of 1637–8 is another example of a virtuoso performance in brick; its fine ornamentation was confidently carved *in situ*. Such unassuming but still impressive and charming buildings formed the noble architectural diet of London in the decades preceding the Civil War, and it is against this mainstream that the designs of London's first architect in the modern sense, Inigo Jones, must be seen in order for the revolutionary character of his work to be fully appreciated.

Renaissance motifs had been employed in England for a long time, in fact since the building of Cardinal Wolsey's Hampton Court at the beginning of the sixteenth century, and they were generously applied in the works of the Artisan Mannerists; but this was merely playing with foreign devices. What Inigo Jones brought to London was the very spirit of the Renaissance. Not content to ape the styles of his Italian contemporaries, he sought counsel in Palladio's *Quattro Libri della Architettura* as a means of access to the original source of early Roman architecture and the theories of the great Vitruvius. Such was the insistence of Inigo Jones on the absolute validity of the work of the ancients that during his year and a half in Italy, 1613–4, in the train of the Earl of Arundel he was generally dismissive of the newer buildings and spent much of his time studying Roman ruins and checking the accuracy of the measurements of the engravings in his edition of Palladio. He was critical of Michelangelo's 'composed ornaments' and expressed his own passionate belief in an architecture that was 'solid, proportionable according to the rules, masculine and unaffected'. His views on the mathematical laws governing perfection, namely the shape of the cube, made him a radical purist even by Italian standards. Set against the cosy decorative schemes of Jacobean London his designs must have been as shocking to many as was Bauhaus to the lovers of Edwardian Baroque earlier this century.

Not surprisingly, Inigo Jones's architectural commissions did not come from the ranks of the men who had been the patrons of Charlton House, Swakeleys and the Dutch House. Instead he relied almost exclusively on the royal patronage of James I and Charles I whom he served in turn as Surveyor General of the King's Works from 1615 until 1642. The stylistic gulf separating Jones's austerely Classical structures from the more comfortable houses of the rising class of wealthy merchants was an apt reflection of the dangerous chasm opening up between the doctrine of absolute monarchy and the groundswell of Parliamentarianism. But for all their vanity it may be said of both James I and Charles I that they resumed the courtly patronage of architecture which had been neglected during the long years of the reign of Elizabeth I.

The Queen's House at Greenwich, the only palace designed by Inigo Jones, was commenced in 1616 but was abandoned on the death of Anne of Denmark in 1619 and was not to be completed until 1635 for Henrietta Maria. This Classical villa must have seemed particularly outlandish to the solid Englishmen of the time. A correspondent of Sir Dudley Carleton referred to it in 1617 as 'some curious devise of Inigo Jones' but the curiosity possibly lay in the fact that the house was designed as two separate halves joined together by a bridge spanning the Woolwich to Deptford road. Two further bridges were added in 1661 by John Webb, creating the squarish form it has today. The lack of external ornamentation, but for an elegant double staircase on the north side and a charming

Queen's House, Greenwich, a Palladian villa by Inigo Jones, is now the centrepiece of the National Maritime Museum.

loggia giving off the *piano nobile* on the south side, is in marked contrast to the theatrical façades with gabled rooflines then in vogue. By comparison the Queen's House was perhaps no more than a modest box of a building. However, it was a strong enough structure to be retained as the focal point of the Royal Naval Hospital of Sir Christopher Wren and the later National Maritime Museum to which it has been joined by a colonnade. The interior is based on the simple geometry of extreme Palladianism, the entrance hall being a perfect forty-foot cube framed by a carved wooden gallery. The square floor contains a magnificent circular pattern of black-and-white marble. The Queen's House was in truth only a minor palace of pleasure but it has a dignity of purpose beyond its playful function and its modest dimensions.

The Banqueting House of 1619–22 in Whitehall was a more ambitious fulfilment

The Banqueting House, Whitehall, was London's first real taste of the Palladian style.

of both the architect's and the monarch's dreams. Built as a vast reception room for court audiences and the performance of masques (in fact it was as a 'picturemaker' or stage designer that Jones initially made his name), the Banqueting House gave Jones his most prestigious commission and the Stuart dynasty its most poignant memorial. The Whitehall façade of the building merits close scrutiny, for it reveals how Jones's Classicism was not mere copying but a subtle adaptation to English conditions of the Roman and Italian models he chose. He decided against the use of a pediment to provide a focal point and opted instead for small devices such as the balustrading in front of the three middle windows and the insertion of rounded columns, which stand out against the flat pilasters at the side, in order to give cohesion to what is essentially a horizontal composition. Just enough vertical importance is imparted by the two tiers of columns, the lower order Ionic and the upper Composite. The discreet use of naturalistic carving of masks and swags as a continuous frieze hints at the theatrical and ceremonial purpose of the building. It should be noted that when the Banqueting House was entirely refaced in the eighteenth century it lost its original aspect composed of three different types of stone, since Portland was then employed throughout. In detail and overall design it is completely authentic but for the substitution of sash windows in place of the previous casement type.

At first glance the interior of the Banqueting House is impressive on account of its stunning emptiness. The only architectural feature is the gallery which relieves the rather frightening void of a double cube 110 by 55 by 55 feet. If in such geometric perfection the architect realised his vision then the ceiling was reserved for the monarch to live out his own fantasies. The 'Apotheosis of James I' is the subject of a series of heroic canvases by Peter Paul Rubens installed in the ceiling in 1635 by Charles I. These nine huge panels represent the nearest England came to the idea of absolute monarchy. They are also London's most blatant display of political allegory, showing a corrupt and ineffectual king as the dispenser of the gifts of wise government. The Banqueting House is thus an important historical as well as architectural landmark. The symbolism of the building was evidently not lost on the Parliamentarians who condemned Charles I to death by beheading in 1649; for this hapless monarch was obliged to step directly from the *piano nobile* of the Banqueting House to the scaffold erected outside in Whitehall. Inigo Jones had not provided an entrance at this level, a departure from strict Palladian practice, so a window had to be demolished for the occasion. Inigo Jones, then in his seventy-seventh year, must have reflected on the transience of mortal man's achievements.

As Inigo Jones faced his own death in 1652 it might have seemed to him that he had been working in an artistic vacuum as far as the Palladian doctrine of palatial building was concerned. Apart from John Webb, his assistant and relative by marriage, there was no obvious successor to carry on his ideals. Seen in retrospect the Queen's House in Greenwich and the Banqueting House in Whitehall appear as marooned specimens of Palladianism, premature productions which would have been more at home in the second half of the eighteenth century. Yet Inigo Jones did exert some influence on the more illustrious Surveyor General Christopher Wren in the realm of church building. It is known that Wren tried hard to save Jones's Classical west portico of St Paul's Cathedral and that its design helped Wren substantially to

Queen's Chapel, Marlborough Gate, a clear departure from the Gothic style.

St Paul, Covent Garden, was an integral part of a Classical urban development.

arrive at his own. In the Queen's Chapel at St James's of 1623–5 Inigo Jones presented to the outside world not the recognisable shape of a Christian church but that of a temple, thereby paving the way for a later generation of churches constructed according to Classical precepts. But, as with his palaces, so with his churches his message was not immediately taken up. Restoration London was to fall under the graceful, less rigid, more entertaining spell of the Baroque works of Sir Christopher Wren.

Inigo Jones's church of St Paul in Covent Garden occupies a special place in the history of London. This powerful and original work employed the less noble Tuscan order to transform the east end of the church into an imposing portico with huge projecting eaves which still dominates its 'forum' of Covent Garden. Since the actual entrance to the church is by the opposite, west end this amounts in effect to a piece of pure architectural charade, signifying that the sturdy Tuscan columns relate to the open space rather than to the structure of the building itself. This shift away from the actual function of an individual building towards the exigencies of the townscape was a revolutionary leap forwards in the evolution of London's urbanism. At Covent Garden in 1631 the notion of a coherent urban plan made its first appearance in London; for Inigo Jones's church was not merely inserted into a vacant plot but was designed as the centrepiece of a novel development, no less than the comprehensive planning of an entire neighbourhood.

The Covent Garden scheme arose from the economic opportunities offered by the rampant growth of London. The families who benefited from the 'redistribution' of monastic lands by Henry VIII were now in a

Lindsey House, Lincoln's Inn Fields, bears the clear imprint of its Classical inspiration.

position to cash in on their luck by promoting residential developments close to the overcrowded city. The area known as the Convent Garden (*sic*) was part of the estate that had fallen to the fortunate Russell family. It was the fourth Earl of Bedford, descendant of this line, who obtained a licence to build as many 'houses and buildings fit for the habitations of gentlemen and men of ability' as he should think proper. This amounted to the first deliberate attempt to create an élitist enclave for the 'quality' in London and helped further a process of social stratification by area with the wealthy clustering in exclusive settlements in the West End, while the East End became the repository for the less well endowed. This was partly caused by the deteriorating physical environment of London, but the flight to the west was also motivated by the growing aristocratic snobbery directed against tradesmen in general.

The influence of Inigo Jones was present in Covent Garden not only in the design of the church. As Surveyor General he had a shaping hand in the overall scheme, and the idea of the square, based on the piazza at Livorno in Italy, was almost certainly his. The design of the houses built along the north and east sides of the square showed the clear influence of the Place Royale of 1609 in Paris (now the Place des Vosges). The church of St Paul on the west side was originally flanked by noble mansions, and the south side remained open for the time being, but for the wall of the Earl of Bedford's garden. It was here that the selling of fruit, flowers and vegetables began in the area. This casual trade was put on a commercial footing in 1671 when a licence for a proper market was obtained, much to the dislike of the aristocratic residents of the square who gradually resumed their westward migration. The sudden arrival of hordes of raucous countryfolk with their produce must have disturbed the much praised 'uniformities and decency' of the area. Of the original scheme only the church survives, completely but faithfully rebuilt in 1795. The houses in the northwest corner, also rebuilt, date from around 1880. Although not quite accurate they do convey the general effect of the originals of 1631 with their delightful vaulted arcades at street level offering a rare opportunity in London of a covered promenade. The present market buildings are from the nineteenth century.

The most important relic of Inigo Jones's Covent Garden is arguably the open space or 'piazza' itself, which unlike other innovations of the architect was to set the style immediately for London's new districts. It may be claimed that this was the birthplace of London's most successful urban creation: the square. Inigo Jones's work as London's first urbanist also included the housing development around Lincoln's Inn Fields from 1638 which was the first thoroughly commercial and non-aristocratic large-scale development in the city, promoted by a Mr William Newton. This square arose, however, more from the public pressure to maintain an open space for recreation rather than from any abstract principles of town planning. But it was architecturally significant in that it continued the idea of a unified development with a Classical formality. Of the original housing only one stately residence, Lindsey House on the west side, remains. It is attributed to Inigo Jones with more justification than many other buildings of this era accredited to his name, and has been described as the single most important townhouse in London on account of the seminal influence of its Palladian features. Inigo Jones should be remembered, however, as more than an architect of distinction in London's building history, for his pioneering creation of the formal square at Covent Garden had a revolutionary impact on the ideas of future generations of urbanists, notably in the Georgian era, who were consistently to use the square as the basic component of London's dynamic expansion with the result that it has become a hallmark of the metropolis.

The Age of Wren

London's architecture from the Restoration of the Stuart monarchy in 1660 until its demise in 1714 was dominated by one man, Sir Christopher Wren, to an extent which has never been equalled in any other age. During almost half a century as Surveyor General from 1669 to 1718 Wren's artistic and administrative gifts found constant application. The Restoration gave fresh impetus to both royal and lesser projects after the destructive hiatus of the Civil War; and the Great Fire of 1666, which devastated 436 acres or 80 per cent of the old City of London, including 87 parish churches, 45 halls of the livery companies, the cathedral of St Paul and all the apparatus of commercial and civic government, provided a unique opportunity for a new architectural and metropolitan vision. Wren's capacity for work was enormous and he took on the lion's share of the commissions, so that his personal style has become synonymous with the buildings of two entire generations of London architects. He was still designing well into his eighties and reached the venerable age of ninety-one before expiring in 1723. But his longevity was no unmixed blessing, for he lived long enough to see his concepts and creations criticised by the prophets of the new age, such as the Earl of Shaftesbury who wrote in 1712: 'Thro' several reigns we have patiently seen the noblest publick Buildings perish (if I may say so) under the Hand of one single Court Architect; who, if he had been able to profit by Experience, wou'd long since, at our expence, have prov'd the greatest Master in the World. But I question whether our Patience is like to hold much longer.' It must therefore be borne in mind that Wren's pre-eminence was by no means always comfortable or undisputed. Far from being an omnipotent dictator of style, Wren suffered the painful defeats of all architects whose most cherished projects have remained on the drawing-board or have been compromised beyond recognition. In retrospect Wren may appear to loom large as a towering monolith; but, like the Monument he himself designed, he was in reality much hemmed in by London's conservatism and entrenched interests.

The fifty-two City churches he designed are a case in point. According to the account given by his son in *Parentalia*, it had been Wren's intention to rebuild 'all the Parish Churches in such a Manner as to be seen at the End of a Vista of Houses, and dispersed in such Distances from each other, as to appear neither too thick, nor thin in Prospect'. The reality was that Wren was obliged to adhere to the existing confined sites wedged into odd spaces between the houses. Accordingly, very few Wren churches present an ornamental façade to the street since they were mostly tucked away behind other buildings. Notable exceptions are the magnificent Corinthian columns and pilasters of the east front of St Lawrence Jewry by the Guildhall and the ornate entrance in Cheapside of St Mary-le-Bow. More usually the exterior of a Wren church is not unlike a box with windows. But what Wren was forced to concede in noble vistas he created above the rooftops with an extraordinary array of steeples ranging from the Gothic of St Dunstan-in-the-East to the Baroque of St Vedast. Wren's powerful vision of a skyline of spires and steeples, now best seen in old engravings since over half have been lost and the rest dwarfed by the buildings of the nineteenth and twentieth centuries, was arranged as a diverse but coherent composition around the great bulk of the dome of St Paul's. One can only steal, as it were, fragmented glimpses of this aerial symphony from specific vantage points such as the Stone Gallery of St Paul's itself, from which it is possible to see the relation between the west towers of the cathedral, the slender spire of St Martin Ludgate and the wedding-cake tiers of St Bride in Fleet Street. Wren is the only architect of London to have devised and accomplished an exhilarating and harmonious skyline to give cohesion to the City.

Towers and steeples were, however, really only embellishments where a fair measure of whim and fancy could be allowed to play. Church interiors had to follow a stricter discipline. Yet even in the most restrictive and unpromising of spaces Wren contrived to create a magical interplay of tension and repose so that there is usually a pleasing visual stimulation behind the unassuming façade of a Wren church. In many cases he has broken completely with the traditional longitudinal alignment of the church which focused all attention on the furthest point of the sanctuary, opting instead for a square, centralised layout, in which the altar is counterbalanced by the new poles of the pulpit and the lectern. In this, Wren was providing the Church of England with a new generation of churches which were specifically adapted to the current Protestant liturgy. In the words of the architect himself:

> In our reformed Religion, it should seem vain to make a Parish church larger, than that all who are present can both hear and see. The Romanists, indeed, may build larger Churches, it is enough if they hear the murmur of the Mass, and see the Elevation of the Host, but ours are to be fitted for Auditories . . . with Pews and Galleries . . . and all to hear the Service, and both to hear distinctly, and see the Preacher.

St Bride, Fleet Street, one of Wren's many varied spires to grace the London skyline.

Wren's City church interiors were revolutionary in more than layout. Huge, clear windows were designed to admit as much light as possible, to create a luminous upper half in contrast to the dark wood of the wainscoting and the high box-pews which contained the congregation. The symbolism of the bright celestial realm above and the sombre world of man below could not be more powerful. This almost scientific division of the church into its essential parts reflects the spirit of the age of rationalism. The deity is still present but the building of the church has been demystified; it is as functional as a public library and as comfortable and orderly as a drawing room, the very antithesis to the ecstatic vision of Gothic architecture with its dark recesses full of medieval mysticism and

St Mary-at-Hill, one of the best-preserved Wren interiors, with its dark box pews and bright walls and ceiling.

distant sources of coloured light. Sadly, the Victorians destroyed the clarity of many Wren churches by introducing stained glass, and disrupted the auditory structure by cutting down the box-pews and removing the galleries. The most authentic interiors in the City are those of St James Garlickhythe and St Mary-at-Hill for their clear light and excellent woodwork. St Mary Abchurch, and St Anne and St Agnes, both show how Wren could create a stunning sense of space by inserting round ceiling shapes into square structures; but St Stephen Walbrook, with its central dome perched on slender columns to enclose a square space, stands out as the most daring and complex achievement of all. It is often interpreted as a preliminary version of the technical ingenuity of the dome of St Paul's.

Wren's variations on the centralised plan were not his last word on the subject, for in St James's Piccadilly he returned to the more conventional scheme of nave and aisles with parallel galleries, which he described as the most convenient form for Anglican churches. Neither was Wren dogmatic in his artistic preferences. Although personally committed to his own brand of freely inventive Classicism, he could when required even turn his hand to Gothic, which he considered 'not ungraceful but ornamental', an apt description of his own version of Gothic at St Mary Aldermary with its mock fan-vaulting executed in plaster. But Wren was not at all interested in the style of the Middle Ages when he first began to devise a rebuilding of St Paul's prior to the Great Fire of 1666. His idea was to refashion the nave 'after a good Roman manner' and to replace 'the Gothick Rudeness of ye old Design'. In the event, Wren was very quickly relieved of the necessity of a complex conversion of the existing fabric by the Great Fire which broke out within two weeks of the ordering of estimates for the work on St Paul's and presented him with the chance to make a completely fresh plan for London's cathedral.

The painful evolution of St Paul's from 1675 to 1711 was for Wren an epic struggle with the eventual users of the cathedral; and the much acclaimed building, as it exists today, is really quite a compromise of the architect's own preferred version. The Great Model of 1674 represented Wren's ultimate statement of intent for the rebuilding of St Paul's. It is essentially in the form of a Greek cross with equal arms but with an elongation of the west end under a domed vestibule and a lofty Corinthian portico. It is worth studying the Great Model, which is on permanent display in the crypt of St Paul's, and comparing it to the building as constructed. It is hard to deny the Great Model its noble proportions which achieve more grandeur with simpler means; but the conservative-minded clergy would have none of it, since it was too radical a departure from the hallowed form of the longitudinal Latin cross. Wren was obliged to give the clergy what they wanted, but devised a rather ugly building which has become known as the Warrant Design. Rather craftily, Wren then obtained a discreet promise from the King that he be allowed to make revisions as the work progressed; and this royal dispensation was to be exploited to the full. It is indeed hard to discern much relation between the Warrant Design and the final building. In order to conceal the full extent of the changes he intended, Wren did not publicly expose his drawings and he even resorted to such secretive measures as the covering of completed parts behind wattle screens. The most radical innovations introduced were the Baroque west towers, the false upper storey which concealed the flying buttresses, and of course the great dome itself, far grander than the small rotunda with its curious projecting spire as in the Warrant Design.

Although not conforming to Wren's ideal, St Paul's is imposing by any standards. Its huge bulk, it must be imagined, really dominated the City and indeed the London region for miles around before a rash of high-rise offices completely ruined its effect from all quadrants of the compass. From the inside, the gaze is drawn involuntarily upwards into the dome and the soaring lantern. The original decor has been altered by the lavish Victorian mosaics in the Byzantine manner, but the superb ironwork by Jean Tijou and the carved wooden choir-stalls by Grinling Gibbons are authentic examples of the cathedral's furnishings when first completed. London may have lost the chance of an artistically more satisfying piece of architecture but St Paul's does express the energy and confidence of the City of London that had risen from the ashes of the Great Fire.

Notwithstanding the demands of St Paul's and more than fifty parish churches Wren still found time to work on a vast range of royal commissions, including a never-to-be-realised scheme for a complete rebuilding of Whitehall Palace which

The west front of St Paul's Cathedral is composed of two tiers of Classical columns to attain the great height required by Wren.

retained only the Banqueting House of Inigo Jones. Work on Wren's new palace at Winchester was abandoned on the death of Charles II. It is significant that although the Baroque style was, within reason, considered acceptable for a cathedral, it was definitely inappropriate for the residence of an English monarch in an age in which England had come to stand for the sober values of a Protestant parliamentary democracy as opposed to the Catholic absolutism of Louis XIV. In the palatial projects which Wren actually accomplished for William and Mary this essential difference between royal architecture in England and France at the time is most dramatically underlined. With the move from Whitehall to Kensington in 1689 William and Mary distanced themselves from the parade of their Tudor and Stuart predecessors, electing to reside in what was no more than a very comfortable conversion of an

Fountain Court, part of Wren's extension to Hampton Court, is a pleasing combination of white stone and red brick.

unremarkable Jacobean mansion. It is in fact maintained by some that Kensington Palace should really be called Kensington House for it was essentially a modest country home by comparison with some of the stately mansions of the nobility of the day. The unassuming lines of Wren's domestic exterior of Kensington Palace appear almost bashful. Inside there is a vivid contrast between the rooms still in the decor of William and Mary's choosing and the later embellishments featuring the decorative murals of William Kent. The Queen's Staircase and the Queen's Gallery with their plain wood panelling are a world apart from the contemporary pomp of Louis XIV's Versailles.

Even at Hampton Court, where the gardens laid out for Charles II provide the most striking example of formal Baroque planning in London, the Wren buildings around Fountain Court and along the south and east fronts are almost reticent in this context. The majestic Long Water, an extension of the central one of three radiating avenues, which is nearly a kilometre in length, demands something more imposing than the pedimented stone centrepiece with which Wren attempted to give some thrust to what is essentially a very sedate range of brick buildings. Likewise the rather fussy and cramped stone ornamentation around the windows facing into the courtyard is pleasing enough but somewhat repetitious as an architectural composition. It is quite clear that the English monarchy was keen to avoid any dramatic massing of building forms which might be interpreted as an attempt to emulate the Baroque palaces on the continent.

Of the royal palaces in and around London only the work at Greenwich can be claimed as truly Baroque, and in this Wren's hand was already committed by the King Charles Block of 1662–9 by John Webb. He responded with a design in the

The Painted Hall of the Royal Naval College, Greenwich, boasts a Baroque décor.

The colonnade at the Royal Naval College is one component of Wren's heroic design.

grand manner where parallel blocks led into a central domed structure but was obliged to keep open the distant view of the Queen's House by Inigo Jones. So emerged the scheme as it exists today, with two domes facing one another across an open space with no architectural climax but the remote prospect of a chaste Palladian villa. However, the colonnades of the Wren buildings are superb, both dynamic and ceremonial at the same time, a grandiose feature for the new role of the palace as the Royal Naval Hospital which it became in 1694. Quite the most regal part of the complex is the Great Hall, known as the Painted Hall on account of its dazzling ceiling and wall paintings by Sir James Thornhill. In this lavish celebration of a Protestant monarchy and its benefits in the persons of William and Mary the artist slips effortlessly into the continental language of Baroque Absolutism with its heroic swirling mass of allegorical figures. In the centre of the huge oval ceiling panel over the main body of the hall William and Mary are enthroned in a tableau which represents the triumph of the English concept of constitutional monarchy over the forces of tyranny and oppression ruling in Europe. There is nowhere better in London to capture the optimism and self-confidence of the age with a new city risen from the ashes and a new England reborn after the Glorious Revolution of 1688 revelling in its Protestant religion and progressive democratic institutions. That Wren and Thornhill used the medium of the Baroque, more associated with autocratic rulers, was not seen in any way as a contradiction. The Royal Naval Hospital was after all simply stunning to behold, equalled in magnificence only by St Paul's Cathedral.

But such grand projects as these were but isolated heroic gestures. Wren had hoped to create out of the destruction of the Great Fire an imposing Baroque cityscape with stately avenues converging on elegant rond-points affording noble vistas in emulation of the Piazza del Popolo in Rome and the projected Place de la France in Paris. In the event the practical needs of the inhabitants of London, whose rights to their private property Charles II was forced to concede, came first and a number of utopian schemes for the City were consigned to the archives. It used to be fashionable to express regret that London's great chance for a geometrically planned city centre was missed; but there is now more awareness that such masterplans, even when offered a *tabula rasa* for their fantasies, are rarely conducive to the emergence of a natural human pattern; and it was precisely the underlying pattern of the City which was salvaged from the ashes and ruins of the Great Fire. As people insisted on rebuilding their homes on their old plots, so the medieval structure of London resurfaced almost in its entirety but for some widening of the streets and the introduction of one scenic route along King Street and Queen Street which opened fine views towards the Guildhall.

The great step forwards in London's urbanism after the Fire lay in the standardisation of house sizes in relation to the width of the streets, and three main types were allowed, depending on the importance of the thoroughfare, with a maximum permitted height of four storeys. Brick became the common building material for all but the wealthiest of clients who could afford stone. Thus there occurred a striking transformation of the physical aspect of London from a huddled mass of half-timbered dwellings into more orderly rows of neat brick. There is a report of 1690 from the Reverend Kirk: 'Since the burning, all London is built uniformly, the streets broader, the houses all of one form and height.' Wren's contribution to the new London as one of the Commissioners behind the 1667 Act for Rebuilding the City of London was in an administrative capacity, determining the guidelines for the reconstruction. But beyond that it was left to private initiative actually to build the houses.

The only Baroque piece of town planning to be introduced in London around this time was the rond-point of Seven Dials near Covent Garden by Sir Thomas Neale in 1694; but this district rapidly fell short of any heroic aspirations and deteriorated into one of London's worst slums, and only the street pattern has survived. Elsewhere there was frantic development to urbanise new areas for the expansion of the city and it was the concept of the square which provided the framework for such schemes. The ancestor of today's Bloomsbury Square was laid out in 1665 by the Earl of Southampton. John Evelyn described it as 'a noble square or piazza and a little town'. In contrast to the Covent Garden of Inigo Jones this was no great architectural unity in the Classical mould but simply terraces of townhouses around a square. The description of 'a little town' indicated that this was designed as a self-contained community with lesser

St James's Square, an expanse of greenery a stone's throw from Piccadilly.

streets for the traders and ordinary folk who served the inhabitants of the 'noble square'. The idea was taken up more effectively in 1684 by Henry Jermyn, Earl of St Albans, who created an entire faubourg of even more aristocratic allure centred around St James's Square. Jermyn's role was confined to the functions of planner and promoter; the business of designing and building the houses was left to those who took up the leases on the plots. This highly successful development, the work of a noble speculator rather than an architectural theorist, illustrates the main trend of London's new urban districts at the end of the seventeenth century. Only Wren's church of St James's remains of the original buildings but the self-contained cohesion of the quarter with its mix of character from the stately square to the courtyards behind and the markets and shops of Jermyn Street is still discernible as the skeleton of the first scheme.

Several other squares in London date back to this period but have retained none of their early houses: for example Leicester Square of 1670, Soho Square of 1681, Hoxton Square of 1683 in Shoreditch and Red Lion Square of 1684 in Holborn. But these were simply residential developments rather than entire neighbourhoods. Kensington Square of around 1700 still has some of the original housing, now much altered, from what was a tiny residential enclave in attendance on Kensington Palace far to the west of London's expansion at the time. New Square of 1685 in Lincoln's Inn has the greatest period character and architectural cohesion, and best conveys the emerging style of London. In the nearby Temple there are some splendid houses of the period in King's Bench Walk, of which numbers 2 to 7 have been attributed to Wren.

There are several examples of the work of London's first notorious speculator and developer, Nicholas Barbon, where we encounter some of the earliest serial

King's Bench Walk, Inner Temple. Numbers 2–7 have been attributed to Wren.

productions of standardised dwellings on a tight budget at such locations as 36 and 43 Bedford Row and 21 to 24 Newport Court. At this time small blocks of uniform housing – the prototypes of the great terraces – made their appearance as far afield as Richmond Green with Old Palace Terrace of 1692, in Chelsea with Cheyne Row of 1703 and in Deptford with Albury Street from 1706 onward, where numbers 21 to 31 and 34 to 40 have managed to retain their impressive carved door hoods. The shell hood was a very popular decorative motif and its occasional survival, as at 1 and 2

Albury Street, Deptford, of 1706, still retains some remarkable original door hoods.

Queen Anne's Gate shows the external woodwork prior to the Building Acts of 1707–9.

Laurence Pountney Hill in the City, evokes a lost world of small-scale urban elegance. One can observe the passing of a house style in Queen Anne's Gate, where some of the houses predate the building regulations of 1707 and 1709 which laid down that the sash windows and door frames had to be set back at least four inches and which banned wooden eaves and cornices in favour of plain brick parapets as a precaution against fire.

London possesses some splendid superior detached houses of the late seventeenth century which are characterised by a hipped roof, long windows flush with the brickwork, a pedimented central door and modillioned eaves cornice. The Deanery in Dean's Court near St Paul's (attributed to Wren), 37 Stepney Green and Fenton House in Hampstead all exhibit the characteristics of a national idiom, albeit with Dutch undertones. Wren has been credited with the invention of the style, even though it may be seen to have preceded him in such buildings as Eltham Lodge of 1664 by Hugh May. Wren refined and distributed his own style not really in domestic works but mainly in larger productions, such as the Royal Hospital in Chelsea which provided an institutional prototype still with us today. In terms of international style Wren spearheaded the triumph in London and in England as a whole of a pleasing blend of Dutch domestic and Classical motifs.

The true flavour of the age can also be sampled in some of the smaller projects, such as the unattributed Trinity House almshouses of 1695 in Mile End for 'decayed Masters & Comanders of Ships or the Widows of such' and the harmonious quadrangular Morden College (attributed to Wren) in Blackheath of the same year for

Fenton House, Hampstead, 1693, now in the care of the National Trust.

Chelsea Hospital, a widely imitated piece of institutional architecture, is still in service as a home for retired soldiers.

'decayed Turkey Merchants'. Possibly the most completely satisfying experience of the Wren style is at the Royal Observatory of 1675 where the charm of the domestic scale is combined with the clarity of light and orderly layout which are the hallmark of his churches. Here, in the Octagon Room, one of the few remaining Wren interiors, one feels that the great architect was truly in his element, for he was Savilian Professor of Astronomy at Oxford before turning his hand to architecture, and he has managed to design in the Royal Observatory a sort of architectural shrine to the spirit of scientific rationalism with the pure geometry of the eight-sided room and its tall, straight windows covering all points of the compass.

Detail of Nash's Marble Arch. This relief on the south side is by Bailey.

3 Georgian Refinement

The foundations were laid during the eighteenth and early nineteenth centuries of what is still a functioning part of today's habitat. Many people still live in Georgian houses, and the period is a vital part of our contemporary awareness, whereas Elizabethan, Jacobean and even buildings by Wren have been consigned by history to the status of museum pieces. Our perception of what is 'modern' may be said to begin fairly precisely with the accession of George I in 1714. The background to the Georgian age in London, which lasted until 1830, was of a tremendous growth in the population and a radical restructuring of urban settlement. Although the first half of the eighteenth century saw London's population static at around 650,000, health improvements and legislation against cheap gin led to a formidable and sustained increase thereafter. By the time of the first census in 1801 the one million figure was in sight, and by the accession of Queen Victoria in 1837 the figure had doubled to almost two million. But behind these rising statistics the City itself registered a decline in overall numbers from an estimated high of 140,000 in 1700 to 128,000 in 1801 and to 123,000 in 1841. Within the expanding conurbation the City thus accounted for an ever dwindling percentage.

The main area of growth was to the west, where a handful of aristocrat-landowners opened up their agricultural estates for housing. Almost overnight, country magnates became urban landlords, and fortunes were established that have lasted to this day. On the map of Georgian London a few names appear as powerful as feudal barons: the Duke of Westminster holding northern Mayfair, Belgravia and Pimlico; Lord Portman and the Duke of Portland owning nearly all of Marylebone; and the Duke of Bedford in possession of Bloomsbury and Covent Garden. One might have expected some autocratic exercises in town planning, but in reality all development passed through the hands of the speculative builders, men of considerable enterprise who took enormous risks as they charted the progress of bricks and mortar through the booms and slumps of the period. What emerged was not grandiose but modest, neat and logical. The tidy gridiron of Bloomsbury and the West End imposed its pattern on the emerging map of London, a geometric scheme in which only the occasional irregularity occurs, such as the meandering course of Marylebone Lane like a palimpsest of the rural past. The squares, which provide relief from the built-up areas, present themselves not as showpieces but as efficient components in the urban machine.

The City remained essentially as it had been reconstructed in the fifty years after the Fire of 1666, a reincarnation in brick along the lines laid down in the Middle Ages. The medieval pattern lived on in the labyrinth of streets and the narrow building plots which still give parts of the City a decidedly ancient character in spite of modern building. Though still the economic power-house, the City came to be regarded as architecturally backward, and it was no longer either fashionable or environmentally congenial to reside there. As for the East End in the eighteenth century, it was a world away from the pleasing elegance of what Defoe described as the 'new world of Brick and Tile' of the West End. London's gaping social divide was already deeply entrenched.

The new streetscape of Georgian London followed a simple but effective formula based on Palladian formality derived from Classical architecture. It was really quite amazing how the style and precepts of the sixteenth century Italian architect Andrea Palladio acted as the hidden hand behind almost all building of the period. There was also an uncanny complicity between the arbitrators of fashion and the legislators of the Building Acts which reinforced the trend towards ever greater austerity and standardisation of appearance. The resulting uniformity was not to everyone's liking, as Boswell confessed after a visit to Wapping; and John Gwynn in his influential *London and Westminster Improved* of 1766 wrote of a street in Marylebone as 'a line of new buildings, which as they at present stand give no better idea to the spectator than that of a plain brick wall of prodigious length'. One has only to look at a street such as Gloucester Place to know what Gwynn had in mind. There is no doubt that Georgian architecture heralded 'an end to gabled individualism' (Summerson) and that it reflected the notion of mass production. In this sense Georgian was essentially 'modern' with its relentless move to uniform façades and steady whittling away at external embellishment – Adam and Nash excepted, of course.

At the top end of the market ideas of style came to be an obsession. Whereas in the seventeenth century architecture was the incidental product of the way people lived, in the eighteenth it became a central issue in its own right. A formidable amount of Classical design theory was digested by builders, architects and patrons alike. The question of the nature of correct taste was a matter for endless discourse and dispute. Architecture became a highly conscious and hotly contested activity, and the style of buildings became almost more important than their practical function.

London dominated the country in the eighteenth century with 75 per cent of the nation's shipping and 10 per cent of the population; its merchants were, according to Defoe, 'greater and richer and more powerful than some sovereign princes', yet the virtues of its architecture were uniformity and reticence at a time when Europe was indulging in an orgy of Baroque and Rococo. Robert Adam brought fanciful decoration to the exterior of the London house, but this was soon to be dismissed as a vain frippery and appears in retrospect as a playful intermezzo between the puristic compositions of the Palladians and the Greek Revivalists. The general rule of the Georgian period may be summed up in the words of the minor architect Edmund Aiken in 1810: 'To be natural and unaffected is the first rule of good taste.' But opulence could be found in abundance behind the self-effacing blankness of the brick walls, where every manner of adornment and embellishment was deployed. Opening the door of a wealthy London house was often like finding a dazzling jewel in a casket of the utmost discretion. That was the self-confidence of the Georgian era which did not need to parade its success too openly to the world.

In the course of the eighteenth century the tide of architectural fashion swept over

The modestly decorated exterior of 20 Portman Square contains some of Robert Adam's most dazzling interiors.

London at regular intervals every two or three decades. There was a short-lived Baroque interlude at the outset which found its highest expression in the dozen churches which actually resulted from the Act of 1711 for 'Building Fifty New Churches'. Such strangely powerful monuments of the English Baroque as Hawksmoor's Christ Church Spitalfields and St Mary Woolnoth in the City, Archer's St John in Smith Square and St Paul in Deptford, and Gibbs's St Mary-le-Strand stand out as erratics in the urban landscape. Their muscular and emotional appeal was alien to the spirit of the refined Palladianism which held sway from 1720 to about 1760. The Palladian supremacy was then challenged by a broad and eclectic Neo-Classical reaction, which resolved itself into a virtual monopoly of the Greek Revival at the beginning of the nineteenth century. However, by 1837 a Regency architect declared: 'It is an architect's business to understand all styles and to be prejudiced in favour of none.' This was a far cry from the single-mindedness of the first generation of Palladians of more than a century before, who were convinced of the universal validity of their ideas. Colen Campbell had indeed acclaimed the Banqueting House of Inigo Jones as 'the first structure in the world'.

In a sense Regency London reaped the last harvest of the Classical tradition which the Palladian movement had inaugurated, but at the same time it sowed the seeds of its own destruction. The Picturesque and theatricality of Nash's Regent's Park was achieved with the stucco known as Parker's Roman Cement which allowed the architect to take all manner of liberties. The 'triumphal arches' of Chester Terrace have been described by Summerson 'as badly detailed as a piece of realism in a provincial production of Julius Caesar'. But as long as the underlying proportions of the building were in line with Palladian principles even such blatant spray-on architecture was acceptable. The age was still 'so imbued with the principles of artistic good manners' (Steegman). However, the Regency period clearly heralds the coming excesses of Victorian architects to whom the Classical tradition was an anathema.

Behind all the wranglings over style the London building trade underwent radical reorganisation. Individual craftsmen were drawn into a structured system. In 1815 Thomas Cubitt was the first to found an enterprise which combined the activities of the contractor and developer. By 1828 he had 1000 men in his employ. Keeping them in work meant a constant stream of projects. Belgravia and Pimlico were to provide the outlets for his energies in the first half of the nineteenth century. Belgravia was reclaimed from marshy ground to the west of Buckingham Palace using spoil from the digging of St Katharine Dock near the Tower, providing a neat allegory of the relationship between the West End and the East End.

The East End was transformed in the early years of the nineteenth century by the creation of the docks, where the genius of Georgian architecture was applied to industrial buildings. The Telford warehouses, now demolished, at St Katharine Dock underlined just how 'modern' the Classical building concepts really were. Some of the late eighteenth-century warehouses of the East India Company have been preserved and successfully blended with modern office buildings in an imaginative development in the City known as Cutlers Gardens. It was in association with the docks that many of the modest Georgian terraces were laid out. The spread of Georgian London was mainly north of the river, for until 1750 when Westminster Bridge was completed, London Bridge had been the only fixed crossing. Blackfriars Bridge followed in 1769, then between 1813 and 1819 Southwark, Vauxhall and Waterloo bridges were opened. This gave a great boost to new housing in Camberwell, Kennington, Walworth and Clapham. London's expansion to the north was held for a while within the bounds of the New Road of 1756 from Paddington to Islington. This was London's first bypass, a precursor of the North Circular and the M25, and is still a vital traffic link under the name of the Marylebone Road and the Euston Road. London continued to grow to the north and spilled out beyond the New Road before the end of the eighteenth century in areas such as Somers Town in 1786, Pentonville in 1790, Camden Town and Kentish Town in 1791. From 1794 there was a new type of villa and semi-detached development on the Eyre estate, now known as St John's Wood.

The physical aspect of London at the end of the Georgian era was overwhelmingly Classical. Most public buildings were in one cut or another Graeco-Roman; and the housing, despite its variety of detailing, was amazingly homogeneous. Order and

Noble front of a house in Bedford Square, a development of the late eighteenth century.

regularity were almost everywhere in evidence, but the noble vision of the metropolis was to fill the Victorians with horror. They saw monotony in the uniformity and the filth and poverty lurking behind the refinement. Already in 1822 William Cobbett defined the new attitude to London. Looking back towards the city on his way from Kensington to Lewes, he noted: 'And these rows of new houses, added to the Wen, are proofs of prosperity are they? These make part of the increased capital of the country, do they? But how is this Wen to be dispersed? I know not whether it be to be done by knife or by caustic; but dispersed it must be.' For some, the great achievement of Georgian London had evidently turned into a nightmare of monstrous proportions.

Noble Ideas of Style

The possibilities of Palladian architecture in London had already been explored in the seventeenth century by Inigo Jones but the Civil War had interrupted a wider acceptance of his ideas. In 1714 at the dawn of the Georgian era the conditions were once more propitious for a new generation of architects and patrons to seek their ideal in the theories and example of the sixteenth-century Italian architect Andrea Palladio. Wren was approaching retirement and his long dominion was openly resented by more than just the Earl of Shaftesbury who had voiced such bitter criticism of him. Although the pleasing Wren formulae of elegant Baroque and an almost Flemish domesticity had satisfied at least two generations of Londoners, this was no longer enough for the newly emerging élite of Gentlemen of Taste, embodiments of the Age of Reason, who required a more substantial intellectual framework to architecture than that it should be merely pleasing to behold.

Slowly the idea had been gaining currency in England that taste was not a subjective idea in the mind of the individual but a physical reality which existed in an ideal form and could be arrived at by understanding and following absolute rules. Now the management of taste was to be taken over by a self-appointed clique eager to lay down those rules, if not for society at large, then at least for the patrons of noble works of architecture. England's tradition of architectural improvisation was to be replaced by an absolutism that is usually more associated with the more rigid systems of the continent. However, to the rational minds of Englishmen in the early years of the eighteenth century an obsession with rules did not appear to be at all unEnglish.

The spread of the chaste, cerebral Palladian principles of symmetry, a scientific belief in correct proportioning according to mathematical ratios and a strict application of the five recognised Classical orders (Tuscan, Doric, Ionic, Corinthian and Composite) was promoted by a steady flood of serious publications. Hard on the heels of the Hanoverian accession there appeared as heralds of the Age of Taste two publications of overwhelming significance at the time. Giacomo Leoni's 1715 edition of Palladio's *Four Books of Architecture* was the first English version of Palladianism; and in the same year the Scottish architect Colen Campbell saw the publication of the first volume of his *Vitruvius Britannicus*, a comprehensive survey of British building practice which had the overt propagandistic purpose of discrediting both Wren and the notions of the Baroque. This represented just the first salvo in what was to be a sustained barrage of books on architectural doctrine. This was accompanied by a growing public awareness of architecture, above all in London, which saw the birth of the academic discipline of architectural criticism as exemplified by James Ralph's *A Critical Review of the Public Buildings of London* of 1734, in which he expressed so clearly the distinctive feature of the new outlook: 'A good taste is the heightener of every science, and the polish of every virtue.' The Age of Taste had arrived.

It was Richard Boyle, third Earl of Burlington (1694–1753), who was responsible for turning words into buildings and relaunching the Palladian style. By about 1720 he had gathered about himself a Palladian coterie which included Colen Campbell, Giacomo Leoni and William Kent, an artist who was to achieve greater renown as an architect and designer. The young Earl's first major work was the transformation of the family home in Piccadilly, an unassuming seventeenth-century mansion, into an advertisement of Palladian practice. The results of the work, which was conducted by Colen Campbell, may still be seen beneath later remodellings of the north range of Burlington House, now the home of the Royal Academy. Some portions of the original interiors by Campbell on the first floor, the *piano nobile* of the true Palladian house, have survived. The magnificent doorcases of the Saloon are the main visible feature of one of London's finest early Palladian interiors, although the cherubs adorning two of the pedimented doorcases are reminiscent of the Baroque.

Burlington was well placed to promote the cause of Palladianism on a larger scale on his land to the north of Burlington House which was then ripe for development, but he appears not to have imposed his vision on the overall shape of the new housing. However, Uxbridge House at 7 Burlington Gardens, originally by Leoni in 1721 but since refaced, and 31 Old Burlington Street by Campbell around the same time still bear witness to the influence exerted by the Earl of Burlington in his own backyard. He was instrumental, too, in

The Saloon of Burlington House dates back to the remodelling of c. *1717–20.*

Lord Burlington's Palladian fantasy of Chiswick House attracted both scorn and admiration.

obtaining for his protégé William Kent the commission for repainting the interiors of the royal apartments at Kensington Palace in preference to the more worthy contender for the job, Sir James Thornhill. Burlington's hand may also be seen as the Palladians wrested control of the Office of Works.

But the Earl was more than a patron and promoter; he was also an aspiring architect in his own right and managed to obtain for himself the commission to design a new dormitory block for Westminster School. This remarkably dignified work in the true Palladian manner, with its orderly rows of pedimented windows, can be viewed from the College Garden which is open for a few hours only once a week. It is, however, at Chiswick House that the architectural and aesthetic ideals of Lord Burlington are most potently and excitingly embodied. The remarkable point about this building, constructed 1723–9, is that it was designed by Burlington uniquely for parade and display, for hosting receptions and for the exposition of works of art. It is an architectural curiosity or a showcase of pure style rather than anything like a house for living in.

The centrepiece is a lofty octagonal space lit by semicircular windows beneath the dome. Four doors seem to compete for attention, inviting the visitor to explore the series of stately rooms which unfold like compartments in a carefully devised cabinet of delights. Most intriguing is the gallery along the west front, which is composed of three parts. An apse-like opening, providing niches for sculptures, leads from each end of the rectangular central area of the gallery into ingeniously contrived spaces. The whole purpose of the interior of Chiswick House, largely designed by William Kent, appears to be nothing less than the creation of a three-dimensional piece of stage scenery which permitted Burlington's Palladian friends and associates actually to enter the theatre of their imagination and to promenade through a world made in their own considered image of themselves. The layout is cunningly planned so that all paths must cross in the Domed Saloon at the centre of the web where stone benches have been thoughtfully and symmetrically placed for the guests to indulge in some enlightened communal discourse on aesthetic matters before resuming their meanderings through the galleries. There are many much grander mansions and palaces than this, for Chiswick House is really a miniature among noble buildings, but there is none so uncompromisingly devoted to the single purpose of the cultivation of taste and with so little concession to domesticity.

It is hardly surprising that such high-flown artistic pretensions could not escape the merciless mockery of eighteenth-century London, notably that of William Hogarth, the satirical artist and a close neighbour of Chiswick House, who described his own humble abode, which still hangs on next to the roaring traffic of the Great West Road, with deliberate irony as a 'villakin' or a 'brick box'. Lord Chesterfield, who considered it beneath the dignity of a fellow aristocrat to practise as a common architect, penned a famous witty verse to ridicule the other-worldliness of Burlington's Palladian premises:

> Possessed of one great house for state
> Without one room to sleep or eat,
> How well you build, let flattery tell,
> And all mankind, how ill you dwell.

Even Alexander Pope, who otherwise hailed Burlington as the spiritual heir of Vitruvius, Palladio and Inigo Jones, sounded a note of caution in his 'Epistle to

The interior of Chiswick House presents a refined Classical environment.

The domed central room of Chiswick House acts as a rond-point giving access to the galleries on all sides.

Lord Burlington' of 1731 against the excesses of 'Imitating Fools' who by seeking to follow Palladian rules:

Shall call the winds thro' long arcades to roar,
Proud to catch cold at a Venetian door;
Conscious they act a true Palladian part,
And if they starve, they starve by rules of art.

However, the revival of the Palladian ideal found many imitators and Burlington and his colleagues certainly succeeded in making the works of Wren appear untasteful to most of his contemporaries. Up and down the land many existing houses acquired a fine Palladian façade but the spirit of the Baroque lingered on behind the new trappings of taste. Lavish Baroque interiors lurk behind the Palladian masks of some of the buildings of James Gibbs, such as Sudbrooke Park in Richmond and the Great Hall of St Bartholomew's Hospital. Even

William Kent, Burlington's closest friend and supporter, produced some interiors of lavish Baroque theatricality, such as the bold staircase at 44 Berkeley Square which Horace Walpole described as 'a beautiful piece of stage scenery'. Another fine example of William Kent's work is in the finely restored mansion at 22 Arlington Street, off Piccadilly, which is now in the care of Eagle Star Insurance.

The Earl of Burlington stands out as the great leader of the first generation of Palladians in eighteenth-century London and his role was crucial in an age when so much depended on aristocratic and royal patronage; but he was not the only nobleman to brave the ridicule of his peers by indulging an architectural urge. Henry Herbert, ninth Earl of Pembroke, collaborated with Roger Morris on the design of his Palladian villa in Twickenham, Marble Hill House of 1724–9. This chaste structure, whose Great Room forms a perfect 24-foot cube, was to provide a more influential model of the English

A lavish staircase is contained behind a quiet housefront at 44 Berkeley Square.

The chaste Palladian style of Marble Hill House found many imitators.

Palladian house than Burlington's unique and eccentric Chiswick House. The restrained façades of Marble Hill House, with their calm air of repose beneath modest pediments, were to be repeated many times in works both great and small.

By the time that the first generation of Palladians expired in the 1750s the main successes of the movement in London had largely been confined to the West End and the surrounding countryside. Although the City was considered architecturally backward, it did not lag behind entirely and the new residence of the Lord Mayor, the Mansion House of 1739–53 by the elder Dance, was doctrinally pure in its great portico of six giant Corinthian columns raised on a rusticated ground floor, if somewhat lacking in presence and authority on account of its cramped site. It was indeed a sign of the times that the Bank of England went Palladian in 1732, but all trace of that disappeared in subsequent rebuilding later in the century. By far the greatest public triumph of the early Palladians was William Kent's work at Whitehall on the Treasury and the Horse Guards. In the latter, designed in 1748, the year of his death, Kent showed all too clearly the limitations of a system of architecture which was ready to sacrifice internal convenience for the desired outward effect. It was the extremely low central arch of Kent's Horse Guards which inspired one of Hogarth's funniest architectural cartoons showing a headless coachman emerging from this curious building with Baroque affinities. There was also a seriously founded disquiet at the growing dictatorship of taste which upheld Palladio as the answer to all problems. Isaac Ware warned in his *A Complete Body of Architecture* of 1756 against the trend 'to transfer the buildings of Italy right or wrong, suited or unsuited to the purpose, in England . . .'

Nevertheless, the Palladian movement continued to dominate the scene, albeit with a considerable degree of artistic licence being exercised in the interiors, as is evidenced by John Vardy's Spencer

House of 1752–4 overlooking Green Park. The works of Sir Robert Taylor (1714–88), the leading representative of the next wave of Palladians, project a greater austerity and purity of expression. There are some telling examples of his style in the charming Asgill House of 1757–8 by the river at Richmond, Ely House of 1772–6 at 37 Dover Street and the imposing Stone Buildings of 1774–80 in Lincoln's Inn. But Palladianism was no longer able to exercise the monopoly of taste which it had once claimed as its right. Already at the time of the accession of George III in 1760 there occurred the flowering of two architects, Sir William Chambers (1723–96) and Robert Adam (1728–92), who were to dominate London – not in harmony but as antagonists in matters of style – during a period that in general saw an escape from the narrow confines of Palladianism.

Sir William Chambers, however, was one who adhered to the Palladian tradition. His work in London, with one notable exception, is now hard to decipher: the façade of the house he built in Piccadilly for Lord Melbourne now conceals the later constructed Albany; Wick House which he designed for Sir Joshua Reynolds on Richmond Hill has been altered; and his Palladian villa in Roehampton now known as Manresa House is partly obscured by later buildings. But Somerset House, his largest project, which was the most palatial government building of its day, survives intact – although the once splendid view of the grand façade from Waterloo Bridge has been impaired by the modern road along the river. The vast edifice used to rise directly from the Thames; and a watergate in the lower storey was a functional part of the original design. Traffic, too, has

The west façade of Spencer House is one of London's prettiest Palladian designs.

penetrated the great quadrangle, which now serves as a car park; but one can still obtain a strong sense of the dignity and propriety of Chambers's design, even though his building falls short of the monumental potential of the large site with its prominent riverside location. It has been suggested that the influence of Chambers on his contemporaries was due more to his publication of 1759, *A Treatise on Civil Architecture*, than to his activity as an architect. He appears in London's building history as a dull, conservative counterbalance to the unbridled innovations of his arch-rival Robert Adam. However, Chambers had also been an advocate of stylistic experiment and of exotic novelties. His Chinese Pagoda in Kew Gardens was founded on his own sketches made during a visit to China, and he published his *Designs of Chinese Buildings* in 1757. He could also turn his hand to Rococo, and his Gold State Coach of 1762, on view in the Royal Mews of Buckingham Palace, is a masterpiece of

Asgill House by the river at Richmond is an attractive variation on the Palladian theme.

The Adam stairwell at 20 Portman Square is a virtuoso accomplishment.

the genre. But these were only regarded as permissible eccentricities outside the mainstream of the serious business of architecture proper, and in the main Chambers operated as a faithful practitioner of the Palladian tradition.

But when Robert Adam installed himself in London after a four-year stay in Italy from 1754–7 he set his sights on a bold assault on the assumptions of Palladian style, with special regard to interior design. His purpose, in his own words, was nothing less than 'a revolution in the whole system of this useful and elegant art'. Adam argued that the houses of antiquity displayed a much greater variety and freedom of decoration than was commonly accepted by the precepts of Palladianism which were those of the temple. This he demonstrated in his *Ruins of the Palace of the Emperor Diocletian at Spalato* of 1764, which was but one of many publications at the time which brought new discoveries at ancient Classical sites to the attention of an avid public of wealthy noblemen desirous of putting on a striking display of taste. The building boom in the 1760s after the Seven Years War (1756–63) helped launch Adam's career, but he was already thriving by the end of the 1750s.

It was generally true that the English aristocrats reserved their best architectural efforts for their country estates. Writing in 1771 J. Stuart noted: 'Many a nobleman whose proud seat in the country is adorned with all the riches of architecture, porticos and columns . . . is here [in London] content with a simple dwelling, convenient within and unornamental without.' Yet as Robert Adam was discovering to his profit, there were some notable exceptions, constituting a healthy demand for palatial accommodation in London. It remains true nonetheless that sober exteriors were the rule, and some of Adam's most spectacular decors were created behind modestly

Somerset House, Sir William Chambers's grandest London building.

There is a pleasing transition from the circular stairwell to the rectangular apartments at 20 Portman Square.

restrained Georgian façades of brick. This is best exemplified at Home House, 20 Portman Square, which Adam designed for the Countess of Home, a septuagenarian widow who decided to indulge one final and glorious extravagance. The amazing extent of the grand reception rooms which Adam provided in a limited space was made possible by the fact that the Countess required only one bedroom of consequence in the house.

The Adam style at Home House is wonderfully ornate and deliciously contrived. He continued William Kent's genius, as shown in 44 Berkeley Square, for installing a grandiose staircase into a modest size of residence, creating here one of his masterpieces which rises dramatically to a dome, diffusing light on the Classical paintings and motifs of the circular stairwell. The most notable of the apartments is the Music Room which displays that feminine delicacy of Adam's design where the pilasters, frieze and cornice are reduced to graceful and slender elements. Here the three-dimensional has been reduced to two and the genius of the scheme has come to reside purely in the decoration of flat surfaces. That Adam was well aware of the working of his style is apparent from his remarks in Volume I of *The Works in Architecture of Robert and James Adam Esquires* (1773): 'The massive entablature, the ponderous compartment ceiling, the tabernacle frame, almost the only species of ornament formerly known in this country, are now universally exploded, and in their place we have adopted a beautiful variety of light mouldings, gracefully formed, delicately enriched, and arranged with propriety and skill.' To which one might add that Robert Adam also took design from a naturalistic portrayal of real objects to a stylistic arrangement of symbolical motifs whose sole purpose was to stimulate the eye.

The Music Room at 20 Portman Square achieves a lavish decorative effect.

The library at Kenwood House is arguably the grandest Adam room in London.

There has been much destruction of Adam interiors in London, notably as a result of the demolition of most of the Adelphi. Lansdowne House, now the Lansdowne Club, in Fitzmaurice Place off Berkeley Square, lost a forty-foot-deep slice along its front when the road was built and the stunning principal drawing room and the dining room were acquired by the Philadelphia Museum and the Metropolitan Museum in New York respectively. Only Adam's intimate Round Room with a Greek frieze is still *in situ*. The picture is rosier in outer London which today contains some fine country houses remodelled by Adam now lying within the confines of the metropolis. There is the spectacular library at Kenwood House of 1767–9, an exhilarating example of his best work; and at Kenwood the fanciful decoration found its way onto the external façade as well. Equally magnificent are the remodelled apartments

The south front of Kenwood House shows the fanciful decoration, a hallmark of the Adam style, recently restored to its former glory.

of Osterley Park House and Syon House where the full repertoire of the Adam style from the colourful 'Etruscan', which was in reality Grecian, to the severe monochrome he introduced into the entrance halls of these houses, may be sampled in a sequence of carefully modulated effects.

Writing in Volume V of *The Works of Robert and James Adam* (1778) Robert was able to make the proud declaration: 'Architecture has already become elegant and more interesting. The parade, the convenience and social pleasures of life being better understood, are more strictly attended to in the arrangement and disposition of apartments.' We must not, therefore, see Adam interiors as mere abstract designs based on theories of aesthetics but as embodiments of a way of life with its social pretensions, elaborate rituals of display and lavish entertainment. Adam designed for a fantastically wealthy class of people who were engaged during the London 'season' on a full-time frantic whirligig of levées, assemblies, tea parties and dinners, recitals and receptions. It was for such an élite that Adam evolved his elaborate stage scenery with such conspicuous success. His career would appear to have taken him in the opposite direction to that of Inigo Jones, who began as a stage designer and progressed to architecture, whereas Robert Adam began as an architect but is chiefly remembered as an interior designer. A taste of the clientele for whom Adam worked may be gained from the reaction of Mrs Elizabeth Montagu of Montagu House in Portman Square (now demolished) in a letter of 1767: 'He has made me a ceiling and chimney-piece, and doors, which are pretty enough to make me a thousand enemies; Envy turns livid at the first glimpsing of them.'

But the triumphant Adam style, although widely imitated in London and elsewhere, inevitably attracted criticism in an age famous for its sharp tongues and cabals. Horace Walpole was contemptuous of what

The entrance hall of Osterley Park House is a relatively austere essay in monochrome.

he termed 'Mr Adam's gingerbread and snippets of embroidery'; and fashion was notoriously fickle too. Even the ecstatic Mrs Montagu brusquely withdrew her enthusiasm from Robert Adam and bestowed it on James Stuart who completed the interiors of Montagu House, which met with the approval of the influential and discriminating Horace Walpole. Adam's decline in popularity was due in part to the nature of the revolution he had helped bring about. He had overthrown the notion of rules and of the oneness of taste in favour of diversity, invention and freedom; and he had broken out of the Palladian mould. The next step was that the idea of taste itself would become nothing more than the product of public opinion. As Walpole noted with irony: 'Nothing so ill-bred as to persist in anything that is out of fashion. Taste and Fashion synonymous Terms.'

When viewed within the overall context of the eighteenth century the Adam revolution in taste appears to have been only a

This ceiling at Osterley Park House shows the Adam taste for colour and variety at its best.

The Adam drawing room at Apsley House is a more restrained décor.

passing phase, but however one may judge the aesthetic value of the Adam style, it was undeniably gay, pretty and entertaining – sheer fun compared to some of the lessons in antiquarianism which passed as correct design. Nor was Adam the only divergence from the Palladian norm. In addition to Baroque, Rococo made an occasional appearance behind the dignified brick façades of Georgian London, as in the exquisite interior of 1 Greek Street in Soho. And there was even a flourishing black market in 'Gothick', often relegated to garden follies and 'bog-houses', but most spectacularly in one London house of amazing audacity. Horace Walpole's Gothic Strawberry Hill in Twickenham, built from 1748 onwards with the assistance of his 'Committee on Taste', may be seen, however, as much as a satirical comment on Palladian presumption as an earnest tribute to the art of the Middle Ages.

The Urban Machine of the Georgians

Perhaps the most remarkable aspect of the Palladian enthusiasm of the eighteenth century was the extent of its influence, from the noble mansions of the aristocracy right down to the humblest of speculative terraces. So complete was the indoctrination of architects and builders by the high priests of Palladianism that the laws of Classical proportion were absorbed and followed almost without dissent. Never in the making of London would there be such a general agreement on how ordinary houses should be designed, and never such a homogeneity in the streetscape. The spirit of standardisation coincided with an energetic expansion of London, which in the course of the Georgian period took the irreversible step from a centralised urban settlement still largely based on its Roman foundations to that of a scattered metropolis, which is the essential pattern of the city today. The demolition of the old city gates in 1760 was a symbolic act.

Palladianism had entered the London streetscape under the influence of Inigo Jones in the early seventeenth century, and Lindsey House of 1640 in Lincoln's Inn Fields is a valuable testimonial of that time. So strong was the model provided by Inigo Jones that almost a century later in 1730 the house next door was built to exactly the same formula. Together they demonstrate how the Palladian building language translated the temple architecture of Classical antiquity into the domestic design which was to set the style for Georgian London. Here one can see the three basic elements of the Palladian scheme which correspond to the front of a Graeco-Roman temple. The podium is represented by the rusticated masonry of the ground floor, giving visual weight and substance to support the columns, here reduced to pilasters, which carry the entablature consisting of cornice and balustrade. So much for the direct borrowings from antiquity; the rest of the façade was invented by Italian Renaissance architects such as Andrea Palladio; for the temple portico did not have to accommodate doors and pedimented windows. These items were then introduced in the voids between the pilasters; and the Palladian emphasis on the first floor or *piano nobile* is reflected in the extreme height of the windows as well as in the higher ceilings inside. By contrast, the windows of the second floor are squarish. This was a dramatic shift from the window dimensions of almost identical height in pre-Georgian houses such as those in Queen Anne's Gate, and it was the insistence on the *piano nobile* which provides one of the essential keys to the new style of façade.

The two houses described above were prominently sited and correspondingly imposing, but when the Palladian syntax was transferred to more modest dwellings, such as a terrace, it was usually the practice to dispense with the pilasters and cornice so that there remained only the imprint of the Classical order in the form of the proportioning, with the solid brick areas representing the columns or pilasters, and the windows in neat vertical groups standing for the voids in between. This 'implied' or invisible order may seem a tenuous connection with the temples of antiquity, but it did establish the cardinal rule of Georgian housing which was the correct and harmonious proportioning of the façade. Just as the architects of antiquity attuned the dimensions of all the elements of their buildings to the particular Classical order they had chosen, so the builders of Georgian London derived the scale of their designs from the breadth of the windows.

The rules of correct proportioning were

Torrington Square in Bloomsbury shows the order of a modest Georgian streetfront.

promulgated through a steady flood of publications, ranging from Isaac Ware's highly regarded *A Complete Body of Architecture* of 1756 to the cruder pattern books such as Batty Langley's *The City and Country Builder's and Workman's Treasury of Designs* of 1740. It is largely as a result of such manuals that Georgian houses acquired their overwhelmingly uniform character. So standardised were the Georgian terraces of housing that one has the impression of an urban machine at work, churning out an endless chain of near identical dwellings. As the century progressed, industrial techniques heightened this overall sameness of appearance, which the Victorians would later denounce as monotonous and oppressive, but which to the Georgians was 'a refined industrial product' (Rasmussen), very much in line with their new vision of society. But within their stereotyped framework the houses of Georgian London

Contrasting colour schemes in Stratford Place off Oxford Street.

demonstrated an amazing variety of stylistic details. To follow some of these trends is like witnessing an architectural fashion show where subtle changes in fenestration and brick colour were as avidly aped as the latest cut in breeches and ballgowns. The parallel with the world of fashion was not lost on William Hogarth, who satirised the Palladian obsession with the Classical orders in his engraving of *The Five Orders of Perriwigs*.

There was a significant shift in the preferred colour of brickwork. The inherited scheme relied on the stunning contrast between red brick and white wood and stone. This was rejected by the more austere taste of the age which preferred the discreet tones of brown and grey. In *A Complete Body of Architecture* Isaac Ware made a reasoned plea for harmonious rather than contrasting colour effects. The move to more sombre hues was taken to the limit in some classy West End façades where the bricks were painted black and the joints highlighted by a chalk line. This formal dressing – the architectural equivalent of the pin-stripe suit – is well illustrated by the houses on the east side of Stratford Place off Oxford Street. As can be seen, the same process could also be accomplished in red, which to the discriminating eye of Isaac Ware would have been thoroughly shocking. But this was an exceptional juxtaposition, for the general trend was towards the muted end of the colour chart with yellowish-grey marl bricks becoming the most common, known as London stocks, by the end of the eighteenth century.

With the overall blankness of the house façade established as the self-effacing rule of the Georgian house, the one great freedom of artistic expression was the doorcase. But even here there was a discernible shift away from the ornate Baroque shell hoods and carved canopies to the Classical

Doorway of 14 Fournier Street, Spitalfields, displays an awkward combination of forms.

columns and pediments, and even within the Classical repertoire there was a move from the elaborate Corinthian to the simpler Ionic and Doric. But fashion was not followed everywhere as assiduously, especially in the City and East End which were regarded as somewhat retrograde, as is evidenced by the doorcase of 14 Fournier Street in Spitalfields which attempted the ungainly combination of Ionic columns with the old-fashioned canopy. This house of 1727 also has a redder brick than was acceptable in the West End as well as the segmental window arches which were in vogue around 1710–30 but were then supplanted by flat arches until the end of the century when the semicircular form came into favour.

With such minute attention to aesthetics it comes as something of a shock to discover that many of London's Georgian houses were jerry-built. The comely façades were sometimes only half a brick deep and often not bonded into the inner skin of cheaper place bricks. Such shoddy methods resulted partly from the leasehold system whereby speculative builders erected houses that reverted to the landlord upon the expiry of the leases which generally ran for 99 years, or originally only for 31 and then 42 years. The builder was thus encouraged to go for a quick return on his investment rather than erect a home for posterity. Isaac Ware lamented that 'some have carried the art of slight building so far, that their houses have fallen before they were tenanted'. Consequently the Building Act of 1774 laid down minimum standards of construction for four defined 'Rates' of domestic buildings. This was the first major legislation since the Building Acts of 1707 and 1709, which had banished unnecessary wood from the façade, thereby reinforcing the general trend towards austerity. But in the second half of the eighteenth century Robert Adam acted as a pioneer for the reintroduction of external ornament such as pilasters, not always in accord with Palladian proportions, and his influence may be detected in the elongated Ionic Order in Stratford Place.

The temptation to view Georgian London purely in terms of taste and the doctrine of Palladianism must, of course, be resisted for there was also a hard-nosed commercialism behind the elegance and charm; and the end product was shaped by the strength of market forces even in the great estates of the West End. The early Georgian schemes at Hanover Square (*c.* 1715), Cavendish Square (*c.* 1717), Grosvenor Square (*c.* 1720) and Berkeley Square in the 1730s failed to realise a grand architectural vision because there was insufficient demand for town palaces. Most aristocrats invested their wealth on their country homes and preferred a simpler style, at least as far as the exterior was concerned, for their urban residences. Planning extended only to the laying out of the squares which were the accepted basic element of Georgian urbanism. Plots were then leased to prospective residents or speculative builders and the terraces of houses would gradually materialise without any grand orchestration. It is significant that Londoners were used to living in individual houses with narrow frontage but extending far back, and the rooms disposed in a vertical arrangement, unlike the horizontal apartments of cities such as Paris. In this sense the internal order of the medieval townhouse was continued within a tidier framework and organised according to a stricter geometry. The squares did not exist as expressions of any real metropolitan magnificence but as efficient and pleasing modules or self-contained units. The new London squares of the West End were essentially inward-looking environments for people of similar status.

This reorientation of London life, albeit impressive, received mixed reactions. Daniel Defoe, writing in 1725 of his visit to Hanover Square, noted: 'In this Tour I passed an amazing Scene of new Foundations, not of Houses only, but as I might say of new Cities. New Towns, new Squares, and fine Buildings, the like of which no City, no Town, nay no Place in the World can shew . . .' But to James Ralph, a more critical observer in 1734, Grosvenor Square was 'little better than a collection of whims, and frolics in building, without anything like order or beauty'. Neither was John Gwynn impressed with London in 1766. He wrote in his visionary *London and Westminster Improved* that the city was 'inconvenient, inelegant, and without the least pretension to magnificence or grandeur'. As for the West End: 'The finest part of the town is left to the mercy of ignorant and capricious persons.' Perhaps this is why so little remains of the original architecture of the first great squares of the West End.

With the creation of Bedford Square from 1776 onwards a more coherent urbanism was to make itself felt in a much finer vision, which has fortunately been preserved intact. This was the first of the

The south side of Bedford Square, a model of Georgian urbanism in the West End.

London squares to emerge as a complete architectural unit, with all the houses brought together within an overall design which gives the impression of four huge ranges of building. Bedford Square is London's most immaculate set piece of Georgian domestic architecture, and it became the model for other schemes in Bloomsbury, which still contains the finest examples of the planning concepts of the period.

The provision of the square as the central unit of the neighbourhood was a practical as well as an aesthetic consideration. London's atmosphere was already badly polluted in the latter part of the seventeenth century, when John Evelyn had described the 'Clouds of Smoake and Sulphur, so full of Stink and Darknesse'; and this was one of the main reasons for the westward migration which continued unabated throughout the eighteenth and nineteenth centuries. A generous expanse of greenery was vital as a lung for any new district, and absolutely essential if the right sort of noble residents were to be attracted. However, Bloomsbury's ambitions as an aristocratic enclave did not last long. As early as 1800 its patron the fifth Duke of Bedford followed the path of fashion and transferred his residence to St James's. A statue of the duke was erected in 1809 in Russell Square and gazes imperiously down Bedford Place where two rows of speculative housing were built on the site of the ancestral home of Bedford House. Bedford Square and Bloomsbury in general managed to survive quite satisfactorily as a respectable 'upper-middle-class' community, but it was uncomfortably close to some of London's poorer and notoriously criminal districts and sought to protect itself against any incursions from less refined neighbourhoods by installing gates in 1830 across its vulnerable openings to the outside world.

Things were only slightly less élitist on the adjacent Foundling Hospital Estate, developed between 1790 and 1830, which aimed to 'comprise all classes of building from the first class down to houses of £25 per annum', but great care was taken in order to prevent 'the lower classes interfering with and diminishing the character of those above them'. The magnificent east side of Mecklenburgh Square, with its palatial stuccoed centrepiece, has its back firmly turned against the Gray's Inn Road and the meaner districts beyond. This was and is still unmistakably the outer bastion of Bloomsbury's defences.

Social segregation was a keynote of Georgian expansion; and fashion was a harsh dictator of terms. Josiah Wedgwood, installed in Grosvenor Square, could not contemplate moving to a larger showroom in Pall Mall slightly to the east 'for you know that my present sett of Customers will not mix with the rest of the World'. Some of the problems faced by the Adam brothers' spectacular Adelphi project from 1772 were due to the fact that they aimed to create a fashionable quarter within a distinctly unfashionable district between the Strand and the Thames, an area once aristocratic but since much in decline. The magnificent houses with their fanciful decoration had to be disposed of by means of a public lottery as the only recourse to avoid bankruptcy. The Adelphi, a series of lofty blocks rising from vaulted cellars, displayed a vertical stratification with the lower orders huddled in lightless quarters well below street level, quite literally an underworld. Most of the Adelphi was demolished in 1936–8, but a few of the original houses remain, notably 7 Adam Street and 8 John Adam Street.

Although the East End was not ignored by the builders, the developments in Stepney, Whitechapel and Wapping were generally much humbler terraces of two- or three-storey houses of little artistic pretension but for the 'artistic good manners' of their Classical proportions. Some of these streets and squares which have survived, such as Albert Gardens of 1803–10 off the Commercial Road, now appear especially appealing by comparison to the post-1945 housing estates which have blighted the area. There were also some attempts in the East End to

Albert Gardens, a modest East End square of late Georgian vintage.

emulate the splendours of the West End, such as Tredegar Square in Bow of 1828–9, but these schemes were subsequently left marooned by the continued retreat westwards of wealth. But even the simpler housing of the East End was not intended for those at the bottom of the social scale. For countless numbers of London's urban poor the only hope of shelter was in the festering communities of ramshackle tenements and 'rookeries' of which a notorious specimen was in the parish of St Giles close to the once-aristocratic Covent Garden which in the Georgian period declined into a refuge for thieves and prostitutes. Soho Square and Leicester Fields had also come down in the world.

According to the laws of economics there was no incentive for speculative builders to cater for the destitute, but the eighteenth century witnessed a generous response from private benefactors anxious to relieve the suffering of the poor. Almshouses were the traditional charitable endowment since the Middle Ages and they continued to be founded in London by philanthropists such as Sir Robert Geffrye. The almshouses he endowed in 1715 in Shoreditch have been preserved and are now occupied by the Geffrye Museum. Hopton's almshouses of 1752 are a charming survival in Southwark's Bankside, wedged between an office block and a power station, and they still fulfil their original purpose as homes for old people. Captain Thomas Coram, a retired ship's commander, broke new ground in 1742 with his Foundling Hospital for abandoned children, a sad by-product of the dens of vice in Covent Garden. Only the entrance arcades remain of this great establishment which counted Hogarth and Handel among its benefactors, but the original Court Room and staircase have been instated in the later building of the Thomas Coram Foundation for Children at 40 Brunswick Square.

The Ironmongers' Almshouses in Shoreditch, founded in 1715 by Sir Robert Geffrye.

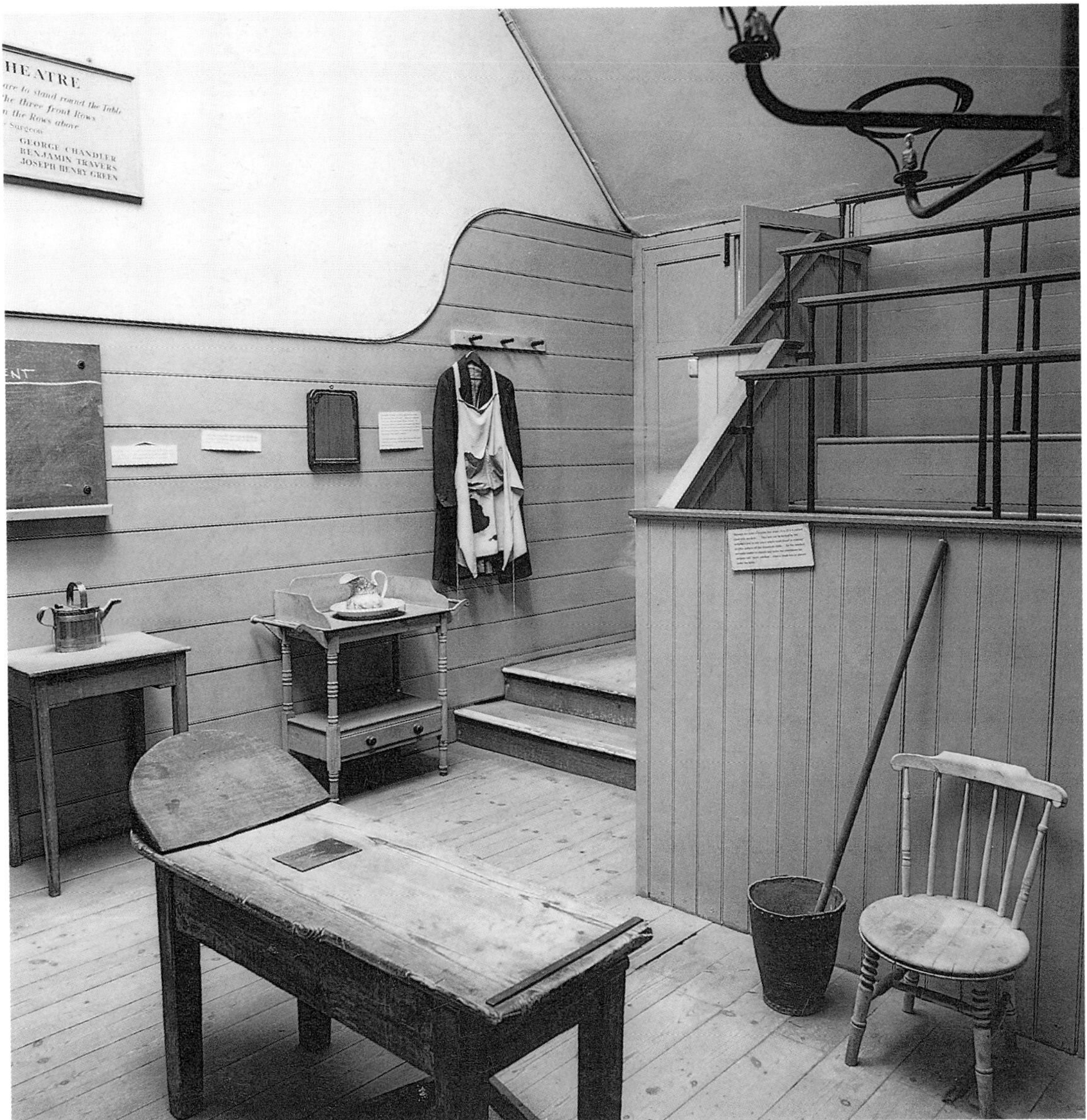

The Old Operating Theatre in Southwark affords a unique glimpse of early medical practice.

Medical hospitals were a particular contribution of the age. New foundations included Guy's in 1721–5, the Westminster in 1719, St George's in 1733–4, the London in 1752–7, and the Middlesex. St Thomas's and St Bartholomew's were extensively rebuilt in the course of the eighteenth century. Fine Georgian buildings are particularly in evidence at St Bartholomew's and at Guy's, the latter possessing a unique survival of the period: a vintage operating theatre which represented the state of the art in 1821. This theatre was shared with the students at St Thomas's Hospital until it was closed down in 1862 and it remained undisturbed until 1957 due to its curious location in the loft of the tower of the Parish Church of St Thomas. The perfect preservation of the operating theatre evokes the less appealing side of Georgian London where surgeons in bloody aprons performed amputations without the aid of anaesthetics

One of the charity children at St Botolph's, Bishopsgate.

or antiseptics. This is a world away from the refined diversions of the Adam drawing rooms of the West End.

Education, not yet the responsibility of the state, was also dependent on charitable institutions which ran special schools for orphans. Already at the beginning of the eighteenth century there were 54 charity schools in London and Westminster with more than 2000 pupils, and their number increased threefold in the course of the century. Such establishments, which were run on spartan lines with uniformed discipline, usually indicated their status by displaying simple painted effigies of suitably pious- and grateful-looking boy and girl 'charity children'. Examples of this type may still be seen at various locations in London, such as in the churchyard of St Botolph, Bishopsgate.

In spite of its philanthropic achievements Georgian London was not noted for its churches, but it did introduce a new and simpler style of edifice as a direct response to the requirements of the growing Nonconformist community. John Wesley's activities as a preacher of the Gospel to the poor eventually led to the foundation of the first Methodist church in 1777 in the City Road. The house next door where he lived from 1779 until his death in 1791 is a typical residence of the period. This area had been of importance to Nonconformists since the seventeenth century, for the Bunhill Fields had been the only place where they could bury their dead without the ministration of an Anglican clergyman. It has been estimated that more than 120,000 burials have been made here, including that of Susannah Wesley (the mother of John), Richard Cromwell, John Bunyan, Daniel Defoe and William Blake. Although the northern part of Bunhill Fields was laid out as a garden following bomb damage in the last war the rest has been retained as it was when the last interment took place in 1854. Here the

Bunhill Fields, burial place for Non-conformists in Finsbury.

Houses in Hanbury Street, Spitalfields, retain the weavers' lofts characteristic of the area.

unfashionable spirits of the Georgian age, mostly from the now anonymous urban masses, may be felt in this rather obscure burial ground which extends between the City Road and Bunhill Row, just to the north of the headquarters of the Honourable Artillery Company, itself a memorial to Georgian military architecture.

Further east, the other side of Shoreditch High Street, lies Spitalfields, a pocket of relative prosperity in the eighteenth century, thanks to the industry of the Huguenot silk weavers who settled here in the aftermath of the persecution of Protestants in France unleashed by the Revocation of the Edict of Nantes in 1685. The Huguenot church, the 'Neuve Eglise' of 1743 in Brick Lane, still stands but it is now a mosque, having also done duty as a synagogue – roles which reflect the ebb and flow of immigration in the East End. There are fine period houses in Fournier and Wilkes Street which show less uniformity than contemporary terraces in the West End. The top storeys of some houses in the neighbourhood were converted into special attics for the weavers' looms, and several good examples may be seen in Hanbury Street. The house at 18 Folgate Street has been wondrously reinstated to evoke the atmosphere and changing living conditions of a Spitalfields family from prosperity in the eighteenth century to destitution in the nineteenth. It is an amazingly moving experience to witness the presence of the past in rooms which appear exactly as they might have been occupied by their erstwhile owners, honest folk of the middling sort who were slightly behind the fashionable chic of the West End.

Elsewhere it is hard to capture quite so vividly the flavour of everyday life in Georgian London. The theatres have all been rebuilt or remodelled but for some early nineteenth-century elements remaining in the Theatre Royal, Drury Lane and the

Dining room at 18 Folgate Street recreates the atmosphere of eighteenth-century London.

portico of the Theatre Royal, Haymarket. Gone are the pleasure grounds at Vauxhall and Ranelagh which figured so prominently in the social life of the city. Gone too are the hundreds of coffee-houses, once the centres of commercial and literary life, which were the tiny cells in an enormous hive of activity. A last vestige of the age lingers on in the taverns of Fleet Street such as Ye Olde Cheshire Cheese, just a short walk from Dr Johnson's house in Gough Square. At the beginning of the Strand there is a charming relic of the period in the premises of Thomas Twining & Co, first established just behind the present site in 1706 as a tea merchant. The present entrance of painted Coade stone, evoking the tea trade with China, dates from 1787. Glass-fronted shops were one of the wonders of the day; isolated examples still exist as in Artillery Lane but more exciting are the bow windows of Goodwin's Court, late eighteenth-century additions to a complete row of houses of 1690 origin, and the

18 Folgate Street presents a vivid tableau of a convivial evening some 250 years ago.

The entrance to Twining's in the Strand is a colourful relic of Georgian commercial design.

beautifully preserved shopping precinct of 1822 known as Woburn Walk, just south of Euston Road.

Such survivals are important for they serve as reminders that there was much more to Georgian London than its highly acclaimed residential squares and neat terraces which have come to represent the genius of the age. However, the serried ranks of Georgian houses with their smart railings and occasional porticoes and balconies in direct contact with the street demonstrate an obvious pride in their urban setting. Although there was already a tendency to settle in the still rural environment of Richmond, Hampstead and St John's Wood, the vast majority of Georgian Londoners were true urbanites at heart, delighting in the manifold diversions of the expanding metropolis. The neat Palladian façades were like a fashionable piece of stagecraft which disguised the fact that the

Goodwin's Court off St Martin's Lane displays late eighteenth-century bowed shopfronts on a terrace dating back to 1690.

familiar medieval organisation of a narrow but deep house extending vertically over several floors had been maintained. The new urban machine of the Georgians was intended purely to be viewed from the front for the backs of the houses have no pretension to order or beauty whatsoever, and the complete blankness of most side elevations when exposed at the end of a terrace is most unappealing. But in spite of the overall sameness of Georgian architecture and street design London at the end of the eighteenth century was a patchwork of individual neighbourhoods fitted together in an improvised manner. It was not until the second decade of the nineteenth century that London was to get a taste of planning in the grand manner at the hands of the Prince Regent and his genial accomplice, John Nash.

Pickering Place off St James's Street is a modest Georgian backwater in the heart of town.

A Grand Design

In spite of the regular planning of the new West End estates, London at the end of the eighteenth century remained essentially untouched by any attempt to impose a masterplan. At the beginning of the nineteenth century the basic character of London's conservative inhabitants can scarcely have been radically different, but the circumstances had changed. The vain and ambitious Prince Regent emerged as the most energetic and visionary royal patron of architecture and urbanism that the country was ever to see. His role was to prove decisive, but of equal importance was the architect John Nash, who rode the tide of royal favour for more than a quarter of a century and was able to turn many of his dreams into reality in what is still unmistakably Regency London.

On the face of it John Nash (1752–1835) was an unlikely candidate for achieving London's most successful grand design. After a failed property speculation in Bloomsbury Square he was obliged to declare bankruptcy, and he retreated to Wales where he gradually re-established himself as an architect of fanciful country houses. He teamed up with Humphrey Repton, who devised the 'picturesque' landscapes in which Nash's stylish villas and mansions would sit so prettily. His sudden rise to fame, fortune and royal favour in one fell swoop has been ascribed to his marriage of convenience in 1798 to the 25-year-old Mary Ann Bradley, who was reputed to be a mistress of the Prince of Wales. Be that as it may, Nash was eminently suited to supply the architectural scenario for the forthcoming royal production. Yet even in 1806, when Nash was appointed in his mid-fifties as architect to the Chief Commissioner of Woods and Forests, there was still no hint of what was to come and he appeared destined for a solid if unspectacular career in the service of the Crown.

However, with the Prince of Wales assuming the Regency in 1811 just as the lease granted to the Duke of Portland on the royal lands known as Marylebone Farm expired, Nash found himself in a uniquely propitious situation. This enormous piece of real estate lay just to the north of London's eighteenth-century expansion and was ripe for development. Here lay great potential both for increasing the revenues of the Crown as well as embellishing the metropolis. Although plans for the area had been sought since as early as 1793 nothing had been advanced beyond the unexciting gridiron of the existing orderly layout of straight streets and neat squares. Nash responded to the challenge with amazing alacrity and confidence of vision, dashing off a scheme so imaginative and audacious, grandiose in conception as well as alluringly lucrative, that his proposals for Regent's Park were accepted, albeit with some modifications, and duly carried out during the years 1812 to 1827.

Nash's central notion was to introduce the elements of Repton's 'picturesque' landscapes, then much in vogue among country noblemen, into London itself. Nash envisaged Regent's Park not as a pleasure garden, as it is today, but as a natural setting for as many as 40 to 50 exquisite private villas arranged, in the words of Nash's submission, 'that no Villa should see any other, but each should appear to possess the whole of the Park'. By an act of what may properly be called environmental awareness the Crown Commissioners ordered the number of villas to be reduced to 26 and eventually to 8. Other items which did not materialise included a pleasure pavilion or 'guinguette' for the Prince Regent and a double circus containing a Valhalla which would have dominated the scene. Had even the villas of Nash's original scheme been built, Regent's Park would have been the very first garden city and doubtless a privileged enclave for the very rich. As it turned out, so few villas were built that they appear as intruders in what became essentially a public park with a lake and ornamental gardens. Regent's Park is thus only a partial realisation of what Nash intended to be the very summit of the Picturesque in a metropolitan context.

The true achievement of Regent's Park lies around the perimeter rather than within. Except for the north side which was left open to protect 'the many beautiful Views towards the Villages of Highgate and Hampstead', Nash was given free rein to erect a succession of noble terraces. The symphonic arrangement of Classical façades created a backdrop of theatrical architecture such as London had never before witnessed and which is unlikely ever to be matched. The splendid Ionic-

Cumberland Terrace, architectural centrepiece to the east side of Regent's Park.

Park Crescent provides the transition from Portland Place to Nash's Regent's Park terraces.

columned Park Crescent is the perfect overture to the grandiose composition of stuccoed fantasies which transforms terraces of standard London houses into a fairytale stage set. In between the larger blocks there are some charming smaller structures such as the Doric Villa, one of the first generation of semi-detached homes, whose false central window gives the illusion that there is no party wall. Such details of sheer artifice would have gone unnoticed in the original scheme because the stucco itself was not the uniform light yellow that it is today but was painted to imitate the effect of Bath stone complete with masonry joints. The residential layout was completed in the north-east sector by the two Park Villages, delightful enclaves of artless rustic character consisting of both detached and semi-detached houses in a variety of styles including Gothic, which have been acclaimed as the prototypes of suburban Picturesque. Unfortunately half of Park Village East was demolished to make space for railway tracks, but Park Village West with its eye-catching Tower House is still intact.

Happily, the substance of Nash's Regent's Park terraces came through the Victorian era relatively unscathed. However, there was severe bomb damage during the last war and the Crown Estate Commissioners inaugurated a works programme in 1962 to give the terraces another lease of life. Perhaps this tribute to the appeal of Nash's work was due not just to the theatricality of the architecture but also to the fact that behind the parade of pseudo-Classical style were concealed the sort of traditional urban homes, arranged as vertical units, so popular with generations of Londoners. Here domesticity and grandeur went hand in hand.

Although now safe in the public's esteem the Regent's Park terraces were not received with unanimous enthusiasm in

Park Village, a delightful small-scale garden suburb.

Sussex Place of 1822, noted for its exotic end pavilions with octagonal domes.

Nash's day. Maria Edgeworth declared herself 'properly surprised by the new town that has been built in Regent's Park – and indignant at plaister statues, and horrid useless domes [Sussex Place] and pediments crowded with mock sculpture figures [Cumberland Terrace] which damp and smoke must destroy in a season or two'. A more reasonable judgement was given by Prince Pückler-Muskau, who observed: 'it cannot be denied that his buildings are a jumble of every sort of style, the result of which is rather "baroque" than original – yet the country is, in my opinion, much indebted to him for conceiving and executing such gigantic designs for the improvement of the metropolis . . . It's true, one must not look too nicely into the details . . . Faultless, on the other hand, is the landscape-gardening part of the park . . .'

Regent's Park was, however, but an element in a much more ambitious project, by which Nash aimed to drive a processional route southwards from Park Crescent to culminate at the Prince Regent's fabulous Carlton House. The proposals for this vast undertaking are contained in Nash's report which conveys the obvious appeal of the scheme. The new Regent Street would provide: 'a boundary and complete separation between the Streets and Squares occupied by the Nobility and Gentry, and the narrow Streets and meaner Houses occupied by mechanics and the trading part of the community . . . those who have nothing to do but walk about and amuse themselves may do so every day in the week, instead of being frequently confined many days together to their Houses by rain . . . the Balustrades over the Colonnades will form Balconies to the Lodging-rooms over the Shops, from which the Occupiers of the Lodgings can see and converse with those passing in the Carriages underneath, and which will add to the gaiety of the scene . . .'

Here one can see Nash's acute and intimate knowledge of the lifestyle of his contemporaries. However, his vision of Regency bucks engaging in idle banter from the balconies was destroyed in 1848 when the colonnade consisting of 145 cast-iron columns of the Doric order was demolished, for it had become a convenient resort for the ladies of the night. Since then all the buildings of Nash's Regent Street have been redeveloped and only the huge sweep of the Quadrant to the north of Piccadilly Circus remains as a testimonial to the scenic planning of the original idea. The sociological divide between Mayfair and Soho, so accurately discerned by Nash, still holds today, and it may be argued that Regent Street is responsible for this strict demarcation. The strategic importance of Regent Street at the time lay in the access it provided to the north, persuading persons

Chester Terrace, with triumphal arches of obvious artifice, on the east side of Regent's Park.

of quality to cross the New Road (Euston and Marylebone Road) and take up residence in one of the Regent's Park terraces.

Notwithstanding its ultimate success, the creation of Regent Street was fraught with financial and administrative difficulties. There was opposition from both traders and landowners such as Sir James Langham whose refusal to sell his back garden obliged Nash to introduce an abrupt change in direction in the course of the road. With his habitual ingenuity Nash made a virtue out of necessity and placed the tapering spire and circular portico of All Souls, Langham Place, like a brave semicolon holding together a twisted sentence. Quite fittingly, it is at this superb vantage point that a bust of Nash is located, commanding the long view southwards over Oxford Circus right down to the distant curve of the Quadrant which Nash financed himself when his other backers, including the ever-optimistic James Burton, were unwilling or unable to take the risk. Beyond Piccadilly Circus, Lower Regent Street was to bring Nash's Grand Design to the gates of the Prince Regent's home of Carlton House but after his accession as George IV the monarch decided to make his palace at Buckingham House. Carlton House was

Bust of John Nash beneath the circular portico of All Souls, Langham Place.

The Royal Opera Arcade is one of the most intimate corners of Nash's Grand Design.

demolished and the Via Triumphalis abutted finally and ingloriously into a broad flight of stairs to the south of Waterloo Place. The two spectacular blocks of Carlton House Terrace have preserved the name of their predecessor. Despite much redevelopment in this southern sector of Nash's scheme there remain several notable survivors, such as the Royal Opera Arcade with its authentic Regency lamp brackets, the proud Corinthian portico of the Theatre Royal, Haymarket, which closes the view from Charles II Street, and some fine housing in Suffolk Place. Nash was also responsible for the new landscaping of St James's Park and for the laying-out of Trafalgar Square, although he had no hand in the design of any of the buildings.

With all this achieved in his sixties and seventies – and much else besides including the Brighton Pavilion – Nash's energies were beginning to fail, but he was urged on by his royal patron to produce one more grand gesture in London. But the conversion of Buckingham House into Buckingham Palace turned out to be a disaster for both men. With the budget well overspent the ailing George IV expired in 1830, leaving the 78-year-old Nash an easy prey for his many critics and enemies. Although he did exonerate himself before a Select Committee of any improper dealings, he was relieved of the commission. His work on Buckingham Palace was obscured by later rebuildings, and only the west front, not visible to the public, is essentially his, along with some of the ornate interiors such as the Blue and the White Drawing Rooms. A further reminder of Nash's work on the palace is the Marble Arch which was removed to its present location in 1847.

Nash's reputation was at a low ebb when he died in 1835; but although he has now been amply vindicated even his most fervent admirers are quick to underline his slipshod habits. Using the new techniques of stucco and cast-iron, Nash was able to sculpt buildings rather than construct them, but his Palladian schooling in the office of Sir Robert Taylor evidently kept him just within the bounds of reasonable architectural behaviour, as he aspired to transcend the scenic limitations of conventional Georgian terraces. In his own home at 14–16 Regent Street, now no more, Nash even managed to break out of the vertical

Carlton House Terrace rising in a stucco-covered crescendo of Doric and Corinthian.

A closer view of the sculpture-filled pediment of Cumberland Terrace shows that it was intended for scenic effect only.

mould of London living and provided himself with what was essentially a grand apartment on one level, albeit of generous scale and lavish decor.

The architect was just one of the multiple roles which Nash filled in his professional life which alternated constantly from estate agent and financier to landscaper and surveyor. He was also a skilful promoter of ideas to excite the interest of such a demanding patron as the Prince Regent, who was reported to have been so enthusiastic about the proposals for Regent's Park as to declare that 'it will quite eclipse Napoleon'. Nash was very much in tune with the spirit of the age and never shrank from the financial rough-and-tumble of his schemes, always risking his own finances in order to further his self-confessed 'earnest desire to complete the plans in progress for the improvement of the metropolis'. His real merit stands on his supreme craft in creating exhilarating urban scenery which also served a practical purpose. His Grand Design – incomplete though it is – represents the greatest individual imprint on the face of the West End and the only masterplan to have been implemented. It was described as 'the last of London's many transformations that has been able to command respect' (Steegman), and its value has been greatly enhanced by all that has since happened and is still happening to London.

Grecian Interlude

The discovery of Italy unleashed by the Palladian enthusiasm of Burlington and his associates at the beginning of the eighteenth century led inevitably in the course of time to a deeper enquiry into the more distant roots of Classical antiquity. At first Greek architecture was but dimly perceived as a merely archaic and primitive form, whose chief purpose was the later sophistication of Roman and Palladian style. With the extension of the Grand Tour into Greece itself there came back news to London of the impressive relics of a distinctly Hellenic civilisation. The curiosity thus awakened was focused through the Society of Dilettanti which, notwithstanding the reputed inclination of its members for copious drinking, encouraged a serious interest in the culture of Greece as well as of Rome. It sponsored a number of notable expeditions as well as erudite publications, of which the most influential was the *Antiquities of Athens* by James Stuart and Nicholas Revett, a fine series of engravings published in five volumes between 1762 and 1830. This was a seminal work in fostering the mania for things Greek which was to sweep the country by the end of the eighteenth century.

James 'Athenian' Stuart put into practice in London some of the lessons he had absorbed in Greece. At 15 St James's Square he inserted columns of the pure Greek Ionic order above a rusticated ground floor into a façade of Palladian discipline. Following a fire in 1779 at the chapel of the Royal Hospital in Greenwich, he used the opportunity to introduce a neo-Grecian interior into the shell of the Wren building. In such works may we glimpse the first experimental steps of the new style at work, yet for the time being Greek designs constituted but one ingredient of a heady cultural cocktail being concocted by Robert Adam under the label 'Etruscan'. The eclectic spirit of the age was well expressed by the Prince of Wales, whose modifications to Carlton House from 1783 before it was demolished in 1827 bore the traces of Greece, Rome, India and China as well as of the Gothic Revival, which was revealing itself as yet another manifestation of what architectural historians have classified as the Neo-Classical movement, a Romantic challenge to the dictatorship of taste maintained by the Palladians.

The growing fascination with Greek antiquities was helped by the existence in the south of Italy and in Sicily of the remains of the Greek colonies of Magna Graecia. At Paestum, Agrigento and Segesta stood the awe-inspiring Doric temples of a remote age, structures of archaic power and simplicity from the dawn of the Classical tradition. Sir John Soane's visit to Sicily in 1779 made a profound impression on him but he was not a Greek Revivalist, for his personal quest for an individual style of architecture was too intense for him to be an imitator of anything. It is noteworthy, however, that caryatids made an appearance in the remarkable interiors which Soane designed for the Bank of England but his work there has survived only as a pale and distorted reflection. Soane's house at 14 Lincoln's Inn Fields gives the truest picture of the man and his times. Here one encounters a serious Neo-Classicist surrounded by the objects of antiquarian interest which speak for the wealth of original material becoming available to architects and designers. Greek items, such as a model of the temples at Paestum, are to be discovered alongside Roman, Renaissance and even Gothic. The Sir John Soane Museum gives an idea of the multiplicity of architectural styles vying for the attention of the age. A further glimpse of Sir John Soane's unique interior arrangements may be gained from his former country residence of Pitshanger Manor which has recently been restored by the Borough of Ealing.

It was, however, the Greek style which left its rivals standing and established itself very soon after 1800 in a position of virtual monopoly. The reasons for its success are complex, but it is clear that Greek had a marked advantage over the other styles such as Gothic, in which the Romantic movement dabbled. To minds trained in the Classical school, Greek implied no more than a shift in emphasis within the framework of antiquity. It might have been a revolution in taste, but it was able to recommend itself as a cultural evolution. Gothic, signifying a retreat to the Middle Ages, was as yet unthinkable as a serious prospect for a generation of rationalists, whose Romantic impulse was for truth or primaeval authenticity in its purest form

The bust of Sir John Soane fits happily into the collection of Classical objects he amassed.

rather than a nostalgic flight from reality. Greek forms came to be perceived no longer as the infantile beginnings but as the not-yet-debased roots of Classicism. The Greek Revival thus stood for the final phase in the search for elegant simplicity and was heralded as the 'modern' movement of its day. The style it pioneered has left London with a bizarre but impressive architectural inheritance which still makes its presence powerfully felt in the chaos of the urban environment today.

The movement really took off in the first decade of the nineteenth century which saw Lord Elgin sending back to London the controversial marbles from the Parthenon. From 1807 these could be viewed at a makeshift museum, prior to their acquisition by the British Museum in 1817. Strictly speaking, the first correct Greek front in London was the Ionic portico of George Dance the Younger's Royal College of Surgeons commenced in 1806, but it was really Sir Robert Smirke's Covent Garden Theatre

The breakfast room of Sir John Soane's house shows a highly original neo-Classicism.

Wren's chapel at the Royal Naval College underwent a Grecian conversion in 1779–89.

of 1808–9, London's first Greek Doric building, which caught the attention and the imagination of the public. Built in about six months, after its predecessor had been destroyed by fire, this stunning innovation of a building, as it appeared at the time, was modelled on the Temple of Minerva at Athens. Sadly this great architectural landmark also succumbed to the flames in 1857, and only the frieze by Flaxman under the new portico by E. M. Barry has survived, along with some statues, in the building as it exists today.

Sir Robert Smirke (1781–1867) and William Wilkins (1778–1839) were the leading lights of the Greek Revivalists, and both enriched London with some major edifices in the new style. Of William Wilkins it was stated by James Elmes in 1847: 'No liberty would he give or take, no line or member would he use, for which he could not find a precedent in some ancient Greek building . . .' His University of London of 1827–9 (now University College) is no direct copy of anything Greek, with its dome sitting rather uncertainly above the pediment, but the portico is a lovely Corinthian affair, to which access is gained via flights of steps arrayed with statues of Greek athletes. No matter that the dome is undecided and that an empty space yawns behind the portico: the total effect is still charming and pleasingly Grecian. Less successful was Wilkins's design for the National Gallery along the north side of Trafalgar Square, dating from 1832–8. A relatively unknown work by Wilkins is St George's Hospital of 1827, whose uncompromisingly Greek stuccoed façade occupies a prominent site at Hyde Park Corner. However, it goes largely unnoticed at London's most frenzied roundabout, and has stood unoccupied since 1980. Like the other Greek buildings by Wilkins in London it does not quite live up to its heroic aspirations.

Those of Sir Robert Smirke, on the other hand, did achieve a robust monumentality despite a certain lack of inspiration. It is the British Museum, commenced in 1823, for which Smirke is chiefly remembered. Here his predilection for the giant Ionic order runs riot across the entire south front and the composition is drawn together by a noble pediment sheltering statuary symbolical of the progress of civilisation. For once the templar style is completely appro-

The west front of University College by Wilkins with statues of Greek athletes.

The south front of the British Museum by Smirke, London's most compelling Greek composition.

priate to the function of the building which may properly be described as a national Temple of Culture. One of the main purposes of the original British Museum was to house the vast collections of books bequeathed by George II and George III, and the King's Library was Smirke's grandiose and effective solution. Running 300 feet along the east side of the British Museum, this is a rare example in London of a vast Grecian-style interior that is neither empty nor oppressive. As for the Grecian aspect of the exterior, it is rather marooned in the narrow streets of southern Bloomsbury, from which the pediment and colonnade rise with magnificence and drama. Nash's plan to link the British Museum to Trafalgar Square was not realised. This would have provided a visual association with another Grecian building by Smirke, the handsome Royal College of Physicians, which survives in the modified Canada House on the west side of Trafalgar Square. The General Post Office at St Martins-le-Grand was another monumental Smirke structure, which has since been demolished, but one of the huge Ionic capitals found its way to Walthamstow village in north-east London, where it offers a unique opportunity to examine at close quarters the stone carving of the Greek Revival.

Decimus Burton (1800–81) was another significant contributor to the Greek collection in London. This son of the prolific builder James Burton is chiefly known for his Ionic Screen at Hyde Park Corner and the nearby Constitution Arch which has been moved out of its intended alignment in order to suit the demands of the heavy traffic. Decimus Burton was also responsible for some of the villas and terraces of Nash's Regent's Park scheme and he left his mark at the southern end of Regent Street with his Athenaeum Club of 1828–30, a fine stuccoed building with a well defined Doric portico and a gilt statue of Pallas Athene announcing the elevated purpose of what was a club for artists, writers, scientists and men of culture. The Athenian frieze is a rare and delightful example of external decoration in London on a grand scale.

A less successful application of the Greek style was to a new generation of London churches. The Church Building Act of 1818 provided £1 million for an unspecified number of churches, and the first half of the 1820s was a period of intense activity with almost thirty large churches under construction in London alone, at an average cost of £15–20,000 each. Although there were no overall guidelines as to style

The Athenaeum boasts a huge gilt figure of Pallas Athene surveying Waterloo Place.

All Saints, Camden Town, of 1822 by Inwood has a circular tower above a semicircular portico of giant Ionic columns.

– and indeed some unhappy Gothic Revival characteristics made a hesitant appearance – this great wave of ecclesiastical building was notable for the preponderance of the Greek Revival adapted to the needs of Christian worship. In the borough of Lambeth alone no less than four grand churches with Greek porticoes were built during the years 1822–4: St Matthew, Brixton; St Mark, Kennington; St Luke, West Norwood; St John, Waterloo Road. These suggest a veritable 'little Greece' in a part of London which had no Classical leanings beyond what happened to be the fashion at the time. Other Greek productions in London included St Mary, Wyndham Place, and St Anne, Wandsworth, both by Smirke, and All Saints, Camden Town, now fittingly a church of the Greek Cypriot community, which was designed by William and Henry William Inwood.

It is to the Inwood father and son partner-

The new St Pancras Church of 1819–22 is a tour de force *of the Greek Revival, complete with duplicates of the Erechtheum caryatids.*

ship that London owes the most spectacular of the Greek Revival churches, the new parish church of St Pancras on the Euston Road, built between 1819–22 for the relatively expensive sum of £76,679. Young Henry William had just returned from Athens and he applied the form of the Tower of the Winds, repeated twice in different sizes stacked one on top of the other, in order to achieve a suitably Grecian steeple. The steeple was a constant problem, never to be happily resolved by the Greek Revivalists, since the Classical temple carried no superstructure other than its roof. The porch is of the giant Ionic order, situated at the west end where most architects were content to mass all their Grecian dressing. The Inwoods, however, took the daring step of adding two purely decorative porches at the east end which were exact replicas of the caryatids of the Erechtheum in Athens. Lord Elgin had taken one of the originals and it may now be viewed in glorious but sad isolation in a gallery of the British Museum. The caryatids of St Pancras are very convincing terracotta copies with hidden iron supports which provide a stunning sight along the Euston

Road and herald the forthcoming craze for architectural artifice of the Victorian age.

Churches, museums and institutes of learning were the most prolific exponents of the Greek mania which raged during the first quarter of the nineteenth century, but the Grecian style was a feature of domestic building as well. In his Regent's Park scheme John Nash deployed the Greek Revival in the Ionic order of Park Crescent as well as Doric on the grander scale of his Carlton House Terrace. In the newly emerging district of Belgravia, created by Thomas Cubitt, the Greek orders found many applications, such as the Pantechnicon of 1830 in Motcomb Street, noted for its giant Doric columns, a motif which recurs in the Pimlico Literary Institute of the same year at 22 Ebury Street, now converted into flats. Even utilitarian buildings in less fashionable areas took on a Greek veneer; indeed, by 1820 it became almost mandatory for new architecture to assume the 'modern' Hellenised style of decoration.

22 Ebury Street, formerly the Pimlico Literary Institute, has a modest Greek frontage.

Statue of Achilles, erected in 1822 in Hyde Park in honour of the Duke of Wellington.

It was inevitable that the love affair with Greece could not last for ever, but it was nonetheless quite remarkable just how quickly it fizzled out at the end of the 1830s and how violent were the expressions of distaste and loathing that followed its decline. A. W. Pugin inveighed against the Greek Revivalists: 'Yet notwithstanding the palpable impracticability of adapting Greek temples to our climate, habits and religion, we see the attempt and failure continuously made and repeated; post office, theatre, church, bath, reading-room, hotel, Methodist chapel and turnpike-gate, all present the eternal sameness of a Grecian temple outraged in all its proportions and character.' And John Ruskin was later to rage against the very idea of Classicism with all the fury of an Old Testament prophet. Smirke lived long enough to hear his work cruelly besmirched by the promoters of the Gothic Revival. It is as well when reading some of Ruskin's comments on Classical architecture – for instance, 'It is base, unnatural, unfruitful, unenjoyable, and impious. Pagan in its origin, proud and unholy in its revival, paralysed in its old age . . .' – to remember that the Greek Revivalists had also seen themselves as impassioned idealists. Smirke, in particular, whom Pugin disparaged as the chief perpetrator of 'the new Square Style', had declared the seriousness of his art in an unpublished treatise of 1815: 'Exterior architecture is a grave exhibition of talent and being always in the public eye, it cannot condescend to trifle. When art chooses to frolic in masonry, the effect is not only unnatural but indecorous.'

The high polemics of the age should not lead us to imagine that the Greek Revival dominated all aspects of style during its brief reign. Just as Baroque had lingered on behind the Palladian façades, so too did a variety of exotic ideas of interior design during the hegemony of the Greeks. In any case, the Greek repertoire did not provide any suitable models for English conditions in this respect. That Greek influence was usually only skin-deep can be seen at what was London's most prestigious private address. Behind the Corinthian portico of Apsley House, the Duke of Wellington added the Waterloo Gallery in 1828–9 and chose a decor that was in complete opposition to the tenets of the Greek Revival. The style of the gallery is in the frivolous, flamboyant and frolicsome manner which we know as the Louis XV or the 'Dix-huitième'. This was perhaps a backhanded compliment to the French, whom the Duke had so recently defeated, but it also served as an architectural pointer towards the fulsome taste of the Victorian age. The Greek theme, however, was taken up by the statue of Achilles overlooking Apsley House, erected in 1822 in honour of Wellington.

Although Smirke's imposing south

Wellington opted for French 'Dix-huitième' decor for his lavish Waterloo Gallery behind the Classical façade of Apsley House.

façade of the British Museum was under construction as late as 1842–7, the Greek Revivalists in London had generally been silenced by the end of the 1830s. Yet one of their last achievements was also perhaps their finest. Philip Hardwick's Euston Station of 1837, completely demolished by British Rail in the 1960s, was a triumphant culmination to the Greek interlude in London's building history. Ironically, it brought the Classical tradition in London to a new type of building which symbolised more than any other the industrial future. Thus the Greek Revival linked up with the Age of Steam: the great Doric Arch of Euston Station became visually synonymous with steam locomotion for generations of Londoners. It was really quite remarkable that the architecture of ancient Greece should have been chosen as the medium for London's first main railway terminus, but that is an indication of the dominion exercised by the Greek Revival for works of monumental character in the thirty years preceding the accession of Queen Victoria in 1837.

Highgate Cemetery, London's Victorian necropolis par excellence.

4 Victorian and Edwardian High Noon

It is quite astonishing how radically London was transformed in the seventy-seven years which elapsed between 1837 and 1914. The population statistics for the nineteenth century as a whole show that the area corresponding to that once administered by the old London County Council experienced an increase from 959,000 in 1801 to 4,425,000 in 1901. Behind the figures there was tremendous turmoil, caused especially by the coming of the railways, which not only slashed almost at will through the metropolis but also drew more and more places into the urban network. The concept of what was and what was not London needed constant revision. Macaulay described Islington on the eve of the Victorian age as 'an island of solitude and poets loved to contrast its silence and repose with the din and turmoil of the monster London'. Very soon it was engulfed by London and emerged as one of the more urbanised parts of the inner city. At the same time the City itself lost its residential status and turned into the commercial enclave which is the reality of today.

London grew as a result of its role as the economic powerhouse and administrative centre of the burgeoning British Empire. Market forces stimulated the expansion of the metropolis; and it was left to private initiative to solve the inevitable problems, such as the provision of adequate housing for those not catered for by the speculative builder. In face of the desperate conditions of life within the booming city there was a general abnegation of responsibility. Indeed, there was a conspiracy of vested interests, notably those of the City and of Westminster, which saw to it that for most of the nineteenth century London was prevented from taking any effective measures to improve the chronic overcrowding of the slums with their concomitants of disease and criminality. When action became imperative London at last acquired the Metropolitan Board of Works in 1855, but its powers were limited to the provision of 'the better management of the metropolis in respect of the sewerage and drainage and the paving, cleansing, lighting and improvements thereof'. This small beginning of municipal government was extremely effective within the limits imposed, but it could not compare with the vigorous régime of a city like Birmingham under the inspired leadership of Joseph Chamberlain. It was as late as 1888 that the democratically based London County Council was instituted, and not until 1890 that it was empowered to provide public housing. By this time London was already long established as the world's largest city.

There was thus no official channel for municipal reform for the first fifty years of Victoria's reign; and it was perhaps not surprising that men of noble vision such as Ruskin and Morris steadily withdrew into an imaginary world of medieval fantasy where the good old values prior to urbanisation and industrialisation were still inviolate. Architects, too, appeared to live in an otherworldliness far removed from the urgent problems of the sprawling metropolis: the 'Battle of the Styles' dominated their thoughts more than any more practical issues. Just how obsessed the early Victorians were with the question of style may be gauged from the flood of pamphlets and books on the subject, written with an intensity usually reserved for great moral causes. The Gothic Revival, as evolved by Pugin, had all the fervour of a religious mission, and the campaign for the Christian pointed arch against the pagan forms of Classical architecture was hard fought. However, both the Classical and the Gothic arguments were deeply rooted in nostalgia; and the opportunity to develop a contemporary style using the new media of iron and glass was largely overlooked in spite of the huge success of the Crystal Palace at the Great Exhibition of 1851.

Behind the stylistic debate lay an understandable desire to make some substantial improvement on what the Victorians perceived as the drab and oppressive appearance of Georgian London. Indeed, it must be borne in mind that London remained essentially a Georgian city until well into the nineteenth century and the Georgian heritage sat heavily and awkwardly on the Victorians. But it was not a simple matter of rejecting wholesale all Georgian values. In fact, the forces of conservatism in the building trade remained obstinately Classical even at the height of the Gothic Revival. It was not until the 1870s and 80s that the eclectic style known as 'Queen Anne', derived from the architecture of the age of Wren, provided a successful alternative for domestic housing. Many of the aspirations of Victorian London were then channelled into the home and the suburb.

Suburban ideals also influenced the design of London's new generation of cemeteries. Healthy locations, green spaces, winding paths and graves with a view characterise the very best, such as Kensal Green and Norwood; but it is above all at Highgate Cemetery where the aura of Victorian London is most potent. Even in the funerary architecture there is a strong echo of the 'Battle of the Styles' with the main contenders Grecian and Gothic, but with the appearance of Byzantine and Egyptian as well. As in the real city below, the best graves seem to congregate in the most agreeable spots, suggesting a form of social segregation in the city of the dead.

Social segregation was a constant feature of London's Victorian suburbs. The aim of the speculative builder was always to attract the highest class of tenant that any particular development was able to sustain. The decoration of Victorian houses demonstrated the attempts to upgrade their status; and the same concern for prestige underlay that curious English compromise of the semi-detached, which required each family to maintain the quality expected by the other. In any case, all the residents of a specific neighbourhood were more than anxious that nothing should lower the tone. Fashion was extremely harsh in its judgement, so that the new areas of Bayswater and Notting Hill, despite their architectural pretensions, were always 'on the wrong side of the park' as far as Belgravia was concerned. Further down the scale, Ealing has always held itself aloof from Acton. Each part of Victorian London knew its place in the social pecking order, and the idea of a mixed neighbourhood became increasingly unacceptable. Gone forever was the old London of aristocratic mansions cheek by jowl with slums and tenements. In this painstaking sorting out of socio-economic groups it

The Prudential, a late flourish in Holborn of the Gothic revival.

usually fell to the speculative builder to guess where the frontiers of fashion should be drawn. Stylish Kensington, at one stage, came to an abrupt halt at Wrights Lane. More significant was the now yawning gulf between the elegant consumer society of the West End and the drab industrious proletariat of the East End. The whole of south London was regarded by some as a sort of no-man's-land. Walter Besant, the novelist, dismissed it as 'a city without a municipality, without a centre, without a civic history'.

Circle of Lebanon, best address in Highgate Cemetery.

Much the same could be said of the far-flung suburbs of north London which had but recently fallen to the inexorable march of bricks and mortar.

As for the notorious rookeries of London, they were gradually expunged, first by the forces of private philanthropy; the grim 'improved' dwellings, a cross between prison and barracks, still mark the spot of the former slums. After 1890 the LCC was able to take up the task of providing homes for the poorer elements of London. Given the energy and imagination which went into the early housing estates, one might well speculate on how different parts of London might have been if the LCC had been given its wings earlier in the century. From housing the LCC extended its sphere to schools, fire and police stations and other new works of the emerging collectivist philosophy. It comes as a surprise to discover so much social commitment behind the accepted carefree image of an Edwardian London bent almost exclusively on pleasure.

In fact, Edwardian London was in many ways still solidly Victorian, and the continental craze for Art Nouveau or Jugendstil was held in low esteem as being vaguely suspect. Taste ran riot in safer, more English directions such as the revival of Baroque as practised by Wren and his successors. After the Entente Cordiale at the beginning of the twentieth century, the architecture of French Classicism became highly fashionable, with its connotations of metropolitan sophistication. As the Edwardian age drew to a close there was an *embarras de richesses* on London's architectural menu, as old stylistic conventions were thrown to the winds and free invention reached fever-pitch. The spectrum ranged from the austere elegance of Ashbee's houses at 38–9 Cheyne Walk of 1899–1901 to the French opera-house fantasy of the Methodist Central Hall in Westminster of 1905–11. The Leysian Mission in City Road, Finsbury, of 1903, with its sumptuous façade and dome of terracotta, might have been a design for a music hall rather than for a charitable work of the Wesleyans. Even the Greek Revival was not despised: the King Edward VII Galleries of the British Museum of 1904–14 continued the giant Ionic theme of the famous south front. Nor was Gothic overlooked, as witnessed by Waterhouse's Prudential Assurance and his University College Hospital, both completed in 1906; and there was also the anachronistic Middlesex Guildhall of 1906–13 in Parliament Square, designed to harmonise with the Gothic of Westminster Abbey. And finally there was a return to English Baroque, in Lutyens's Country Life building of 1904 in Tavistock Street, Covent Garden.

But the underlying message of the Edwardian era was modernity. Michelin House of 1905–11, a daringly innovative French design, and Voysey's Sanderson Wallpaper Factory of 1902–3 in Turnham Green gave an inkling of the future possibilities of industrial architecture. The Stripped Classical look of buildings such as Cooper's Marylebone Town Hall of 1914–21 and of Holden's building in the Strand for the BMA of 1907–8, now Zimbabwe House, prefigure the style of office blocks after the Great War.

Also of great modernity was the new, clean and efficient transport of the electric Underground, which gave a huge boost to London's expansion, to the extent that the overall area of the conurbation almost doubled between 1900–14, as new outer suburbs were drawn into the network. Yet this flight into the countryside did not mean that the metropolitan heartland was undervalued. On the contrary, as one surveys the major achievements of Edwardian London, such as the great set pieces of the Aldwych and Kingsway or the ceremonial rond-point in front of Buckingham Palace, there is the inescapable feeling that the age celebrated an unalloyed delight in the stylish trappings of metropolitan life. Taken together, the Victorian and Edwardian chapters may be reckoned the most prolific in the 2000 years of London's evolution, a period which despite its profound misgivings finally came to realise its destiny as the high noon of urban civilisation on the banks of the Thames.

The Gothic Revival and the Battle of the Styles

It may be argued that the architecture of Victorian London amounted to a systematic and comprehensive rejection of all Georgian values, but the first generation of Victorians shared at least one thing with their forefathers: the same obsession with style that had fired Palladianism and the Greek Revival now espoused the neglected cause of Gothic. The physical results of this stylistic revolution and its aftermath gave Victorian London its predominantly Gothic image, leaving behind a vast architectural legacy which is only now subdued by the works of the twentieth century. The switch from Classical to Gothic coincided neatly with the accession of Queen Victoria in

The Houses of Parliament, London's first major building in the revived Gothic manner.

The House of Lords, London's most sumptuous Victorian Gothic interior.

1837 and became the hallmark for at least the first fifty years of her reign. However, the first major triumph of the Gothic Revivalists preceded the Victorian era when London's – and indeed the nation's – most conspicuous monument went up in flames and had to be entirely redesigned.

The conflagration at the Old Palace of Westminster, which occurred on 16 October 1834, symbolically cleared the ground. For the first time it was stipulated in the terms of the ensuing competition for the new Houses of Parliament that the design had to be in the Gothic or the Elizabethan style, but this was not such a straightforward instance of a new architectural direction as it might appear, for there was concern that the new structure should harmonise with the adjacent Westminster Abbey and the medieval Westminster Hall which had survived the fire. The designs submitted in 1835 by Charles Barry

(1795–1860), who won the commission from a field of ninety-seven competitors, took their inspiration from the Perpendicular Gothic of the Henry VII Chapel. This was a quite remarkable achievement for an architect whose own preferred style was the Italianate *palazzo.* Barry largely owed his success, beyond doubt, to the brilliant Gothic details of the design elaborated by Augustus Welby Northmore Pugin (1812–52), the man who was to provide the inspirational leadership in the forthcoming campaign for the Gothic Revival.

This unique partnership of a Classicist and a Gothicist produced London's most individual and enduring public building of the nineteenth century. Its success lay in the happy symbiosis of the medieval spirit of the ornamentation and the clear layout and symmetrical disposition of the façades. Pugin himself was all too aware of the extent of the artistic compromise, and he is reported to have quipped, 'All Grecian, sir; Tudor details on a classic body.' But, whatever misgivings he may have had, he threw himself without reserve into the minutest detail of the design, producing everything from the stone carvings to the wallpaper, umbrella stands and inkwells. The external aspect of the Houses of Parliament had been marred by the grime of more than a century but is now gloriously cleaned and restored, the difficult magnesium limestone giving a honey-coloured glow in the sunshine to the intricate reticulation of the Perpendicular stonework. Yet the full intensity of Pugin's Gothic vision only becomes apparent inside the building, most spectacularly in the House of Lords which forms the inner sanctum of this shrine to Gothic style. This interior is rich with mural paintings, statuary, mosaics, wood panelling and red leather setting off the gilt reredos behind the throne, and ranks as the most stunning evocation of Victorian medievalism in London, if not in Britain as a whole. But for all the wealth of imagery the Houses of Parliament did not set a new trend in public buildings. The only close relations were Pennethorne's Public Record Office of 1851–66 in Chancery Lane and Hardwick's New Hall and Library at Lincoln's Inn of 1843–5, the former in the Perpendicular style and the latter a Tudor revival. The real contribution of the Houses of Parliament to the Gothic Revival was to refocus attention on medieval building crafts and on Pugin who gave the movement its decisive ethical and religious foundation.

It was Pugin the writer, even more than Pugin the designer, who set the Gothic Revival on its triumphant course. The title of his pamphlet of 1836, *Contrasts; or; A Parallel between the Noble Edifices of the 14th & 15th Centuries and Similar Buildings of the Present Day; Shewing the Present Decay of Taste*, left the reader in no doubt as to the intents of the author, who launched into a virulent attack on the whole theory and practice of Classicism as exemplified especially by Palladianism and the Greek Revival: 'This mania for paganism is developed in all classes of buildings erected since the fifteenth century – in palaces, in mansions, in private houses, in public erections, in monuments for the dead; it even extended to furniture and domestic ornaments for the table.' In the 1841 edition of *Contrasts* Pugin showed the effect of Classical architecture on the appearance of an entire town, setting the urban landscape of 1440 alongside that of 1840. The simplified comparison served to underline just how complete a revolution in urbanism had been achieved by the Georgians: the London inherited by the Victorians had been thoroughly Georgianised. Pugin drove home forcefully the main point of his argument:

> There is no need of visiting the distant shores of Greece and Egypt to make discoveries in art. England alone abounds in hidden and unknown antiquities of surpassing interest. What madness, then, while neglecting our own religious and national types of architec-

New Hall, Lincoln's Inn, a rare specimen of Tudor revival.

ture and art, to worship at the revived shrines of ancient corruption, and profane the temple of a crucified Redeemer by the architecture and emblems of heathen Gods.

The religious implications of the argument were made thoroughly explicit in further pamphlets by Pugin, such as *An Apology for the Revival of Christian Architecture in England* of 1843 and *The True Principles of Pointed or Christian Architecture* of 1853, in which he demolished the pretensions of the Greek temple as a model for Christian worship. Pugin argued that the temple was not designed to hold congregations, that it made no allowance for a bell tower or for windows, and that the pitch of its roof was unsuited to a northern climate. He also stressed the religious spirit and ritualistic symbolism of the traditional Christian church of the Middle Ages. Pugin concluded: 'Let then the Beautiful and the True be our watchword for future exertions in the overthrow of modern paltry taste and paganism, and the revival of Catholic art and dignity.' Pugin saw Protestantism as the source of all moral decay in church architecture and the decline of Gothic, so his conversion to Catholicism would appear to have been motivated by a concern for style rather than for theology.

Behind the polemics Pugin advanced some solid architectural doctrine, most

Ruskinian polychrome decoration of the font at All Saints, Margaret Street.

importantly that ornamentation should result from the essential construction of the building; but his main achievement was to give the Gothic Revival its religious justification, which was also propounded by the Ecclesiological Society and the Oxford Tractarians. How Pugin put his own theories into practice may be judged at his best church in London, St Thomas of Canterbury in Fulham of 1847–9, which is a competent if unexciting composition. The multi-pinnacled design of the high altar in the Church of the Immaculate Conception in Mayfair is a precious example of the energy and devotion he expended on the objects of Catholic ritual. Yet Pugin was the first to express his disappointment at the discrepancy between his ecstatic expectations and his actual productions. His career ended with his premature death in 1852 at the age of forty.

The flame Pugin had lit lived on with even more brightness in the person of John Ruskin. His book, *The Seven Lamps of Architecture*, of 1849, was instantly acclaimed as an oracle of artistic values. Ruskin served up to his public a relentless torrent of aesthetic judgements delivered with the vigour and inspiration of an Evangelist minister: 'I say that if men lived like men indeed, their houses would be temples – temples which we should hardly dare to injure, and in which it would make us holy to be permitted to live . . .' Yet Ruskin's deeper thoughts on the moving spirit behind worthy architecture were largely disregarded. Instead, what became embraced as Ruskinian in architecture was derived from some of his practical recommendations such as the use of structural polychromy: 'The true colours of architecture are those of natural stone, and I would fain see these taken advantage of to the full. Every variety of hue, from pale yellow to purple, passing through orange, red, and brown, is entirely at our command; nearly every kind of green and grey is also attainable; and with these, and pure white, what harmonies might we not achieve?' It might seem that William Butterfield's gorgeous jewel of All Saints, Margaret Street, designed in 1849, was the direct answer to Ruskin's prayers, but the evidence is that this model church of the Ecclesiological Society, with its lavishly ornate, polychromatic interior, evolved parallel to the theories of Ruskin. A later example of Butterfield's work is St Augustine, Queen's Gate, of 1870–7 whose polychromy was considered so overpowering in the 1920s that it was painted over. The original splendour has been partly restored to view. Further notable polychromatic effects of the period can be seen at Street's St James-the-Less in Pimlico, and White's St Saviour, Aberdeen Park.

Ruskin's influence was also keenly felt in the imitation of Venetian Gothic, a direct result of his three-volume work *The Stones of Venice* of 1851–53, which was a celebration of what Ruskin called southern Gothic as well as Byzantine style. These publications marked Ruskin's full espousal of the Gothic Revival, which he confirmed in 1855 in the second edition of *The Seven Lamps of Architecture*: 'In this style let us build the church, the palace and the cottage; but chiefly let us use it for civil and domestic buildings.' This was a marked extension of Gothic from its restricted ecclesiastical base; and Ruskin loosened another tenet of the faith by stressing ornament at the expense of structure, thereby giving his blessing to some of the most extreme showmanship of Victorian architecture. Examples of 'Ruskinian' Gothic began to proliferate; even in that bastion of philistinism and capitalism, the City, there appeared some crazy versions of Venetian Gothic, such as the Vinegar Warehouse of 1868 by Roumieu at 33–35 Eastcheap and the commercial premises at 7 Lothbury, behind the Bank of England, by G. Somers Clarke in 1866. Venetian Byzantine can be seen at 59–61 Mark Lane, at 103 Cannon Street and in Greville Street. Such buildings

All Saints, Margaret Street, most ornate of London's Victorian churches.

were to haunt Ruskin who came to regret his propaganda bitterly. He remarked in the 1874 preface to the third edition of *The Stones of Venice*:

> I would rather, for my own part, that no architects had ever condescended to adopt one of the views suggested in this book, than that any should have made the partial use of it which has mottled our manufactory chimneys with black and red brick, dignified our banks and draper's shops with Venetian tracery, and pinched our parish churches into dark and slippery arrangements for the advertisement of cheap coloured glass and pantiles.

The London area is full of specimens that must have shocked Ruskin's sensitivities. He mentioned in particular his horror at finding a piece of Italian Gothic serving as the porch of a public house somewhere between Ealing and Brentford.

Although Ruskin was to retire wounded from the fray, the central message of *The Stones of Venice* was salvaged by William Morris, who published in 1892 an essential chapter of that work under the title *The Nature of Gothic*. In his introduction Morris described it 'as one of the very few necessary and inevitable utterances of the century. To some of us when we first read it, now many years ago, it seemed to point out a new road on which the world should travel . . . For the lesson which Ruskin here teaches us is that art is the expression of man's pleasure in labour . . .'

Pugin, Ruskin and Morris were then the moving spirits behind the Gothic Revival, but its most prolific architectural practitioner was Sir George Gilbert Scott (1811–78). In keeping with the literary tradition of the age, he too produced a book; his *Remarks on Secular and Domestic Architecture, present and future*, of 1857, proposed the general application of fourteenth-century Decorated Gothic as the universal style to follow. By this time the cause of Gothic had evidently been won. As early as 1851 Francis Cross had reported: 'we have Gothic Houses of Parliament, libraries, halls, churches, aye, even the very Methodist body have been vaccinated into a furor for Gothic . . . The almshouses, hospitals, workhouses, schools, villas, houses, cottages – everything now is Gothic.' But the Conservative Prime Minister Lord Palmerston was to succeed in stemming the tide when he steadfastly opposed the use of Gothic for the new government buildings in Whitehall, notably the Foreign Office.

The story is well known how Scott managed to obtain the commission but then fell foul of Palmerston, who would not accept his resoundingly Gothic designs. The rejection of Gothic was not just blind prejudice, as Palmerston explained in a statement to Parliament: 'We all know that our northern climate does not overpower us with an excess of sunshine. Then, for Heaven's sake, let us have buildings whose interior admits, and whose exterior reflects, what light there is.' Thus the argument that Gothic was naturally suited to the northern climate was turned neatly on its head. Scott sought to outflank Palmerston by producing a round-arched Italo-Byzantine design which Palmerston dismissed with his famous rebuke that it was 'neither one thing nor t'other – a regular mongrel affair'. The Prime Minister could not see a middle way in what he himself described as 'this battle of the Gothic and Palladian styles'. Italianate it had to be, and Scott – according to his own account – 'bought some costly books on Italian architecture and set vigorously to work to rub up'.

What is remarkable here is the extent of the climb-down on the part of Scott. He had described his full conversion to the cause of Gothic as a manner of religious experience: 'I was awakened from my slumbers by the thunder of Pugin's writings . . . What for fifteen years had been a labour of love only, now became the one business, the one aim, the overmastering object of my life. I cared for nothing but the revival of

Gothic architecture.' The results of Scott's temporary recantation may be seen in the Classical elegance of the Foreign Office in Whitehall, in all a competent composition which Scott might not have designed had his artistic mentor Pugin still been alive. As it was, Scott consoled himself that he acted in the best long-term interests of his family and he lived to fight another day.

Compensation for Scott came almost immediately with London's most amazing display of High Victorian Gothic architecture, the frontage of St Pancras Station, constructed 1868–74, of which the dominant feature was the magnificent Midland Grand Hotel. Sadly, the hotel has been closed for more than fifty years and only the soaring great staircase of Baroque character gives an idea of the former glory of the interior. The vigorous design of the exterior, offering a complex display of European styles – notably the picturesque roofline, reminiscent of the great town halls of Flanders – makes a brazen architectural

The Foreign Office in Whitehall, the forced compromise of Scott, the ardent Gothicist.

statement. The New Road had become the gathering place for London's railway termini, and St Pancras was determined to upstage its close neighbours, the Doric Euston and the functionalist King's Cross. In this aim the directors of the Midland Railway and their architect Sir George Gilbert Scott succeeded triumphantly. Scott wrote of it: 'It is often spoken of to me as the finest building in London, my own belief is that it is possibly too good for its purpose, but having been disappointed, through Lord Palmerston, of my ardent hope of carrying out my style in the Government Offices, I was glad to be able to erect one building in that style in London.' However, to some contemporary observers it seemed to be an act of architectural sacrilege to employ the Gothic mode for so mundane a purpose. The architect J. T. Emmett remarked of it: 'There is here a complete travesty of noble associations, and not the slightest care to save these from sordid contact. An elaboration that might

St Pancras Station and the Midland Grand Hotel, triumph of Scott's Gothic vision.

The Albert Memorial, the ultimate expression of High Victorian taste.

be suitable for a chapterhouse, or a Cathedral choir, is used as an "advertising medium" for bagmen's bedrooms and the costly discomforts of a terminus hotel . . .'

Such criticism would explain Scott's own reservation that it was 'possibly too good for its purpose'. In fact the Gothic Revival had come a long way since its initial promotion by Pugin and the Camden Society as the only acceptable style for church architecture. The results of this successful propaganda are to be seen throughout the Victorian suburbs of London where scores of nineteenth-century Gothic churches are scattered as outposts of a beleaguered morality. They are so numerous and so familiar a type that it is easy to overlook how hugely impressive some really are, such as Pearson's lofty and austere St Augustine, Kilburn, and St Michael, Croydon. Brooks's Ascension, Lavender Hill in Battersea, looms majestically and ominously over the surrounding streets; and the rogue architect of the Gothic Revival Edward Buckton

Lamb's startling productions of St Martin, Gospel Oak, and St Mary Magdalene, Addiscombe, have lost none of their disquieting influence on the onlooker. But there is always something stiff and cold in the quality of Victorian Gothic churches, not excepting Scott's own, such as St Mary Abbots in Kensington, despite the evident nobility of intention.

The root of the problem had been defined by Ruskin as a lack of spirituality and true feeling in the craftsman: 'I cannot too often repeat, it is not coarse cutting, it is not blunt cutting, that is necessarily bad; but it is cold cutting – the look of equal trouble everywhere – the smooth, diffused tranquillity of heartless pains – the regularity of a plough in a level field.' One has only to look at the passive statues inserted in the medieval reredos of Southwark Cathedral to appreciate the point Ruskin is making. The same shortcoming was even more painfully evident in the restoration work undertaken by Scott on many churches and cathedrals, most notably on Westminster Abbey, where it was his practice to apply an overall style and to remove any discordant elements, however ancient. Such work aroused the scorn and anger of William Morris and prompted him to found in 1876 the Society for the Protection of Ancient Buildings. Thus Scott, who had devoted himself to the cause of the Gothic Revival under the spell of Pugin, found himself condemned by the latter-day saints of the movement, Ruskin and Morris. There was thus a sad edge to his prodigious career, but he was redeemed and vindicated by his Albert Memorial. This was a monumental version of a medieval reliquary for the holding of saintly relics, resplendent with colour and bright materials, surrounded with exotic allegorical statuary and surmounted with tiers of angels. The religious symbolism was not lost on the widowed Queen Victoria and Scott was rewarded with a knighthood. Scott described the Albert Memorial as his most prominent work and it has certainly become a much loved London landmark. Whatever its artistic merits, there is no denying that it represents the quintessence of High Victorian taste.

Of his several disappointments Scott's greatest was in not obtaining, despite energetic lobbying, the commission for the new Royal Courts of Justice in the Strand, which were built from 1874 to 1882 to the designs of George Edmund Street (1824–81). Street had previously made his mark in London with his highly regarded St James-the-Less in Pimlico and St Mary Magdalene in Paddington's Little Venice, but the Law Courts were his greatest achievement. The picturesque Strand frontage of spired turrets and towers has a magical quality which is surpassed only by the Great Hall inside, possibly the most enchanting Victorian Gothic enclosed space in London. This vast *salle des pas perdus* has the character of a cathedral nave but without the focal point of an altar, offering an air of permanence in contrast to the temporary passage of plaintiffs, defendants and their lawyers who for the past century have borne their triumphs and disasters beneath its lofty pointed arches. A memorial to Street is located in the south-east corner, a fitting tribute to the architect who died in the course of his exertions on the project. The Law Courts represent the high-water mark of the Gothic Revival; in fact all eleven designs submitted by the best practitioners, such as Scott, Burges and Waterhouse, were in that style. But this great public building also marks the beginning of the decline of Gothic in London, for although the style continued to be practised until the end of the century and beyond, occurring in such unlikely guises as Waterhouse's amazing Prudential Assurance of 1899-1906, it was no longer the dominant mode but just another element in the increasingly cacophonic architectural composition of late Victorian London.

Eclecticism had been present all along, most noticeably in the grand railway stations which the private companies had

Street's Royal Courts of Justice in the Strand contain a cathedral-like main hall.

built with the prime intent of upstaging their rivals. *Building News* reflected on the situation in 1875 on the occasion of the opening of Liverpool Street Station: 'One monster station or hotel after another has risen in the metropolis, each vieing, it would seem, to eclipse the others either in point of size or in architectural pretensions. Every style has been tried to captivate and draw the attention of the travelling public, from Egyptian and Greek to Gothic.' To which one might add the French Renaissance 'château style' of the Loire Valley, as represented by Victoria Station's Grosvenor Hotel of 1860–1 by Knowles. *Building News* continued: 'Railway termini and hotels are to the nineteenth century what monasteries and cathedrals were to the thirteenth century. They are the only truly representative kind of buildings we possess . . .' But with the exception of King's Cross there was no stylistic relation between the architecture of

The Albert Hall strikes an imposing note at the northern end of Albertopolis.

the buildings and the engineering of the railway shed. The real achievements of the age in constructions of iron and glass were not adequately appreciated at the time.

The most varied assemblage of Victorian styles in London is to be found in the area of South Kensington sometimes referred to as Albertopolis, due to the great initiative shown by the Prince Consort in the promotion of culture and education. This collection of buildings, which arose out of the profits of the Great Exhibition of 1851, is a repository of Victorian taste. From the sumptuous Gothic of the Albert Memorial one passes to the Italianate amphitheatre of the Royal Albert Hall. All that remains of the extravagantly exotic Imperial Institute, a late Victorian fantasy of 1887–93, is the soaring tower of the edifice which now resembles a disembodied chimney. The southern limit of Albertopolis is formed by the Victoria & Albert Museum (originally the South Kensington Museum). The early parts of this complex are to be seen from the Main Quadrangle and in the Huxley Building facing Exhibition Road, all in a dashing style of bright red brick and terracotta which has been aptly described as

Lombardic Renaissance in appearance.

A close neighbour to the west is the Natural History Museum, the most original and powerful conception of all. It owes its design to Alfred Waterhouse (1830–1905), who was commissioned in 1872 to complete an Italian Renaissance scheme prepared by Captain Fowke, architect of the Royal Albert Hall and part of the V & A. Like Scott before him, Waterhouse designed round arches as a compromise between Gothic and Classical. Thus we have an instance here of a committed Gothic Revivalist working in the manner of the German Romanesque. Of equal note is the material chosen by Waterhouse, for this was the first building in London, if not anywhere, to be entirely fronted with terracotta. In fact, only the front half of the building was ever completed. Terracotta not only had the advantage of a washable, acid-resistant surface; it also permitted at an economic outlay the most spectacular relief work. The beautiful grey-blue and light brown façade

Waterhouse's Natural History Museum makes bold use of terracotta.

seethes with naturalistic statuary of beasts both living and extinct. There is hardly a space which does not provide a convenient perch for a sculptured animal. Adam, as the superior being in the creation, used to occupy a pedestal on the gable above the main entrance – in glorious isolation for there was no room for Eve – but he disappeared in mysterious circumstances during the last war. The theme of terracotta and animal portrayals continues inside the building where the dramatic main hall – not vaulted but with a roof of iron and glass – provided the most exciting permanent exhibition space of its age.

In South Kensington the battle of the styles is thus transformed into a sumptuous stylistic banquet. Indeed, the bitter antagonism between Gothicists and Classicists was really only at its most acute over the emotive question of church architecture and in the disputes which arose around the Houses of Parliament and the Foreign Office.

There is an impressive list of London buildings of the Victorian era which may be cited as upholders of the Classical tradition: Charles Barry's *palazzi* of the Reform Club and Bridgewater House; the Museum of Mankind, the Royal Opera House, the Royal Exchange, and even the Metropolitan Tabernacle at Newington Butts. But the most significant defector from the Gothic camp must surely be the London Oratory, designed by Herbert Gribble in 1876, which is a full-blown pastiche of a Roman Renaissance church of the very type that Pugin had denounced as a heathen profanity. One shudders to think how he might have reacted.

The lesson to be drawn is that the eloquence of the polemicists in the battle of the styles creates a distorted picture of a clear division through the ranks of the architectural world. Even the most fervent Gothic Revivalist, Sir George Gilbert Scott, was ultimately prepared to abandon his ideals rather than relinquish a commission; and Pugin's design masterpiece of the House of Lords was contained in a space corresponding to a perfect double cube of impeccable Palladian lineage. But it is true to say that Victorian London was obsessed with the search for styles. The mad scramble for a bold style at the expense of any serious quest for truthful construction was the main characteristic of the age. It is not the styles that were advocated but how they were interpreted which provides the key to Victorian ideas; and it does not require the distance and perspective of the present day to spot the general thrust of Victorian design. Looking back with some pride in 1898 *Building News* commented:

> Wherever we go-we find the once dominating dingy brick front, with its neat pointing and gauged flat arches, is gradually disappearing, or its solid complacency, so characteristic of the eighteenth-century English character, broken through by the stirring activities of commercial competition. Everywhere we find a restless desire to introduce something new, occasionally very excrescent and erratic; not only a variety of material, but a diversity of feature.

It has been argued that the sometimes laughable excesses of Victorian architecture resulted from a need to cover up a deep well of self-doubt and anxiety, but it is also fair to say that the economic energies unleashed by the age outstripped the artistic capacity to respond. The Victorians were the first to be confronted with the entire rich menu of international style along with the means of mass-production to indulge themselves most liberally. Certainly, there was confusion and gluttony, but the aesthetic anguish must have been reserved for the more sensitive spirits of Pugin, Ruskin, Morris and associates. For all its shortcomings, Victorian architecture was self-confident enough to make brashness a kind of virtue. It was an age when the epithet 'pretentious' had not yet acquired a totally pejorative meaning. Only one year into the reign of Queen Victoria there was a comment about Adam's Adelphi, expressing surprise 'that such a paltry gingerbread piece of architecture should ever have been admired, for now-a-days many of the gin-palaces about town exhibit quite as much grandeur, and far more consistency of design'. This is perhaps an accurate reflection of the general level of popular taste of Victorian Londoners. If so, it would help to explain both the fervent protests of Pugin, Ruskin and Morris as well as the reasons for the failure of their cause. For they had all been at pains to point out that the spirit of Gothic in the Middle Ages was a direct result of the religious and social values of society at the time. Right at the beginning Pugin had written in his *Contrasts* of 1836: 'The mechanical part of Gothic architecture is pretty well understood, but it is the principles which influenced ancient compositions, and the soul which appears in all former works, which is so lamentably deficient; nor, as I have before stated, can anything be regained but by a restoration of the ancient feelings and sentiments 'tis they alone can restore Gothic architecture.' As it turned out, Pugin's exact statement still held good at the very end of the Victorian age, for the Middle Ages were, in spite of the elaborate architectural stage sets prepared in such profusion, quite beyond any recall.

The memorial to the architect G. E. Street in the main hall of the Royal Courts of Justice.

Metropolis

The phenomenal growth of London in the nineteenth century was not just a statistical achievement in terms of population and acres under urban occupation; it was a metamorphosis from a large town to a metropolis or indeed a world city, as its status was perceived at the time. Although London's expansion was built on the profits of trade and industry, its metropolitan character was not expressed in the sort of palatial factory buildings which were the glory of Manchester or Glasgow. The industrial archaeologist will find only isolated examples of the genre in London. Instead, the soul of the Victorian metropolis must be sought in an urban apparatus of ever-increasing complexity and sophistication, where it was the engineer rather than the architect who set the pace and provided the key to progress.

Probably the most dramatic change in the basic structure of London was the concentration of the institutions of business and finance into the original square mile of the City which had constituted the whole of London in the Middle Ages. This was in a sense a continuation of the medieval practice of grouping trades into their own exclusive areas, but it now happened on a scale which would have been beyond the wildest imagination of the Middle Ages. What occurred was no less than a total transformation of the historic heart of town from a collection of mixed neighbourhoods into an enclave devoted almost entirely to commerce. The population statistics show the extent and rapidity of the process. The City had sheltered 123,000 residents in 1841, but this declined gradually to 112,000 by 1861, then dropping sharply to a mere 51,000 in 1881 and just 27,000 by the end of the Victorian era in 1901. This represented a minute 0.6 per cent of London's 4,425,000 inhabitants at the time.

What emerged from the labyrinth of obsolete residential properties in the City in the course of the nineteenth century was a new generation of imposing commercial premises, still aligned to the medieval street pattern, but boldly proclaiming the virtues of Victorian capitalism. Commenting on the new face of the City in 1863 *The Builder* noted: 'there is one prevailing idea – something large, coarse, showy, thick, clumsy, would be grand, but not an idea of any of the tradition of England's sweet poetic loveliness and littleness . . .' The economic powerhouses of Leadenhall and Lombard Street had little use for such niceties. But there was a measure of respect as well in the media coverage. In 1868 *Building News* remarked that 'buildings worthy of notice' were to be found 'at almost every step'. 'There is the graceful Grecian style, the palatial Palladian, and the gimcrack Gothic . . . the student may be fitted with his favourite style of architecture anywhere between St Paul's and the Aldgate Pump . . .' In addition to the parade of banks and insurance companies the City introduced a completely new form of building which has since come to dominate the urban landscape: the office block. Two fine examples of the genre are to be found in Queen Victoria Street, Mappin & Webb of 1870 and Albert Buildings of 1871. After years of neglect there was belated recognition of the merits of such Victorian commercial architecture when in 1986 public opinion went in favour of the Mappin & Webb building and against the proposed Mies van der Rohe modernist block.

If the new buildings of the City were a sign of London's dominance of the world financial markets, then the Docks were physical evidence of the international trade based on the British Empire's control of a quarter of the land surface of the globe. It

Butler's Wharf, Shad Thames, one of many Victorian warehouses which once crowded London's riverfront.

was in London's Docklands that the imperial net of commerce disgorged its catch, and visitors were encouraged in no uncertain terms by the new Baedeker guides: 'Nothing will convey to the stranger a better idea of the vast activity and stupendous wealth of London than a visit to the warehouses, filled to overflowing with interminable stores of every kind of foreign and colonial products.' The first impetus to dock building had occurred in the late Georgian period, and the Victorians continued the process further downstream with such enormous enterprises as the Royal Victoria and the Royal Albert. Following the advent of containerisation Tilbury has now become the nearest seaport facility to London and the original docks face an uncertain future with no prospect of commercial shipping. Some, such as the Surrey Commercial Docks, have been filled in and thus removed from the map. Many of the magnificent warehouses have been destroyed, although the trend is now to convert them into luxury flats. With the rapid development of Docklands now in progress there remain almost no undisturbed corners. Until recently Shad Thames on the south bank just down from Tower Bridge was one such place, still redolent of the nineteenth century.

Docklands and the City were the twin levers of London's economic power, but the making of the metropolis involved the interests of the entire region, which was drawn together by the new communications system introduced by the railways. It was the spread of steam locomotion in all directions which gave force and cohesion to a scattered urban growth, shaping what is recognisably the Greater London of today. The railway first came to London in 1836, the eve of the Victorian era, with the line from Greenwich to London Bridge. This was a remarkable undertaking, built at enormous expense on a majestic sweep of brick viaducts which carried the tracks at roof height over the huddled streets and out across the open fields which still existed between Deptford and Greenwich. The engineers of the time were still imbued with Classical principles; some of the cast-iron Doric supporting columns are in evidence under the arches where the line crosses Spa Road and Abbey Street. This line was also notable as a suburban service, for most of the pioneering railways of the next decades were essentially main lines which established London's communications with the provincial towns and cities. The shining railway tracks which soon reached out like the threads of a web were a symbol of London's supreme role in the life of the nation: the metropolis sat at the centre like a huge, voracious spider.

The City was the focus of the railway companies' ambitions, and if they had reached their goal then the 'square mile' would have played host to nearly all the termini. As it was, the New Road and the conservatism of the Bedford estate acted as an effective barrier, with the result that the stations at Euston, St Pancras and King's Cross had to settle for their present locations. The lines from the south had more success, throwing bridges across the Thames to Cannon Street, Blackfriars and Charing Cross. To lovers of steam locomotion it was certainly a noble sight to see a train crossing the railway bridge at Ludgate Hill with the dome of St Paul's providing a picturesque backdrop, but many Victorians recoiled at this incursion in the same way that we now resent urban motorways. Samuel Butler described the view from Waterloo Bridge in the 1880s in quasi-apocalyptic terms: 'huge wide-opened jaws of those two Behemoths, the Cannon Street and Charing Cross railway stations . . . See how they belch forth puffing trains as the breath of their nostrils, gorging and disgorging incessantly those human atoms whose movement is the life of the city.' This fine evocation of the very essence of metropolis contains more than a hint of the menacing aspects of the big city which came to haunt the Victorians and undermine their faith in the future. The entrance to Cannon Street station with its monumental flanking towers, although spruced up and sanitised, is still a daunting and awesome vision. As for the 'human atoms' transported by the railways, there were tens of thousands others made homeless by the building of the railways who had no alternative but to add to the misery of the slums which survived.

Rapid communication with the provinces was an absolute necessity for the growing metropolis, but ease of access from one district to another proved to be equally important. The first great advance in urban transport in London was provided by the appropriately named Metropolitan Railway which in 1863 linked Paddington with Farringdon, with an extension to Moorgate in 1865. This was a vital link between the new suburbs in the west and the workplace in the City, which later served all the mainline termini north of the river as the Circle Line.

Paddington Station, the start of London's first underground railway, opened in 1862.

This first generation of the Underground ran just beneath street level and was constructed by the method of 'cut and cover' which caused great disruption at the time. Some of the stations along the route have recently been restored to their original condition, and the nineteenth-century appearance of Baker Street, Great Portland Street and Paddington has re-emerged from beneath the grime and accretions of more than a century of use.

Much attention was paid to the architecture of the principal station buildings and their hotels, but to our present perception there is often more merit to be discerned in the engineering of the trainsheds than in the hyperbole of the frontages. Surfeited as we are by the bombast of Victorian architecture, we are still uplifted by the technical beauty of its structural creations of iron and glass. The railway companies led the field in this new building technology, endowing

The western trainshed of Liverpool Street Station, a perfect fusion of engineering and design, was built in 1875.

London with some magnificent examples of the engineer's artistry, such as Brunel's trainshed at Paddington and the daring 240-foot span of St Pancras, whose pointed arch is a structural necessity rather than a salute to the spirit of Gothic. At the time of its opening in 1875 Liverpool Street Station's western trainshed was hailed as 'decidedly the most successful attempt to combine iron and brick construction to be seen in London'. A GLC report of 1976 referred to its undeniable cathedral-like qualities. It would appear, however, that Victorians were split between admiration for the technically advanced structures which they devised and a nostalgic belief in the value of historical style. All London's termini, with the exception of the brave functionalism of King's Cross, demonstrate the same basic dichotomy between architecture and engineering. The confusion of the age was well expressed by *Building*

News in 1875 apropos of Liverpool Street station: 'Our metropolitan termini have been the leaders of the art-spirit of our times, however loath we may be to admit it, and despite our declaring them to be the works of engineers without artistic merit except of the lowest order.'

The new technology of iron and glass also featured prominently in some notable market buildings which reflected London's metropolitan status. The Coal Exchange of 1849 was the first of these, but this highly individual rotunda was senselessly demolished in 1962. There are three fine survivors, all designed by the official architect to the City of London, Sir Horace Jones, which represent the best features of this class of structure: the markets of Billingsgate, Leadenhall and Smithfield. The two latter are still in operation, rare reminders of the basic requirements of human existence in what is now a hot-house environment of economic activity. Leadenhall is a particularly pleasing specimen of Victorian

Leadenhall Market, in the heart of the City, is a Victorian gem of iron and glass.

design in which architecture and engineering have come together in terms of style and harmony. In the Royal Arcade of 1879 glass is used as the roof of the charming Victorian shopping passage running between Old Bond Street and Albemarle Street. Probably the most public, yet least perceived example of nineteenth-century iron and glass construction in London is the original exhibition hall at Olympia which predates by half a century its 1930s façade.

But the greatest of all the glass and iron structures of Victorian London was the Crystal Palace, since hailed by one eminent architectural writer as a 'ferrovitreous triumph' and by another as the only one Victorian building which was 'a total and absolute success'. Its first location was in Hyde Park where it housed the Great Exhibition of the Works of Industry of All Nations of 1851, an event which crowned London's rule as the leading metropolis of the age before an international audience. Of equal importance to the metropolitan status of London was the permanent role

The Royal Arcade, opened in 1879, shows the increasing sophistication of the West End.

A sphinx guards the now deserted terrace where the Crystal Palace once stood on the heights of Sydenham.

the Crystal Palace played as a sort of national symbol throughout the Victorian and Edwardian period at its new home on the heights of Sydenham, south of the river. It formed a great London landmark until its destruction by fire in 1936.

Nothing remains of the Crystal Palace itself, but the steps leading up to the now empty terrace where it once stood have survived, along with some portions of the balustrade and some exotic items of statuary such as the sphinxes. The most eloquent testimony to past glory is the disused subway which linked the site to the former Crystal Palace High Level station. This passage for visitors to the Crystal Palace, partially vandalised as it is, still conveys a keen impression of the sophisticated urban culture which created it. The brickwork of red and cream of the vaults and their octagonal columns was accomplished by a team of Italian cathedral bricklayers, well versed in the secrets of combining structural strength and artistic beauty. Not officially accessible at present, this subway merits better care and preservation as a precious relic of one of the glories of Victorian London.

As for the Crystal Palace itself, although it caught the public imagination, it was not taken up seriously as a school of design, since iron and glass were not considered yet to be proper materials for architecture in general. Ruskin, not surprisingly, condemned their use and dismissed the Crystal Palace as 'a cucumber frame between two chimneys'. Nevertheless glass and iron were introduced as new elements in the street scenery of London, and found

Italian craftsmen created this underpass from the railway station to the Crystal Palace.

particular application in huge shop windows of plate glass where the weight of the building fabric was supported on slender columns of iron. The technique was deplored by Scott and Pugin as a misdemeanour of structural deception. There is a magnificent specimen of the type in the vast shopfront of Asprey's in Bond Street.

A dramatic increase in traffic was one of the inevitable side-effects of metropolitan expansion. Horse-drawn carriages ruled the streets until the end of the Victorian era and the traffic jams were more intractable than those of today. Thus there began the process of sacrificing buildings to road schemes in order to ease the flow of vehicles through the city. New Oxford Street of 1843–7 and Victoria Street of 1851 cut great gashes in the urban fabric. In both cases the streets were directed knowingly through some of London's most notorious rookeries. Thus slum clearance and road improvements went conveniently hand in hand; but it was not until the creation of Shaftesbury Avenue in 1877–86, and Charing Cross Road in 1887, that any measures were taken to rehouse the displaced inhabitants of the rookeries. One of the great achievements of the Victorian road engineers in London was the Holborn Viaduct of 1869, a mighty bridge which spared the horses the strenuous descent and ascent of the Fleet valley. However, this fine piece of urban engineering, rampant with allegorical figures representing Commerce, Agriculture, Science and Fine Art, and its attendant buildings in the Florentine version of Italian Gothic with statues of City worthies, made an estimated 2000 Londoners homeless. At the time there was a heavy human price to pay for the attainment of the required metropolitan amenities.

Without any doubt the most beneficial of all the Victorian road schemes in London was the Victoria Embankment of 1864–70

Holborn Viaduct, a stately road bridge to facilitate east-west traffic, opened in 1869.

by Sir Joseph Bazalgette of the Metropolitan Board of Works. This mighty feat of land reclamation clawed back thirty-seven acres from the stinking mud flats of the Thames, enclosing the territory gained within a river wall of uncompromisingly solid granite. Here there emerged a public garden, a wide thoroughfare and a scenic riverside walk which boasted the best in Victorian street furnishings. The coiled dolphins of 1870 which form the base of the lampposts and the crouched camels which serve as ends to the iron benches are delightful signs of a highly confident urban culture. Similar schemes were accomplished by Bazalgette with the Albert Embankment of 1866–70 and the Chelsea Embankment of 1871–4, and he also designed both the Hammersmith and the Battersea Bridge. The attractive Albert Bridge of 1871–3 by R. M. Ordish provided a link between the Chelsea Embankment and the increasingly popular Battersea Park which was opened in 1853. Some thought was also given to the East

Dolphin lamppost on Albert Embankment, one of the great urban schemes by Bazalgette.

End with the creation of Victoria Park in Hackney in 1845.

But the true significance of the Victoria Embankment lay concealed below ground where alongside the tunnel of the Metropolitan Railway was a brick sewer eight feet in diameter, one of three running from west to east, designed by Bazalgette to carry effluent which had previously been discharged raw directly into the Thames. This was a belated measure to combat the shockingly unsanitary conditions of Victorian London which had become a scandalous disgrace to the self-image of the 'world city'. Journalists had described the Thames as 'a sewer with a tide in it'. During the 'Great Stink' of 1858 the sitting of Parliament could continue only with the aid of sheets soaked in chloride of lime hung over the windows to combat the stench. Such circumstances show that the forceful language of John Ruskin needed no discounting for poetic licence when he wrote of 'that great foul city of London – rattling, growling, smoking, stinking – a ghastly heap of fermenting brickwork, pouring out poison at every pore'. The outbreaks of cholera of 1848 and 1849 were the most obvious results of the complete neglect of the basic necessities of urban sanitation prior to the works carried out by Bazalgette.

Victorian belief in private enterprise left the supply of water to London's growing population in the hands of about nine companies, most of which drew water from the polluted Thames. A sign of the times was the transfer of the pumping station of the Grand Junction Waterworks Company from Chelsea to Kew by 1842, but legislation in 1852 forced all companies to draw their supply from the non-tidal fresh water above Teddington. The Kew Bridge pumping station managed to continue in operation by extending its intake to Hampton. Miraculously, the great Cornish beam engines which filled the Campden Hill reservoir serving the new suburbs of west London have been preserved *in situ* within a striking piece of industrial architecture dominated by the lofty standpipe tower dressed up as a sort of Italianate *campanile*. Of even greater architectural fascination are the buildings designed for sewage disposal at Abbey Mills in West Ham by the indefatigable Bazalgette. This pumping station, which is still in operation, is possibly the most surprising stylistic hybrid in London. A contemporary commentator wrote in 1869 that 'the building might be taken for a Turkish mosque or a Chinese temple . . . no music-hall in London can be compared with it'. A more recent account compares it to a Byzantine church interior under a Slavic dome. Whatever stylistic derivation one might detect, the significant fact remains that the Victorians saw fit to disguise in so florid a manner such a workmanlike item of sanitary engineering. One might argue that the Metropolitan Board of Works saw its pumping station as a great engine of urban civilisation and endowed it accordingly with the most lavish symbolism it could borrow; or it may have been that Victorian architecture had not responded to the spirit of the new technology.

The same dilemma underlies London's crowning piece of metropolitan engineering, its watergate to the world, Tower Bridge, which was opened towards the end of the Victorian era in 1894. Bazalgette's functional design, produced as early as 1879, was passed over in favour of a partnership between the engineer John Wolfe-Barry and the architect Sir Horace Jones. The Act which authorised the bridge required it to be in the Gothic style in order to accord with the antiquity of the Tower. Thus there resulted a typical Victorian product which perfectly reflected the confusion between architecture and engineering, historicism and technology, so characteristic of the age. Tower Bridge is really a cladding of medieval stone imagery over a steel frame which contains what was the most advanced system of hydraulic power at the time. Contemporary reaction expressed by *The Builder* in 1894 is revealing:

Tower Bridge represents a curious blend of historicism and advanced technology.

What strikes one at present is that the whole structure is the most monstrous and preposterous architectural sham that we have ever known of, and is in that sense a discredit to the generation which has erected it. Far better would it have been to have built simply the naked steelwork, and let the construction show us what it really is; the effect, if somewhat bare-looking, would have been at least honest, and we should have been relieved from the spectacle of many thousands spent on what is not the bridge at all, what is no part of the structure – but an elaborate and costly make-believe.

Here we stand at a stylistic crossroads, with the spirit of functionalism waiting in the wings. Tower Bridge, almost a hundred years old, now has more of the intended air of antiquity than it possessed for our great-grandparents; and, while they were perhaps shocked by the historicism of the exterior, we are taken aback to discover within the marvellously efficient steam engines which powered the bascules for the raising of the bridge. Tower Bridge, that last great flourish of Victorian London, thus encapsulates the deep and unresolved ambiguity engendered by the conflict between the historical spirit of the Gothic Revival and the new horizons of science and technology.

But there was an even greater ambiguity in the general attitude of the Victorians to the metropolis they had created. The banks might pose as palaces, a railway hotel as a fairytale castle, a drinking fountain as a medieval reliquary, and a pumping station as an exotic temple; the authorities might be proud of the eighty-two miles of sewers constructed by Bazalgette and of the gleaming railway tracks both above and below ground which provided an urban transport system second to none; the Crystal Palace might appear as a heavenly apparition on the heights of Sydenham, and Tower Bridge a miracle to guard the entrance to the 'Great World of London'. But the mighty metropolis was also the largest repository of human misery, and was held in deep suspicion as a potentially evil force by nearly all decent folk. William Morris described the urban sprawl as a 'spreading sore . . . swallowing up in its loathsomeness field and wood and heath without mercy and without hope, mocking our feeble efforts to deal even with its minor evils of smoke-laden sky and befouled river'. And Morris was expressing the subconscious aspirations of many of his contemporaries in his poetic fantasy 'The Earthly Paradise', in which he wrote with such feeling:

Forget six counties overhung with smoke,
Forget the snorting steam and piston stroke,
Forget the spreading of the hideous town,
Think rather of the pack-horse on the down,
And dream of London, small, and white, and clean,
The clear Thames bordered by its gardens green.

The Buxton Memorial Fountain of 1865, a minor essay in Gothic.

These sentiments provide the background to the various forms of housing in which nineteenth-century Londoners sought to lead a decent life in a metropolis that in spite of its achievements was always a threatening force. What Henry James described as 'the rumble of the tremendous human mill' could, it was feared, rise at any time into a mighty roar. Accordingly, home was conceived as the ultimate refuge which gave full and unashamed expression to a deep romantic nostalgia.

House and Home

For all the impressive metropolitan achievements of Victorian London, the most passionate concern of the age was reserved for that most elementary unit, the home. The challenge of providing appropriate housing had strong moral as well as practical implications for nineteenth-century Londoners, as may be seen from Disraeli's remark: 'I have always felt that the best security for civilisation is the dwelling. It is the real nursery of all domestic virtue and without a becoming home the exercise of those virtues is impossible.' Victorian London saw the birth of a variety of new domestic concepts whose overriding effect was to place the individual dwelling firmly at the focal point of city building; and the underlying trend of the period was a shift away from the primacy of grand architectural façades – as represented by Nash's noble terraces – to the rule of the single house as an entity in its own right, which was the dominant feature of Victorian suburbs of a certain quality. But development was patchy, and there was no direct and orderly progression from Regent's Park to Hampstead Garden Suburb. Nor was there equal and identical treatment of the domestic theme across the wide and highly differentiated social spectrum of Victorian London.

In such superior developments as Cubitt's Belgravia, commenced in the 1820s, the influence of the Regency lingered on well into the 1850s and ensured the continuity of Georgian Classical values in the new aristocratic and upper-middle-class suburbs of the West End. The formal schemes of Italianate stucco extended like slabs of ornate wedding cake across Bayswater, Paddington and Notting Hill to the north of Hyde Park as well as engulfing Pimlico and Kensington to the south. The style of the houses declined steadily from the relative grace and elegance of the pioneer scheme in Belgravia to an ever coarser and heavier type characterised by over-lavish window mouldings, excessively bold columns and an increase in height which produced an alienating and overbearing effect. The degeneration of the style was criticised repeatedly in the architectural press of the day, as in a report of 1876 in *Building News*: 'We suffer a sense of oppression as we cast our eyes down the miles of stereotyped perspective of Cromwell Road or Queen's Gate, in which balustrade and hackneyed fenestration in stock brick and stucco are supreme, the flat stretch of wall being only broken by Ionic porches, which look like sentry boxes in the lengthened vista.'

In fact *Building News* had been less than enthusiastic about Belgravia back in 1857 which the writer dismissed as 'only a few degrees less insipid than Baker, Harley and Gower Streets', these being the *bêtes noires* of Victorian architectural criticism. It must be remembered, however, that the first generation of Victorian building speculators were pulled in two directions. On the one hand they were still imbued with the principles of Classical formality, but they were catering for a public that demanded more brazen ornamentation. The addition of clumsy terracotta window embellishments to the Georgian façades of Russell Square was a symptom of the new aesthetics of the age.

Although the style dubbed as 'Kensington Italianate' by Osbert Lancaster continued to find favour with the conservatively minded building trade until the middle of the Victorian era, there were signs of a break with precedent in the relaxing of the rigidly formal layouts in the more picturesque curving streets of Notting Hill and Holland Park as well as in the elliptical

The military regularity of Belgravia, as exemplified by the north side of Eaton Square.

circus, The Boltons in Kensington. Here the Victorian ideal of the detached house, and of the semi-detached posing as such, is strongly asserted. Holland Park, Pembridge Square and other streets nearby are so crammed with rows of identical villas in the grand *palazzo* manner that there is scarcely any space left between the houses, and the visual effect is really that of another terrace.

The Victorian suburban villa found its highest expression in the larger and more spaciously sited mansions of Kensington Palace Gardens, which also demonstrated a refreshingly playful individuality of style, ranging from Islamic domes and Perpendicular Gothic to the more common Classical arrangement. The mania for villas also spread south of the river in a string of suburbs conveniently situated for a carriage ride to the City; the homes of bankers and financiers are still in evidence in Clapham, Brixton and Wandsworth · which was

Holland Park. Its serried ranks of huge palazzi *were the ultimate Victorian houses.*

London's original stockbroker belt in the nineteenth century. Cedars Road, running north from Clapham Common, was once a particularly imposing avenue containing forty-two grand detached villas dating from 1869, but today only a handful remain, along with the associated mews, to serve as reminders of those pioneering commuters. Further fine examples of stockbroker-style villas may be found in Herne Hill and Denmark Hill, which used to be south London's equivalent to Kensington. The most impressive feature of such houses was their tremendous size: they were veritable strongholds of privacy, bastions of family life. Nowadays in the age of mini-flats and bedsits there can be up to sixteen separate door-bells under the porches of such establishments where previously just one would have sufficed.

The businessman's villa in effect took over from the aristocrat's mansion as the summit of domestic refinement in London. Apart from a few grand town palaces such as Bridgewater House and Lancaster House – of which Queen Victoria remarked to the Duchess of Sutherland, then mistress of the place, 'I have come from my house to your palace' – Victorian London belonged firmly to the new financial meritocrats. However, some of the most lavish and original houses were created for the successful society artists of the day, whose talents could earn considerable fortunes. Frederic Lord Leighton, raised to the peerage just before he died in 1896, showed to what great heights an artist might aspire. His studio-house at 12 Holland Park Road in Kensington is a magnificent example of the taste and opulence of a grand Victorian London home. The crowning glory of this vast and generously proportioned mansion structured around the Great Studio is the exotic Arab Hall. This is a uniquely Victorian production in its artful combination of authentic and sham features. The tiles

The Arab Hall at Leighton House, a glimpse of the nineteenth-century taste for the exotic.

are originals from Cairo, Damascus and the cities of Persia, and the overall design of the hall, built by George Aitchison 1877–9, is based on drawings of the twelfth-century palace of La Zisa in Palermo; but to this heady cultural mix Aitchison added Corinthian capitals according to his own design and the mosaic frieze was the work of Walter Crane. Although the arrangement is therefore far removed from any Islamic model, the overall impression is remarkably successful and effective. Leighton's Arab Hall represents just one of the many attempts of Victorian London to transpose and concoct a variety of foreign styles from distant lands in its tireless search for novel expressions. This is the most accessible of the few exotic interiors to have survived in London.

A good idea of the more average taste in interior design of a well-to-do Victorian house in London may be gained at 18 Stafford Terrace, a development of 1869–74 in the familiar Italianate manner just north of Kensington High Street. The house has four storeys and a basement and a relatively narrow frontage; its windows, devoid of glazing bars due to the use of plate glass, are framed with moulded stucco dressings which provide a pleasant contrast to the exposed grey Suffolk brickwork. Behind this modest frontage lies a wondrously preserved series of rooms as originally furnished by the cartoonist Linley Sambourne, who lived there from the early 1870s until his death in 1910. The entire house is now in the care of the Victorian Society as a unique testimonial of the lifestyle and décor of the period.

The first and lasting impression is of a homely clutter of furniture and ornaments; the sensation of an Aladdin's cave of shining objects is heightened by the relative gloom. Daylight penetrates with difficulty as it is absorbed by the sombre walls and heraldic displays in stained glass. This is in marked contrast to the interiors of the eighteenth century which delighted in sunshine. In the former age there was more concern with order and elegance than here, where disorder and a certain clumsiness are the rule. Scores of pictures cover the walls and countless objects jostle for space on the shelves, mantelpieces and tables. It is as if the products of industrial manufacture have imposed their presence on the scene; and indeed the relative cheapness of machine-made articles had the effect of filling drawing rooms less wealthy than that of number 18 Stafford Terrace. How the cumbersome shapes of crinoline skirts managed to pilot a safe course through the shoals of ornaments is not easy to imagine. But for all that, there is a cosiness and homeliness which is more appealing than the artistic formality of the Georgian house.

There is also a lingering sense of the discrepancy between the regularity of the Italianate façades of streets such as Stafford Terrace and the haphazard domesticity which existed within. It is quite remarkable how the Italianate terrace continued to find favour in face of the Gothic Revival which had been promoted with such fervour since the eve of Queen Victoria's accession. Pugin indeed was not alone in complaining of the 'restless torrent of Roman-cement [stucco] men, who buy their ornaments by the yard, and their capitals by the ton', but the style of speculative building adhered doggedly to the manner handed down by Nash and Cubitt. Thus there occurred the curious phenomenon in the new suburbs of Kensington, Paddington and Bayswater of many neo-Gothic churches with their lofty steeples trapped like the masts of sailing ships in a pack-ice of Italianate stucco.

An obvious reason for the late flourishing of the Classical tradition in London's housing was the lack of any suitable Gothic models which might have been borrowed for the purpose. It is also possible that the puristic zealots of the Gothic Revival were so critical of all new Gothic architecture that it was easier to avoid the style altogether. There are nevertheless many interesting examples of domestic Gothic in Victorian London, ranging from the Tudor

Sunlight filters into the crowded interior of 18 Stafford Terrace.

façades of Islington's Lonsdale Square of 1838–45, and the medieval Germanic effect of Scott's range of houses of 1853 in Westminster's Broad Sanctuary, to the uncompromisingly dour Scottish aspect of the Tower House of 1875–80 in Kensington's Melbury Road by William Burges. The Gothic style was generally applied to vicarages of the period, and there is a fine specimen of the genre by Butterfield at 14 Burleigh Street in Covent Garden which was formerly attached to St Michael's. A rare example of a Gothic townhouse in London is 4 Cadogan Square by another great exponent of the Gothic Revival, G. E. Street. Possibly the most curious assemblage of domestic Gothic in London is the bizarre Holly Village in Highgate which was designed in 1865 by Henry Darbishire for the noted philanthropist Baroness Burdett-Coutts. This group of self-consciously medieval cottages, originally built for the

The décor of 18 Stafford Terrace reflects the Victorian love of stained glass and rich colour.

retainers of the Baroness, is arranged in a picturesque manner about a green, but the pleasant informality of the setting does not offset the gloomy character of the dwellings which have much in common with the ambience of the adjacent cemetery. Indeed, the ecclesiastical and funereal associations of Gothic were one of the major drawbacks of the style in a domestic context; but it was employed nonetheless with regularity in Victorian houses of all shapes and sizes, even as late as 1895 in a brooding block of flats called Artillery Mansions in Victoria Street.

Not overtly Gothic but deeply medieval in spirit is Philip Webb's Red House in Bexleyheath of 1859. This was Webb's first independent commission and the only house to be designed especially for that great champion of the Arts and Crafts movement, William Morris. Although Morris considered the Red House to be 'in the style of the thirteenth century', it was also very much a product of the nineteenth century as an early expression of the search for lost domestic values. Here the idea of the house is redefined within the tradition of the English vernacular as a reassuring and richly symbolic composition with its pitched roof, pointed gables and prominent chimneys, which convey the emotional values of home much more potently than the rational scheme of a brick box with windows, so characteristic of the Georgian era. However, this highly significant expression of the new awareness of what an Englishman's home should aspire to was not taken up as a model to be copied; and the only other domestic works by Webb in London which point in the same direction were the house at 1 Palace Green in Kensington and the row of shops and dwellings at 91–101 Worship Street in Finsbury. Ironically, Morris was to spend only five years in his 'medieval' Red House, preferring to make his permanent London base in

Webb's Red House in Bexleyheath pays tribute to the Middle Ages.

a comfortable eighteenth-century house by the river on Hammersmith's Upper Mall. Morris surrounded himself with his beloved Arts and Crafts furniture and décor within Kelmscott House, but the fact remains that he was quite content to live in a Georgian home. In this paradox he was not alone, for many adherents of the Gothic Revival set up home in classical surroundings: Pugin in Great Russell Street, Ruskin in Denmark Hill, Scott in Hampstead and Butterfield in the Adelphi. Perhaps this phenomenon signifies an unspoken admission that Gothic was not really the answer to the Classical ascendancy in urban domestic.

As it turned out, the answer to the problem of finding a new style of architecture for the townhouse was to come from quite another quarter. It resulted from the Victorian disenchantment with both urbanisation and industrialisation and took the form of a romantic quest for an idealised traditional manner which would provide the spiritual solace and sense of belonging which neither the alien 'Kensington Italianate' nor the unfriendly neo-Gothic had been able to supply. At last in the 1870s the basic urban machine of the Georgians was convincingly replaced by an alternative vision in the eclectic 'Queen Anne' style. This was an attractive medley of picturesque features such as Flemish gables, Elizabethan chimneys and oriels. The irregular windows were composed of small panes, marking the return of the white glazing bars which made a charming contrast to the bright red brickwork, which was decorated with carved panels of sunflowers, swags and cherubs in the jolliest manner of the seventeenth century. The scenic individuality of the style was best expressed in the detached house such as Lowther Lodge of 1872–4 in Kensington Gore by the greatest practitioner of the genre, R. Norman Shaw. The picturesque features of the 'Queen Anne' style are also much in evidence in the house Shaw designed for his own occupation at 6 Ellerdale Road in Hampstead, where the staircase divides the structure into two distinct halves with teasingly different floor levels. Shaw also experimented with an 'Old English' style with fake half-timbering, as may be seen in his country mansion of 1870–2 in Harrow Weald known as Grim's Dyke.

The most fertile ground for more modest houses in the 'Queen Anne' style was the 45-acre site by the new Underground station of Turnham Green, developed by Jonathan T. Carr from 1875 onwards, which achieved international renown as a progressive and enlightened community. This early encapsulation of the suburban ideal, with its detached houses with pretty front gardens, meandering roads and mature trees, was a determined attempt to bring rural values to town life. Bedford Park, as it was named, was epoch-making in that it became a model for so many subsequent suburban estates as well as prefiguring many of the features of the Garden City movement. It is also significant as the place where the smaller English house was pioneered, for the new homes of Bedford Park as designed by Norman Shaw, Edward Godwin and others were not aimed at the large house-holds with many servants of the wealthy 'carriage folk' but catered for people of simpler lifestyle. The pervading Arts and Crafts spirit of the place is most apparent in the contrived village centre with its 'Old English' Tabard Inn and parade of shops, and the 'medieval' church of St Michael and All Angels, all the work of Norman Shaw. The first inhabitants of Bedford Park were artists, intellectuals, writers and journalists who shared the common aspirations of the Arts and Crafts movement, so neatly summed up in the formula 'sweetness and light' (Girouard) which lay at the heart of the 'Queen Anne' style, and the need to find something of enduring worth beyond the brashness and materialism of the Victorian city. The original identity of Bedford Park is still surprisingly intact because the houses were designed to be run without the usual hierarchy of ser-

Bedford Park made the 'Queen Anne' style available for people of the middling sort.

vants and thus they provide convenient family homes for today's requirements.

'Queen Anne' was to show the way forward and to be received with great enthusiasm by the wealthy middle-class clients able to afford the luxury of an architect-designed house. Shaw obtained commission after commission for his expressive houses, which, although obviously all from the same drawing-board, were at the same time strikingly individual in their composition and arrangement. Shaw's distinctive 'Queen Anne' style was especially popular in artistic Chelsea, and a number of his eloquent houses grace the Chelsea Embankment, most spectacularly the famous Old Swan House, number 17, noted for the unexpected symmetry of its three generous oriels on the first floor. 'Queen Anne' also found favour in nearby Tite Street, which became the aesthetic nerve centre of Chelsea towards the end of the nineteenth century; and 44 Tite Street by Edward Godwin is a particularly fine example of the palatial studio-residences then in fashion. The red-brick 'Queen Anne' even penetrated that stronghold of Italianate stucco, Queen's Gate, where Shaw designed numbers 170 and 196, as well as 180 which has unfortunately been demolished. Cadogan Square in Chelsea was another happy hunting ground for Shaw, and he was responsible for numbers 60a, 62, 68 and 72.

It was also in Cadogan Square, at number 52, that one of the most colourful derivatives of 'Queen Anne' made an appearance. This Flemish-inspired extravaganza with lavish use of terracotta represents the style of London's most flamboyant interpreter of the terraced townhouse, the architect Ernest George. His most amazing creation is surely number 39 Harrington Gardens of 1882–3, an incredibly rich frontage topped by a gable of nineteen steps. This is the centrepiece of a row of speculative houses

Norman Shaw's Old Swan House of 1875 on the Chelsea Embankment.

The search for theatrical effect reached new heights at 39 Harrington Gardens.

extending from 35 to 45 Harrington Gardens to which Ernest George transferred details of the rich burghers' houses he had sketched in places such as Amsterdam, Bruges and Ghent in order to enliven the customary uniformity of the London street. This has more of the quality of a fantastic stage set than even Nash's scenic terraces. Harrington Gardens would need only a canal to replace the street for the transposition of the Low Countries to London to be complete. The scheme continues on a slightly more restrained note with the adjacent development of 1–18 Collingham Gardens. In this complete reversal of all the tenets of Georgian urbanism each house proclaims its individuality; and even the idea of the square is turned inside out, forming a communal back garden rather than the usual expanse of greenery to be viewed from the front window. Nowhere in London is the rejection of Georgian values by the Victorians so much in evidence, although the plans of the houses adhere to the convenience of the Georgian layout.

Of course there was a heavy dose of sham in this conscious evocation of a historical past which had not actually existed, but Bedford Park, in particular, responded to the needs of the age in the search for a reassuring 'traditional' environment. Its success was largely due to the skill of architects such as Norman Shaw in devising a completely new style of house, but one which gave people the impression of familiarity. A similar spirit underlies that other great patch of *rus in urbe* in London, Hampstead Garden Suburb, which was laid out from 1907 onwards by Raymond Unwin on behalf of Dame Henrietta Barnett, an active philanthropist in the East End. Dame Henrietta's social mission went much further than that of the founder of Bedford Park. Hampstead Garden Suburb was intended as a morally positive as well as healthy environment for a broad cross-section of society from the upper-middle down to the artisan class. But today Dame Henrietta's dream of attracting ordinary working folk to the leafy groves of Hampstead has evaporated, and the residents of the Garden Suburb have turned out to be decidedly middle-class. For all its attractive architectural and environmental features the pleasant purlieus of Hampstead Garden Suburb are pervaded by a curious dullness, especially in the 'village centre' which is an empty space with neither shops nor pub.

Although Hampstead Garden Suburb was not able to alleviate the grim living conditions of London's poorer inhabitants, the second half of the nineteenth century was marked by the more successful efforts of a wide range of philanthropists to provide a solution to the abject slums in which so many Londoners were obliged to live. Octavia Hill, who had studied art under Ruskin, devoted her life to the improvement of housing for London's poor. Her career began with the purchase and refurbishment of a group of tumbledown houses in 1864 in Paradise (now Garbutt) Place, a slum pocket off Marylebone High Street. Another relic of Octavia Hill's work in that area may be seen in the Gothic block of 1877 in St Christopher's Place, just north of Oxford Street. There are two charming examples of her activities in Southwark in the wonderfully intact Redcross Cottages in Redcross Way and the nearby Gable Cottages in Sudrey Street; these are like oases of village peace in a rather bleak inner-city environment. In the East End another lady philanthropist, the Baroness Burdett-Coutts, took matters a stage further. In addition to the four blocks of housing in Columbia Road, Shoreditch, she sponsored the construction of the ambitious Columbia Market whereby she hoped to provide employment for her tenants. The market has been demolished but the blocks remain.

Victorian London was especially indebted to the American benefactor George Peabody, who endowed a trust with £500,000 of his personal fortune to provide dwellings at low rents in the worst parts of town. Between 1862 and 1897 the Peabody Trust managed to house nearly 20,000 people. The distinctive architecture of the Peabody buildings, mainly designed by Henry Darbishire, has a prison-like quality, with its tiers of iron galleries around an inner courtyard and its barrack-like exterior which seems to keep the outside world at bay. This was probably the intent, for Peabody dwellings were usually planted directly in the heart of slum areas and acted as bastions of respectability to protect the occupants from the depravity which still lurked on the doorstep; it was decidedly a back-streets architecture not intended for public view. Inner London abounds in examples of Peabody Trust buildings, such as Old Pye Street in Westminster, Peartree Court in Clerkenwell, Greenman Street in Islington and a vast complex to the west of Bunhill Row occupying several blocks between the Barbican and Old Street. Grim as they are, such dwellings were a considerable improvement on the slums.

Hampstead Garden Suburb, suburban dream in a sham pastoral setting of enduring charm.

The work of public-spirited individuals was also channelled into the efforts of the voluntary organisations, such as the Metropolitan Association for Improving the Dwellings of the Industrious Classes of 1841 which aimed to provide 'the labouring man with an increase of the comforts and conveniences of life, with full compensation to the capitalist'. In fact dividends were restricted to 5 per cent which gave birth to the handy formula of 'five-per-cent philanthropy'. The effect of this basic objective was that it excluded those at the bottom of the heap who could not afford even the reasonable rents of the improved dwellings. The Society for Improving the Condition of the Labouring Classes followed a similar policy. Its first block of 'Model Houses for Families' of 1849 still maintains a discreet presence in Streatham Street just off Tottenham Court Road. The galleries of flats were arranged to provide the essential

Gable Cottages in Southwark, sponsored by Octavia Hill, form an unexpected village enclave.

privacy of separate front doors, which must have represented a luxury beyond price for the first occupants, used to the communal squalor of the notorious St Giles rookery. The architect was Henry Roberts, who also designed the smaller unit of Model Dwellings which were displayed at the Great Exhibition of 1851 under the patronage of Prince Albert. The quaint dwellings were subsequently removed to Kennington Park where they may still be seen. An early exercise in cottage housing for the poor was launched in Wandsworth in 1872 by the Artisans, Labourers and General Dwellings Company on the 40-acre Shaftesbury Park estate. This pioneering project of neat terraced cottages of Gothic character has a number of pleasing architectural features, such as corner turrets marking the entrance, and the building fabric is still largely intact. In all some 1,135 houses, a block of flats and 30 shops were built. The

Company followed up with a similar venture on a 76-acre site in north London from 1875, known as the Queen's Park estate.

It is a remarkable fact that for almost the entire span of the nineteenth century the provision of housing in London for the poorer elements in the community was left to the conscience of the private sector. Not until 1890 with the Housing of the Working Classes Act was the fledgling London County Council empowered to provide public housing for the residents of the metropolis. The first generation of LCC architects set to work with the high ideals of the Arts and Crafts movement and created the imaginative Boundary Street estate of 1894–1900 in Shoreditch on the site of the disgraceful 'Jago' slum as well as the vast Millbank estate of 1897–1902 behind the Tate Gallery. In both schemes the picturesque qualities of the 'Queen Anne' style are deployed on five-storey blocks which combine the requirements of high-density urban accommodation with

The forbidding architecture of the Peabody Trust estate in Clerkenwell.

some of the stylistic niceties such as pitched roof, pointed gables and white glazing bars, so popular in the fashionable suburbs.

Between the efforts of the philanthropists and the LCC on the one hand and the developers of schemes such as Cadogan Square and Harrington Gardens on the other, there were an enormous number of houses built for that vast market of people of the middling sort, such as clerks and the more prosperous artisans. It was for such

The Boundary Street Estate of 1900 set new standards of social housing.

folk that the greatest acreage of Victorian suburbia in London was developed. Huge areas were engulfed in brick and mortar where the railways at last offered cheap workman's fares to places such as Edmonton, Tottenham, Lewisham and Walthamstow which were among the fastest growing suburbs towards the close of the century. The general exodus from the inner city to the outer suburbs was greatly accelerated from 1900 when the LCC was permitted to develop housing estates beyond its own boundaries. The first of such cottage estates was at Totterdown Fields in Tooting.

Thus the Englishman's dream of his own home became a reality for hundreds of thousands of Londoners of all classes during the latter half of the Victorian age, a phenomenon which it took a perspicacious foreigner to define and describe to those concerned. Hermann Muthesius noted in the 1904 English edition of his monumental survey *The English House*: 'The Englishman sees the whole of life embodied in his house. Here, in the heart of his family, self-sufficient and feeling no great urge for sociability, pursuing his own interests in virtual isolation, he finds his happiness and his real spiritual comfort.'

Given the truth of the observation and its applicability, even to the inhabitants of the great metropolis of London, it is not surprising that there was considerable resistance to the idea of apartments. The fourteen-storey Queen Anne's Mansions of the 1850s in Victoria Street, now demolished, was London's first skyscraper but it did not set a trend. Other notable early apartment blocks were the French Renaissance-style The Cedars in Clapham of 1860, an attempt to lure the West End south of the river, and the equally French-inspired Grosvenor Place of 1868 by Thomas Cundy II. It is doubtless significant that English architects turned to France due to the lack of a native metropolitan style. The aversion to blocks of flats may have been partly caused by associations with the forbidding dwellings which middle-class philanthropists were quite content to impose as models on the industrious classes but not choose for themselves. But there was also real concern that the communal entrance represented an unacceptable intrusion on the privacy of the family and a potential danger to its morals. Nevertheless, the success of Norman Shaw's Albert Hall Mansions of 1879–81 helped make apartments fashionable and more respectable; and there followed some very grandiose developments such as the extravagant Whitehall Court of 1884 by Jonathan T. Carr. He, it must be remembered, had been the originator of Bedford Park, so that this was a quite remarkable change of direction from the promotion of *rus in urbe* to that of an intensely urban lifestyle.

The suspicion of flats was also part of the strongly anti-urban sentiments of the Victorians who, although they made London the world's largest and most powerful metropolis, recoiled from their own creation and sought refuge in a suburban illusion of a lost world of pastoral innocence. In spite of all its many splendours there was a loss of faith in the city, and Victorian Londoners tended to flee from the monster metropolis. Thus the soul of the place came to be scattered around in the suburbs rather than be expressed in the centre. But even the suburban dream was followed by disenchantment as the idyllic enclaves of the nobler suburbs fell prey to the meaner developments that followed, described by *Building News* in 1900 as 'the fungus-like growth of houses'. Thus one cannot escape the conclusion that Victorian Londoners had been reluctant urbanites from the start, and that all their energies had been directed at dissipating the inherent evil of the big city rather than developing a true metropolitan culture for its own sake. But that might also be the secret attraction of Victorian London, not a conventional metropolis but a conglomeration of aspirant village communities held together by a network of train and tramlines.

Edwardian Exuberance

It might have been expected around the year 1887 when Queen Victoria was celebrating fifty years on the throne, that Victorian London, like the monarch, would also be declining in strength and vitality. In fact, quite the opposite turned out to be the case, for from about this time there was a distinct uplift in energy, creativity and exuberance which has left an indelible mark on the character of London. The charisma of the Prince of Wales, crowned in 1901 as Edward VII, was such that the Edwardian era actually predated his accession by more than a decade and continued beyond his death in 1910 until the outbreak of the Great War in 1914. The lingering image of this Edwardian Golden Age is of balmy days of style and elegance, artistically vibrant with a piquancy of *fin de siècle* decadence. All that is true, but as far as the making of London is concerned, this was a period of quite exceptional archi-

Albert Court, one of London's many Edwardian mansion blocks.

8 Addison Road by Halsey Ricardo, noted for its pioneering use of blue and green glazed tiles, probably London's most spectacular Edwardian house.

tectural, civic and metropolitan achievements. Edwardian London was no mere frivolous epilogue to the weightier Victorian chapters but a brave and imaginative attempt to create a resplendent urban culture. There was a change of emphasis from the passive Victorian approach of stemming the evil effects of the big city by private philanthropy to an active collectivist sense of responsibility. Whereas the Victorians had been profoundly uneasy about London and suffered a dose of guilt for any pleasure they derived from it, the Edwardians appeared to relish and cultivate the possibilities of the urban machine. The Victorians had been reluctant makers of the metropolis, but the Edwardians were not afraid to enter into their inheritance and sought to endow their capital city with status and style.

Although Victorian dreams of idyllic suburbia as the answer to inner-city squalor continued to hold good and even to reach new heights of idealism in such schemes as Hampstead Garden Suburb and the White Hart Lane estate, there was also a new awareness of the benefits of more urban housing forms. On the Duchy of Cornwall estate in Kennington around Courtenay Square there appeared in 1913 a small development of two-storey terraces in the Regency style arranged in the strict Georgian manner so much despised by the Victorians. Far more revolutionary and far-reaching in its effects was the spread of the once decried 'continental' habit of apartment living which occurred in the 1890s. Not surprisingly, there was a considerable divergence of opinion as to the propriety of such a public form of accommodation. While the *Architectural Review* commented in 1900 on the 'wonderful development of Flatland during the last decade', *Building News* in the same year upheld the old prejudices: 'The apartment house has disadvantages: among them the gregariousness of the occupants. It is very doubtful, we think, whether the English race will ever abandon their own small castles.' In London, however, the trend towards blocks of flats was already in full flood. The increasing cost of building land was one factor; another was that a building style both fashionable and respectable was devised. The English Baroque created the concept of the mansion block as a noble edifice which imitated the prestige and splendour of the stately home. London is still studded with these grand Edwardian buildings with mock baronial façades; columned and pedimented porches, imposing bay windows and generous balconies are the hallmarks of the best specimens of the genre. In the early years of the new century French Classical also became highly desirable as a style for the mansion block.

For the rich a town mansion in Mayfair was still very much *de rigueur*, as is evidenced by the stately Baroque residence at 54 Mount Street by Fairfax B. Wade of 1896–9, built for Lord Windsor. The style is reminiscent of Wren, a sign of the renewed popularity of the great architect which amounted to a movement which has been neatly dubbed 'Wrenaissance'. In another London mansion in the slightly more suburban setting of West Kensington at 8 Addison Road, there was a return to a design of more Classical proportions; but the chief claim to attention of this residence, Debenham House by Halsey Ricardo of 1905–7, is the gorgeous dressing of the exterior with glazed bricks and tiles of blue, green and white. Ricardo promoted this technique as a way of introducing colour to the drab cityscape of London. Not only was the glazed surface resistant to acid pollution but it also had the advantage of being easily washable. The exotic decorative scheme is continued inside the house, and the highlight of the interior is the dome, which sits atop a central atrium with galleries on three sides; Byzantine-style mosaics were added to it in 1913. This is quite the most remarkable Edwardian house in London, although not a trend-setter, for Ricardo's polychromatic glazed bricks were not generally taken up in domestic buildings.

One of the most enthusiastic users of coloured tiles was the new Tube or underground electric railway pioneered by the American entrepreneur Charles T. Yerkes. The ox-blood-red stations of the Northern, Central and Piccadilly lines in particular have survived in large numbers to be still a hallmark of the London Underground. In fact, this new, clean and efficient method of transport, which contributed significantly to the cohesion of the fragmented structure of central London, was very largely an Edwardian achievement. As for the steam railways, their great expansion was over in London, but for the arrival of the Great Central at Marylebone Station in 1899, a curiously provincial backwater sheltering behind its hotel of the same date. There was a measure of Edwardian improvement lavished on grandiose, new façades at Victoria Station in 1906–8 and at Waterloo

Selfridges introduced American neo-Classicism to London on a monumental scale.

from 1907. The latter was not completed until 1922 and was altered to serve also as a memorial to the men of the London and South Western Railway who died in the Great War.

However, the looming spectre of death in the trenches could not be perceived during the heyday of Edwardian London where energies were concentrated on the more pleasurable amenities of the great metropolis. The new concept of the department store, introduced from America, was pioneered in London as early as 1880 by William Whiteley with his store in Bayswater. As an architectural form the London department store came into being during the first decade of the twentieth century. The premises of William Whiteley, now newly refurbished, date back to a rebuilding of 1909–12. The previous building of Debenham & Freebody in Wigmore Street, as constructed in 1906–9, still exists, with

Highlight of the interior of 8 Addison Road is the mosaic-covered dome.

its huge recessed columns and curved pediments faced with white tiles. More illustrious, and still functioning, is Harrods in Knightsbridge, a building of 1901–5 of undecided style, but undeniably pretentious with its domes of terracotta and very much the symbol of the grand emporium. The shell of Waring & Gillow's Oxford Street store of 1906 has been preserved, although it now contains offices. This grandiloquent Baroque façade was inspired by Wren's work at Hampton Court which it surpasses in the wealth of its fanciful stonework, including ships' prows emerging from the corners of the building. But the huge commercial palace of Selfridge's, built in 1907–9 and extended in the same style until completion in 1928, left the others architecturally in the shade. This was indeed the aim of its founder Gordon Selfridge, who introduced a truly breathtaking vista of American Neo-Classical style to the jumbled medley of Oxford Street. Such department stores provided the ladies of Edwardian London with almost equivalent amenities to those offered to the gentlemen in their clubs. The Royal Automobile Club made its dramatic appearance in Pall Mall in 1908–11 in the garb of the French Classical style and exercised a similarly stunning effect in clubland to that of Selfridge's in Oxford Street.

There was also a spate of theatre building, with the result that Edwardian is still the dominant tone of the West End. Of particular note are the large stucco angels at mansard level on the Apollo of 1900. Prominent London landmarks by Frank Matcham, the most prolific of all theatre architects are the Hippodrome in Leicester Square of 1899–1900 with its splendid chariot and horses on top of a crown, and the curious Baroque tower of the Coliseum of 1904. Pubs too underwent dynamic growth in London in the 1890s, when there occurred a notable shift from an open layout to a

The Black Friar is the finest Arts and Crafts pub in London.

subdivision of private booths and drinking compartments framed in glass and mahogany; these suggest a mixture of secrecy, intimacy and social segregation at the same time. London abounds in late Victorian and Edwardian pubs from the Red Lion of 1880 in Duke of York Street to the Old Shades in Whitehall of 1898, in which the successive refinements of drinking are reflected in a multitude of fixtures and fittings. Pub design was a specialist discipline, often independent of the general trends, but the Black Friar in Queen Victoria Street of 1903–5 displays in its richly decorated interior many of the principles of the Arts and Crafts movement. The exterior is notable for the statue of a jolly friar placed on the sharp end of the wedge-shaped building like a galleon figurehead. In Edwardian London pubs were more abundant in certain areas than today: in place of some twenty pubs in Oxford Street there is now only one, the Tottenham, as a reminder of the period.

Some of the most distinctive buildings of Edwardian London were sponsored by private charity, as illustrated by three works of the architect Charles Harrison Townsend, who brought into action a higher degree of individual creativity, drawing on some of the principles of the Arts and Crafts movement. His Bishopsgate Institute of 1892–4 displays on its narrow frontage a bold frieze of naturalistic foliage motifs above the round entrance arch flanked by twin towers. Townsend's Whitechapel Art Gallery of 1899–1901 makes great play of the mysterious interaction of round and square forms, but the intended mosaic panel was never realised due to lack of funds. Townsend's masterpiece in London is without doubt the Horniman Museum of 1897–1901 in Forest Hill. A brilliant mosaic by Anning Bell on the subject of Humanity in the House of Circumstance dominates the façade, held in balance by a highly original tower where square and circular shapes merge ambiguously into one another, and the mysterious symbolism is heightened by the outlines of trees carved into the stone. This is one of the most original buildings in London and still retains its power to entrance and surprise.

There was a boom in hotel building around the turn of the century when London saw the construction of establishments such as Claridge's in 1895–9 and the Connaught in 1901. The Savoy goes back in part to 1887–90 but was extended along the Strand in 1903–4. To the same date belongs the rebuilding of Simpsons-in-the-Strand, a rare example of an authentic Edwardian restaurant lovingly maintained in its original dignified style. The Ritz of 1903–6 in Piccadilly brought Parisian elegance to London, concealing between its dazzling Louis XVI interiors and its Norwegian granite exterior, one of the first steel frames to be employed in London. Its arcades are extremely reminiscent of the rue de Rivoli. The Waldorf Hotel of 1906–8 is also a French composition, an elegant component in the sweeping curve of the Aldwych; it contains a magnificent Palm Court, that lasting symbol of the Edwardian era. Norman Shaw's Piccadilly Hotel of 1905–8 is an ambitious Baroque conception, originally intended to be part of a grander scheme to be extended along Regent Street. The Russell Hotel of 1898 in Russell Square survives as a relic of the wilder excesses of Edwardiana. Its façade of terracotta and red brick is a riot of embellishment including regal statues, heraldic shields, miniature columns and round-arched forms which have been likened to the style of a François I château.

Such exuberance belonged very much to the spirit of the age: grandiose ideas were even pursued on buildings of quite small scale, as in the amazing façade of 1896 by Beresford Pite on the modest front of 82 Mortimer Street in the West End. Michelangelo-type male and female figures carved in stone are placed on one pediment and combine their strength to support another. This is but an extreme example of the Baroque invention lavished on a whole series of small commercial premises. The

The Horniman Museum of 1901 by Townsend displays a wonderfully fresh style.

partnership of Treadwell & Martin was responsible for several fine buildings in the Bond Street area displaying a high degree of artistic fancy, most notably 7 Dering Street of 1906, which uses the Gothic form of the ogee arch to encompass the ground-floor showroom window and to provide visual support for two oriels on the first floor. Such buildings generally go unremarked, partly on account of their smallness but also because they were carefully inserted into the existing Georgian and Victorian structures and respected both the street-line and the roof-line of the other structures. In Torrington Place in Bloomsbury there is a more ostensible Edwardian commercial block of a striking Flemish type of Gothic designed in 1908 by FitzRoy Doll, the architect of the Russell Hotel. This was once a small parade of shops but is now occupied entirely by Dillon's Book Store. In Sicilian Avenue there is a delightful and more substantial piece of Edwardian urban design: the stylish shopping street of 1905 runs diagonally from Southampton Row to Bloomsbury Way with an elegant Classical colonnade as a screen at either end. The shops and accommodation are contained in an architecture of brick and terracotta with pretty turrets, creating as charming a piece of planning, albeit in miniature, as to be found anywhere in London. With such insouciance could Edwardian London show its almost playful delight in the business of commercial architecture and provide a graceful interpretation of the functions of the metropolis.

Much of Edwardian London, however, bears the stamp of a considerable monumentality deemed appropriate to the world's largest city at the time and the centre of the British Empire. As the nineteenth century drew to a close, so the imperial spirit found architectural expression in a revival of the Baroque as practised by Wren, Hawksmoor, Vanbrugh and

Sicilian Avenue, an imaginative scheme of 1905 to create a traffic-free shopping street.

The Port of London Authority in Trinity Square, a bombastic expression of self-confidence.

Gibbs, which was acclaimed as a true national style rooted in the English tradition prior to the intrusion of the corrupt Palladian doctrine. Larger businesses in particular espoused the style as a symbol both of their patriotism as well as of their power. The rise of the great insurance companies and financial institutions led the way. Belcher & Pite's Institute of Chartered Accountants of 1888 in Great Swan Alley off Moorgate has been recognised as the precursor of the style, but for its crowning accomplishment one must look to buildings such as Moncton & Newman's Pearl Assurance of 1906–12 in High Holborn.

Edwardian Baroque was also eminently in favour for public buildings such as the hugely impressive Central Criminal Courts by Mountford of 1900–7, of which the dome is clearly based on Wren's design for the Royal Naval Hospital. The headquarters of the Port of London Authority in Trinity

Square of 1912–22 is perhaps a case of Baroque gone berserk, for its Edwardian exuberance is overpowering, with the massing of the tower and monumental statuary; but it speaks eloquently of the enormous optimism of the era, and in particular of the pride in London's docks which were then at the very centre of world trade. With the demise of its docks, the PLA has moved to a less boastful headquarters and the original building is now occupied by an insurance Company. *Sic transit gloria mundi.*

It was above all in civic architecture that the rediscovered bombast of the Baroque was most in evidence. The old part of Chelsea Town Hall of 1885–7 by Brydon set the style and prefigured the more extravagant productions to come, such as Battersea Town Hall of 1892–3 (now an arts centre) by Mountford, which makes lavish display of allegorical statues of Labour, Progress, Art and Literature as the tutors of

County Hall, London's most prominent example of Edwardian Baroque.

The surprising façade of a small commercial building at 82 Mortimer Street.

the young Battersea. Woolwich Town Hall of 1903–6 by Thomas makes its statement mainly through an array of broken segmental pediments and an imposing tower, favourite devices of the Edwardian Baroque. Both impressive and endearing is Deptford Town Hall of 1902–7 by Lanchester & Rickards; it is not huge in scale but is extremely rich in content, with its great oriel window borne by caryatids and with statues of admirals stationed in niches as reminders of Deptford's ancient naval traditions. These were all surprisingly grand buildings for some of London's poorer boroughs at the time.

As for County Hall, the new seat of the London County Council on a prime riverside site diagonally opposite the Houses of Parliament, the competition for its design was won in 1908 by Ralph Knott. The choice of the winning design was influenced in part by the power politics of the day, for although imposing, Knott's County Hall was not as overbearing as the lofty Baroque tower proposed by Rickards which would have represented a direct challenge to the primacy of Westminster as symbolised by Big Ben. But County Hall was certainly grandiose, even forbidding; and this flagship of municipal achievement in London still makes a powerful statement across the waters of the Thames, although stripped of its functions since the abolition of the Greater London Council in 1986.

Other palaces of bureaucracy appeared in Whitehall at around the same time, and these too showed a preference for the Baroque. The best examples are the War Office of 1898–1906 and the government offices extending from Parliament Square to St James's Park, completed in 1912, which are now mainly the home of the Treasury.

Church architecture did not stand still during the Edwardian period, but London was not greatly endowed with much in the way of Arts and Crafts design, in the way that many parishes in the country were. The church of Holy Trinity of 1888–90 by Sedding is a magnificent exception. Situated in the highly urban setting of Chelsea's Sloane Street, it is a glorious repository of Arts and Crafts devices, notably the east window designed by Burne Jones and the altar rails and railings by Henry Wilson. More typical of the period was the continuation of the Gothic Revival in such churches as another Holy Trinity in Prince Consort Road, Kensington, of 1902–4, which captures in its interior the soaring qualities of medieval Gothic. Baroque was hardly used at all for churches, but there is a notable exception in Holy Trinity in Kingsway of 1910–12 by Belcher and Joass.

A full-blooded return to the style of Byzantium was made by John Francis Bentley, whose Westminster Cathedral of 1895–1903 towers both literally and artistically over all other ecclesiastical works of the period in London. The style was chosen to give London's new Catholic cathedral a distinctive but Christian identity which would avoid any emulation of the Gothic of Westminster Abbey. Now that the vista from Victoria Street has been opened it is possible to admire the great power as well as the surface beauty of Westminster Cathedral. This mighty structure of brick banded with stone, with its towering *campanile*, is strongly reminiscent of northern Italy, and the Byzantine references of its huge round arches and domes are unmistakable. Yet for all that, it is still a profoundly original building whose proportions are equally effective when viewed from the restricted vantage point of the narrow streets behind. There is an echo of the Byzantine style in Beresford Pite's Christ Church in Brixton Road, Lambeth, of 1899–1902, but Westminster Cathedral is in a class of its own.

It is not individual buildings alone – abundant and interesting as they are – that constitute the essence of Edwardian London, for this was also a period of some notable exercises in urban planning, such as the creation of the Aldwych and a new road, Kingsway, which from 1900 was driven through one of London's infamous rookeries and provided a grand link between the Strand and Holborn, with an extension further north to Russell Square. Despite inevitable alterations, Aldwych and Kingsway still contain a wealth of Edwardian commercial architecture, ranging from the Parisian-style offices of the *Morning Post* at Inveresk House of 1907, now occupied by the Aldwych branch of Lloyds Bank, to the epoch-making Kodak Building of 1910–11 by Sir John Burnet at 65 Kingsway. This surprisingly modern structure still owes its basic form to the Classical heritage but is stripped of the usual embellishment, and it was to set the style for countless other office blocks which followed in the 1920s and thereafter. It was also during the Edwardian era that Regent Street acquired much of its present appearance, according to designs prepared by Sir Reginald Blomfield which were executed with considerable delay so that completion was not achieved until 1930. And so Nash's stucco buildings were gradually replaced, and only the enticing curve of the street now remains of the original scheme.

The Mall, another crucial element in Nash's Grand Design, also attracted the attention of Edwardian urbanists. Sir Aston Webb, architect of the new front section of the Victoria & Albert Museum of 1899–1901, was entrusted with the improvement of the approach from Trafalgar Square to Buckingham Palace. This involved the design of the

The Victoria Memorial of 1911 represents the highpoint of Edwardian London.

Admiralty Arch of 1908–9 to provide a ceremonial entrance to the Mall, which now terminated at a rond-point completed in 1913. The final item in the scheme was a new façade for Buckingham Palace, a dignified if unexciting Neo-Classical composition of 1913. Pride of place in this attempt to give London a monumental avenue worthy of her imperial destiny was reserved of course for a statue of Her Majesty. The Victoria Memorial of 1911 in front of Buckingham Palace is an Edwardian tribute to the monarch who had reigned over one of the most glorious chapters in the nation's history. The Victoria Memorial, much disregarded in spite of its prominence, stands not only as a symbol of British self-esteem but may also be regarded as the high-water mark of London's self-confidence and metropolitan aspirations.

The Queen Alexandra Memorial of 1932 by Alfred Gilbert, the sculptor of Eros, marks the continuation of a sentimental Edwardian romanticism.

Epilogue

The First World War marked the end of London's Edwardian exuberance, but the style lingered on after the cultural climate which had engendered it had changed. The stately imperial tradition continued to find acceptance well into the 1930s, notably in the works of Sir Herbert Baker such as at the Bank of England (1921–37), India House (1928–30) and South Africa House (1935–7), and those of Sir Edwin Lutyens such as Britannic House, Finsbury Circus (1924–7), the Midland Bank headquarters in Poultry (1924–39) and the façade of Reuters and the Press Association in Fleet Street (1935). Arthur J. Davis, architect of the Ritz, designed an elegant Classical garb for the Westminster (now the National Westminster) Bank in Threadneedle Street. Sir John Burnet progressed from the Egyptian monumentality of Adelaide House of 1924–5 at the northern end of London Bridge to the grand manner of Lloyds Bank headquarters of 1927–30 in Cornhill, and finally to the exaggerated Baroque of Unilever House of 1930–2 facing Blackfriars Bridge. Thus did commercial and governmental buildings seek the reassuring forms of the Edwardian era, demonstrating a marked reluctance to move into the modern age. Many of the buildings in the City which were built in the 1920s and 1930s shared this conservatism and now appear much more antiquarian than they really are.

London's few truly modern buildings of the period show up in stark contrast. The black glass and steel of the *Daily Express* office in Fleet Street of 1931 and the retail stores of Simpson's in Piccadilly of 1935 and Peter Jones in Sloane Square of 1936–8 still strike a decidedly modern note more than fifty years after their conception. The new cinema cult of Hollywood has left some bizarre relics in London in such unashamed fantasy pieces as the Gaumont State in Kilburn High Road of 1937 and the Granada in Tooting of the same year. The spirit of the ultra-modern electrical revolution in industrial technology of the 1930s is expressed by two contrasting London buildings. The gleaming Hoover Factory in Western Avenue of 1932–5 holds out the promise of a bright clean future where manufacturing is almost fun. The uncompromising bulk of Battersea Power Station, on the other hand, of 1929–35 looms ominously as a more forbidding industrial monument which expresses the sheer force of physical energy. This chilling but compelling vision of human subordination to nature still commands respect. A similar mood of raw strength comes through in the larger buildings designed by Charles Holden such as the London Transport headquarters in Broadway of 1927–9, and especially in the Senate House of 1932 for London University, a rude but powerful excrescence in Georgian Bloomsbury.

Holden was the one British architect to have emerged from the Arts and Crafts movement into the dawn of Modernism, which in London did not break until the 1930s. London owes most of its small stock of original Modernist buildings to Berthold Lubetkin and his Tecton group. Domestic architecture underwent the most dramatic conversion in such structures as the block of flats in Highgate of 1933–5 known as Highpoint One. Its successor, Highpoint Two of 1937–8, shows how the Modernist ideal of straight lines, unadorned surfaces and structural simplicity was not so doctrinaire that it could not allow itself a satirical gesture, cocking a snook at the language of Classicism, by including a set of caryatids to support the porch. It may be seen as a sign of Modernism's confidence that it could indulge in a Post-Modernist joke without undermining its own position. Indeed, confidence and optimism appear as the underlying characteristics of the 1930s Modernist architecture in London, which ranged from the geometrical *élan* of the Penguin Pool at London Zoo to the symbolically radiant Finsbury Health Centre of 1938–9 in Pine Street. There was also a substantial dose of optimism in some flat-roofed suburban houses of the period, whose white façades and spacious balconies called for the climate of California rather than that of the Thames Valley.

However, the impact of Modernism in London between the wars was limited, and more important than the new style was the fact of London's continued expansion as the metropolitan area doubled in extent during the 1920s and 1930s. As the drift to the outer suburbs gathered momentum, so the inner city entered its long phase of decline, which has only recently shown signs of lifting. The process was greatly accelerated by the LCC which followed a deliberate policy of social engineering with the transfer of the inner-city population to soulless estates in the middle of nowhere such as Becontree in Essex and Borehamwood in Hertfordshire. Growth along the periphery left a void at the centre.

The Second World War brought London's evolution to a halt for just over a decade. The widespread devastation of the Blitz, particularly in the City and the East End, left behind huge areas of dereliction and presented a *tabula rasa* for planners on a scale unprecedented since the Great Fire of 1666. The possibilities of a radical reorganisation of the City, which had been denied to Wren, were now partially realised as London re-emerged from the ruins. The resulting achievements of the period from 1945 to 1975 were thus accomplished under the positive banner of reconstruction but sadly they represent perhaps the most negative, certainly the most traumatic period of London's development. The old spectre of intolerant architectural dogma reappeared in the shape of a shabby Modernism, just bearable in such buildings as the Royal Festival Hall expressing the brave spirit of the Festival of Britain in 1951, but soon to become oppressive and tyrannical as Modernism was hijacked by what has been so aptly named as a new Brutalism. Seen in retrospect, it appears quite amazing that London, still with vivid memories of the war, should willingly select the bunker-style architecture of the South Bank as the medium of its fresh urban vision.

Similar brutalistic developments posing as modern and progressive replaced the old streetscapes with an open wilderness studded with tower blocks, a tendency which may be experienced in many parts of London but particularly in East End districts such as Stepney. The tower-block estate proved slightly more attractive on the slopes of

Roehampton but the notion of providing unrelated expanses of parkland was essentially anti-urban, as if the planners had decided that the very idea of placing people in a communal environment was somehow suspect. The same phenomenon of high-rise buildings anxious to keep their distance from one another may be observed at its worst along the street in the City known as London Wall. This desolate thoroughfare, so overtly hostile to human beings, represents a complete rejection of the crowded sociability of the once populous medieval London within the walls. Victoria Street, for all its mediocre architecture, is still a street with some visual cohesion; and the Barbican Centre, despite its much decried Brutalism, is a brave attempt to create an urban community in an area which had become a sort of no-man's-land. But so many of the post-war public housing estates in London have done little more than introduce a new dimension of inner-city despair and alienation. One doesn't have to look to the lands behind the Iron Curtain to find examples of a totalitarian, collectivist utopia.

Yet it must be assumed that these onslaughts on the face of London were conceived in good faith, springing from a conviction that people would ultimately benefit. However, the actual result of the planners' and architects' endeavours in the thirty years following the Second World War has been to make Londoners only more aware of the virtues of earlier periods which better served the needs of communities. Even some of the grim philanthropic dwellings of the Victorian age are now being perceived as potentially superior in social quality to many more recent housing developments. The general dissatisfaction with the works of the 1950s to 1970s has brought about a loss of faith in the architectural and planning professions. Never before has there been such public suspicion of the implications of new schemes, and never so much energy expended on a better understanding of the true potential of the urban machine. It is a sign of the times that the media more often invite proposals for the demolition of the most hated buildings than they bestow praise on the more popular edifices. In all, 1945 to 1975 has been an inglorious and painful chapter in London's building history which has left psychological as well as physical scars.

The 1980s have witnessed a revival of the metropolitan spirit and a healing of some of the wounds. The suburban dream is as potent as ever but there is emerging an equivalent cult of the inner city and a positive commitment to revitalise urban qualities. The birth of the conservation movement in the 1960s has broadened into a wider demand for residences in the run-down terraces of Georgian and Victorian London. The public perception of districts from Hackney and Islington to Clapham and Wandsworth has shown a radical improvement. The regeneration of Covent Garden marked a turning point in urban attitudes with its message that people prefer to see a rehabilitation of the old rather than risk another shock from the new. Perhaps the most significant building in London of recent years is one that was not put up: the rejection of the proposal to erect a Mies van der Rohe Modernist block at Mansion House in favour of the conservation of a hitherto unremarked Victorian commercial complex was a sign of the times. The 1980s also brought the famous remark of the Prince of Wales condemning a proposed extension to the National Gallery as a 'monstrous carbuncle'.

There is now greater respect for the inherited building stock; the new design for the extension to the National Gallery and that for the Tate both pay tribute to their parent structures. The Tate Gallery extension by James Stirling has brought Post-Modernism to public architecture following its successful application to such private commercial projects as Terry Farrell's TV-AM in Camden Town and Quinlan Terry's 'Queen Anne' office block in Soho. In addition to its love of stylistic references and gratuitous decoration, Post-Modernism appears to show concern for a harmony of scale and adherence to the street-line of the existing structures. Lovat Lane, the most medieval street in the City with its cobbles and central gutter, has retained its authentic spirit of place although now playing host to London's most concentrated collection of smaller contemporary buildings. On the other hand, there are no such proprieties behind the romantic, technological vision of Richard Rogers's Lloyd's building which is a bold challenge to those enamoured of the past. It remains to be seen whether its exciting shapes and surfaces stand the test of time; making a design feature of air-conditioners, lift shafts and even toilet cubicles may well be rejected as a gimmick.

As London approaches the close of the twentieth century there is something stirring. The eclectic approach to architecture embraces an excitement for the new which does not preclude a love of the old. But the real shaping force in London's future appearance is less concerned with the aesthetics of style than with the imperatives of economics. The expansion of the City into Docklands and the audacious scheme to create another 'square mile' at Canary Wharf promises not only to reverse London's traditional growth to the west but also to upstage the City itself whose office blocks are mostly unsuitable for the new communications technology required by the international financial institutions. There is thus a question mark over the unloved 'shoe-box' buildings of the 1960s and a chance to correct some of the ills of contemporary London. The opening of the M25 London Orbital Motorway in the mid-1980s poses another challenge to the inner city as the possibility emerges of a belt of satellite communities developing a commercial base of their own, largely independent of the great metropolis at the centre. London's inherited radial network, first created by the roads and strengthened by the railway, must now contend with a new force. London's dramatic growth under the Romans some two thousand years ago resulted from its strategic location on the Thames which made it the focal point for transport between regional centres. There is no more commerce on the river and London can now be by-passed on land in all directions, yet it continues to thrive as an international centre dependent on business and subject to the demands and fluctuations of market forces. In this sense London is still fulfilling its historic destiny as a living metropolis which can never be static.

Bibliography

Barker, Felix and Hyde, Ralph, *London As It Might Have Been*, John Murray, 1982

Barker, Felix and Jackson, Peter, *London: 2000 Years of a City and its People*, Macmillan, 1983

Brooke, Christopher, *London 800–1216: the Shaping of a City*, Secker & Warburg, 1975

Byrne, Andrew, *London's Georgian Houses*, The Georgian Press, 1986

Cherry, Bridget and Pevsner, Nikolaus, *The Buildings of England, London (South)*, Penguin Books, 1983

Cruickshank, Dan and Wyld, Peter, *London: the Art of Georgian Building*, Architectural Press, 1975

Dalzell, W. R., *The Shell Guide to the History of London*, Michael Joseph, 1981

Fletcher, Geoffrey, *The London Nobody Knows*, Penguin Books, 1962

French, Ylva, *Blue Guide to London*, A. & C. Black, 1986

Godfrey, Walter, *A History of Architecture In and Around London*, Phoenix House, 1962

Hibbert, Christopher, *London, The Biography of a City*, Penguin Books, 1980

Hobley, Brian, *Roman and Saxon London – A Reappraisal*, Museum of London, 1986

Home, Gordon, *Medieval London*, Ernest Benn, 1927

Jenkins, Simon, *Landlords to London, the Story of a Capital and its Growth*, Constable, 1975

Jones, Edward and Woodward, Christopher, *A Guide to the Architecture of London*, Weidenfeld & Nicolson, 1983

Marsden, Peter, *Roman London*, Thames & Hudson, 1980

Meller, Hugh, *London Cemeteries*, Godstone, Gregg International, 1985

Metcalf, Priscilla, *Victorian London*, Cassell, 1972

Merrifield, Ralph, *The Archaeology of London*, Heinemann, 1975

Merrifield, Ralph, *London, City of the Romans*, Batsford, 1983

Morris, John, *Londinium – London in the Roman Empire*, Weidenfeld & Nicolson, 1982

Olsen, Donald J., *The Growth of Victorian London*, Peregrine Books, 1979

Olsen, Donald J., *Town Planning in London: the Eighteenth and Nineteenth Centuries*, Yale University Press, 1982

Pearce, David, *London's Mansions*, Batsford, 1986

Pevsner, Nikolaus and Cherry, Bridget, *The Buildings of England, London City and Westminster*, Penguin Books, 1973

Pudney, John, *London's Docks*, Thames & Hudson, 1975

Rasmussen, Steen Eiler, *London – The Unique City*, The MIT Press, 1982

Rudé, George, *Hanoverian London 1714–1808*, Secker & Warburg, 1971

Saunders, Ann, *The Art and Architecture of London*, Phaidon, 1984

Schofield, John, *The Building of London from the Conquest to the Great Fire*, Colonnade, 1984

Schofield, John and Dyson, Tony, *Archaeology of the City of London*, City of London Archaeological Trust, 1980

Service, Alastair, *The Architects of London from 1066 to the Present Day*, Architectural Press, 1979

Service, Alastair, *London 1900*, Crosby Lockwood Staples, 1979

Sheppard, F. H. W., *London 1808–1870 – The Infernal Wen*, Secker & Warburg, 1971

Summerson, John, *Georgian London*, Peregrine Books, 1978

Summerson, John, *Victorian Architecture*, Columbia University Press, 1970

Sykes, Christopher, *Private Palaces – Life in the Great London House*, Chatto & Windus, 1985

Trease, Geoffrey, *London – A Concise History*, Thames & Hudson, 1975

Trent, Christopher, *Greater London*, Phoenix House, 1965

Weightman, Gavin and Humphries, Steve, *The Making of Modern London 1815–1914*, Sidgwick & Jackson, 1983

Weinreb, Ben and Hibbert, Christopher, *The London Encyclopaedia*, Macmillan, 1983

Index

Numbers in italics refer to illustration captions

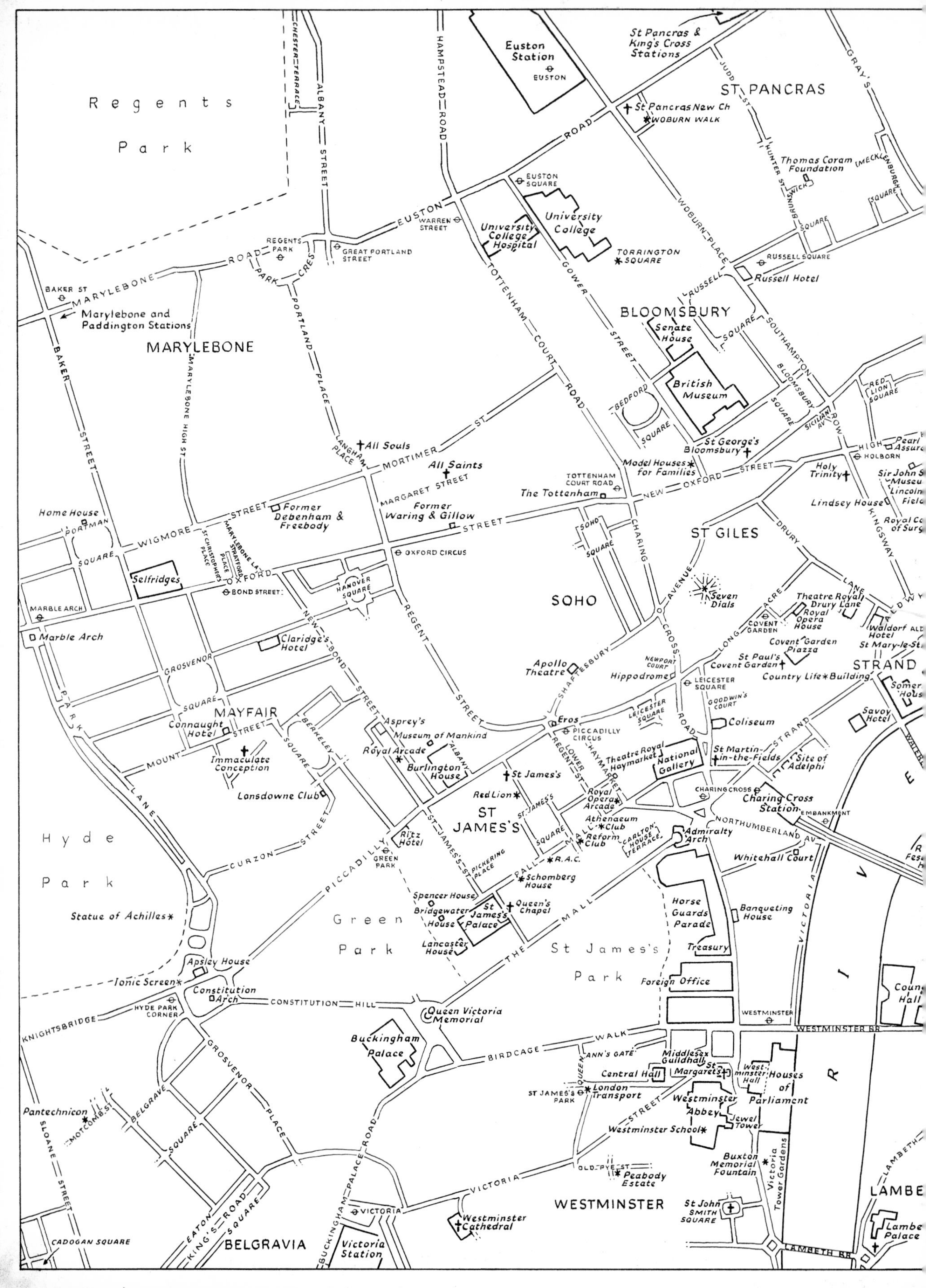

Regents Park
Euston Station
EUSTON
St Pancras & King's Cross Stations
ST PANCRAS
St Pancras New Ch
WOBURN WALK
Thomas Coram Foundation
EUSTON SQUARE
University College
University College Hospital
TORRINGTON SQUARE
RUSSELL SQUARE
Russell Hotel
WARREN STREET
REGENTS PARK
GREAT PORTLAND STREET
BAKER ST
Marylebone and Paddington Stations
MARYLEBONE
BLOOMSBURY
Senate House
British Museum
St George's Bloomsbury
Model Houses for Families
TOTTENHAM COURT ROAD
The Tottenham
All Souls
All Saints
MARGARET STREET
Former Waring & Gillow
Former Debenham & Freebody
Home House
PORTMAN SQUARE
WIGMORE STREET
OXFORD CIRCUS
Selfridges
BOND STREET
MARBLE ARCH
Marble Arch
HANOVER SQUARE
SOHO SQUARE
SOHO
ST GILES
Seven Dials
Pearl Assurance
HOLBORN
Holy Trinity
Lindsey House
Theatre Royal Drury Lane
Royal Opera House
COVENT GARDEN
Waldorf Hotel
St Mary-le-Strand
Covent Garden Piazza
St Paul's Covent Garden
Country Life Building
STRAND
Claridge's Hotel
GROSVENOR SQUARE
MAYFAIR
Connaught Hotel
Immaculate Conception
Lansdowne Club
Apollo Theatre
Hippodrome
NEWPORT COURT
LEICESTER SQUARE
GOODWIN'S COURT
Coliseum
Savoy Hotel
Asprey's
Museum of Mankind
Royal Arcade
Burlington House
Eros
PICCADILLY CIRCUS
Theatre Royal Haymarket
National Gallery
St Martin-in-the-Fields
Site of Adelphi
St James's
Red Lion
ST JAMES'S
Royal Opera Arcade
Athenaeum Club
Reform Club
CARLTON HOUSE TERRACE
Admiralty Arch
CHARING CROSS
Charing Cross Station
EMBANKMENT
NORTHUMBERLAND AV
Ritz Hotel
GREEN PARK
R.A.C.
PICKERING PLACE
Schomberg House
Whitehall Court
Hyde Park
Statue of Achilles
Green Park
Spencer House
Bridgewater House
St James's Palace
Queen's Chapel
Lancaster House
Horse Guards Parade
Banqueting House
Treasury
St James's Park
Foreign Office
Apsley House
Ionic Screen
Constitution Arch
CONSTITUTION HILL
HYDE PARK CORNER
KNIGHTSBRIDGE
Queen Victoria Memorial
WESTMINSTER
WESTMINSTER BR
County Hall
Buckingham Palace
BIRDCAGE WALK
ANN'S GATE
Middlesex Guildhall
St Margaret's
Central Hall
London Transport
ST JAMES'S PARK
Westminster Hall
Houses of Parliament
Westminster Abbey
Jewel Tower
Westminster School
Pantechnicon
MOTCOMB ST
BELGRAVE SQUARE
GROSVENOR PLACE
Buxton Memorial Fountain
Victoria Tower Gardens
OLD PYE ST
Peabody Estate
VICTORIA
WESTMINSTER
St John SMITH SQUARE
LAMBETH
Westminster Cathedral
Lambeth Palace
LAMBETH BR
CADOGAN SQUARE
BELGRAVIA
Victoria Station
EATON SQUARE
KING'S ROAD
BUCKINGHAM PALACE ROAD
SLOANE STREET
PARK LANE
CURZON STREET
PICCADILLY
THE MALL